Blind
Cartridges

Also by William Colt MacDonald
in Large Print:

Alias Dix Ryder
The Comanche Scalp
Powdersmoke Range
Restless Guns
Ridin' Through
Sunrise Guns

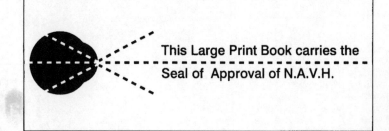

This Large Print Book carries the
Seal of Approval of N.A.V.H.

Blind Cartridges.

William Colt MacDonald

G.K. Hall & Co. Thorndike, Maine

Published in 2000 by arrangement with Golden West Literary Agency.

G.K. Hall Large Print Paperback Series.

The text of this Large Print edition is unabridged.
Other aspects of the book may vary from the original edition.

Set in 16 pt. Plantin.

Printed in the United States on permanent paper.

Library of Congress Cataloging-in-Publication Data

MacDonald, William Colt, 1891–1968.
  Blind cartridges / William Colt MacDonald.
    p. (large print) cm.
  ISBN 0-7838-8937-2 (lg. print : sc : alk. paper)
    1. Cattle stealing — Fiction. 2. Frontier and pioneer life —
Fiction. 3. Large type books. I. Title.
  PS3525.A2122 B58 2000
    813′.52—dc21   99-058226

Contents

Dead Wrong

Where the afternoon sun slanted through the dusty-paned window it fell brightly on the wide spiderweb stretching across one corner of the frame shack and turned the silken strands of the web to red, shimmering gold when the captured fly struggled to escape. There were other insects, flies and moths, entangled in the web, but these were already dead, some partly devoured by the thick-bodied black spider resting in the center of its web. Only this one fly remained, a huge bluebottle type, to buzz frantically and beat futile wings in its effort to escape the ensnaring cable-like strands.

The man seated on the chair a distance of three yards away had been watching that particular fly for three days now, such time as the sun came through lighting up that corner of the shack. He'd seen other insects trapped and promptly eaten, but this bluebottle had proved unusually tough. So far the spider had made no move to approach it.

"It's likely," mused the man on the chair, "Mister Spider's plumb gorged himself. He's saving up that bluebottle for a time when he's got more appetite —"

7

He broke off. The fly had renewed its struggles. One strand of the web gave way, then another.

"Fight, boy, fight." The man spoke encouragingly. "You'll make to break out yet."

Then his face fell. The spider had moved quickly out from the center of its web to repair the damage brought about by the fly's struggles. New strands were quickly spun, wrapping the fly's wings tightly to its sides. It buzzed angrily, but the sound grew fainter and fainter as the spider worked. Finally the fly fell silent altogether, and the black spider once more retreated to the center of its web.

"Dammit, you're done for now, boy," and there was a hopeless tone in the man's soft voice. "I was hoping —" He paused, then added, "Hell, I should know better than to hope."

Under some circumstances even a bluebottle entrapped in a spider's web can hold an absorbing interest for a man. For three days now, when the sun shone on the web, the fly's struggles to escape had held the man's attention, helping him to pass the time, a time that dragged past on weighted feet. He had felt a certain kinship with that particular bluebottle; unconsciously he had been identifying its fate with his own. And with fairly good reason: the man on the straight-backed wooden chair was as much of a prisoner as ever the bluebottle had been — and with only slightly less chance of escape. Tight ropes bound his arms to his sides and passed around the back

8

of the chair. Another rope bound his feet tightly to the chair legs. He, too, had struggled, in the beginning, to break his bonds, but had long since relinquished that method of gaining freedom; the ropes were far too stout to be broken. How long was it since he had been brought here, to this cabin, at the point of a gun? Two weeks? Come to think of it, it was nearer three.

He was a tall, thin man with leathery lined features; gray had commenced to appear above his temples, and his otherwise dark hair was becoming sparse. His name was Steve Wyatt and he was — had been — an operative for the Artexico Cattlemen's Association. For some time now he'd been unable to do any operating for the Association. He'd been too good at his job. That had brought about his downfall. He'd not been quite good enough, not careful enough. He'd made only one slip, but that single lapse of mind had been enough to apprise the enemy of his intentions, and the enemy had acted with quick, ruthless force. Perhaps he had reason to identify himself with the hapless bluebottle.

On a bare table behind Wyatt lay his cartridge belt and holster, though the holster was now empty. The brim of his battered gray sombrero covered one edge of the belt buckle. There were various other objects on the table: a bit of broken harness, one rusty spur, a candle stuck in the neck of a whisky bottle, a two-months-old newspaper. There was a second chair in the room and a couple of overturned wooden boxes also to serve as seats. A bunk was built against the back wall on which lay some rumpled blankets. There was a rusty iron stove with above it, nailed to the pine uprights, a wooden shelf holding some canned goods. The single door was closed and there was but one window.

"Well," Wyatt told himself with attempted cheerfulness, "that bluebottle told me one thing — it don't do no good to struggle. Not in a fix like mine. I'll have to think of some other way. Anyhow, can't say I've been downright mistreated yet. Howsomever, my present position is mighty confining — just like that ol' bluebottle." He stared moodily at the floor, littered with old cigarette butts and dust, and slowly shook his head. "Steve," he warned himself, "you might just as well face the facts. This cow-thief web that's holding you won't give you any more chance to get free than that black spider is giving that bluebottle." He drew his breath in a deep sigh. "Lord, if I only had a fightin' chance when my time comes. That's all I'm asking now — but I don't reckon I'll get even that much —"

His meditations were broken off by the sound of creaking saddle leather beyond the closed door and the thumping of horses' hoofs. His features stiffened. "I wonder if this is it," he mused, and an involuntary shudder coursed his spine. "They don't generally come afternoons."

The voices of two men reached Wyatt's ears as they dismounted. A booted foot stumbled near the front of the shack. Then the door was kicked open and the two entered. Wyatt said sarcastically, "Come in, gentlemen. Or maybe I'm wrong, now I see the spider himself has come visiting. Ain't seen you in a couple of weeks —"

"What the hell you meanin' — spider?" the foremost man rasped, glancing quickly at Wyatt's bonds. He was tall, unprepossessing, with a lean lantern jaw and a very dark complexion. His hair was as black and straight as an Apache's. His companion was thicker through the shoulders, with pale blue eyes set too closely together. The two were in cowmen's togs and carried holstered sixshooters.

"You wouldn't understand," Wyatt said quietly, "even if I explained what I meant when I called you 'spider.' Visiting early today, aren't you?"

"There's a reason," the light-complexioned man said nervously. "Look here, Wyatt, you haven't any kick on the treatment we've given you, have you?"

Wyatt eyed the speaker soberly. "Aside from being held here against my will, no. Some of your men have visited me mornin' and evenin'. I've been fed and watered regular."

"All right," the speaker went on, "then you ain't got any real grudge against us. Supposing we let you go, would you keep your mouth shut?"

Wyatt laughed scornfully. "Now you hombres know better than to ask me anything like that.

11

Certainly I won't keep my mouth shut — not with what I know about you two."

"Didn't I tell you, pard?" the dark man with the lantern jaw said wearily. "You can't make these cattle dicks listen to reason."

"I'm not through yet," the light-complexioned man went on. "Look here, Wyatt, we'll make you a proposition. You're no yearlin' any more. It must be about time for you to retire. Maybe you've got a mite of acreage you figured you could retire to shortly. Let's say we let you go, you keep your trap closed, and we'll see that you get a nice roll of cash money to shore you up in your old age."

Wyatt shook his head contemptuously. "I'm not interested in bribes, in the first place. In the second, I know pretty much how you're fixed hereabouts. I can't imagine you having much cash money to throw around —"

"But we will have, when our plans go through," the speaker said eagerly.

"I'm not interested." Wyatt spoke in short tones. His voice changed. "There is something that interests me though. I'd like to know just how you learned who I was — where I made my slip."

Lantern-jaw laughed coarsely. "You sent weekly reports to your association. Oh, sure, I know" — as Wyatt interjected a phrase — "sure, most telegraph operators are honest. Don't blame that dot-and-dash man. But when we saw that you made regular trips down to the depot

12

we got curious. It was a simple matter to reach through an open window one night, when the operator had his back turned, and lift your message off a spindle after he had sent it. That address — Artexico — spelled dynamite to us, Wyatt, and we've had a man trailing you ever since —"

"Then," the light-complexioned man broke in, "we fixed it so you'd catch one of our men brand-blottin'. You never realized the rest of us were so near —"

"And so you grabbed me and brought me here," Wyatt said coldly. "And now you've got the bull by the tail and don't know how to let go. You don't dare to kill me." This last was sheer bluff.

Lantern-jaw guffawed. "The hell we don't! And what makes you think we don't?"

"Artexico expects weekly reports from me. When they stop, somebody gets suspicious. There'll be another man sent down here, into the Holster Basin. Probably my chief has already —"

"Don't build up any hopes, Wyatt," Lantern-jaw's companion cut in. "Those weekly reports are still being telegraphed to Artexico headquarters. One of our hands brings 'em to the telegraph operator and says you sent 'em in. You're supposed to be roamin' the country, too busy to get into town. You sent telegrams whenever you happened to run across a rider out on the range some place."

Wyatt's lined features tightened. "You can't keep that up forever."

"We don't intend to," Lantern-jaw sneered. "Artexico will shortly receive a telegram to the effect that you're mistaken about any suspicions you might have had here, and that the trail is leading you down into Mexico. We got friends across the border, too, and there'll be more wires sent from time to time. Artexico may think it mighty queer if you go skippin' around, but they'll be stalled off from gettin' suspicious for a long time."

"Until," Wyatt said grimly, "my body is found dead some place."

"You're one hell of a good guesser —"

"Look here," the light-complexioned man interrupted, "Wyatt will listen to reason. There's no need of killing —"

The quick rasping sound of metal against leather cut in on the words. Lantern-jaw's gun was out of its holster. He fired once, shifted aim slightly, then fired a second time. The heavy detonations of the Colt's forty-five shook the rafters overhead. Dust sifted down from the ceiling. Black powder smoke swirled through the room and drifted through the open doorway.

Wyatt groaned once, twisted his body in agony, then his head slumped on his chest. The light-complexioned man turned frightenedly on his companion.

"My Gawd! Did you have to do that?"

Lantern-jaw plugged out his empty cartridges

14

and reloaded while he spoke. "Anybody but a damn' fool would realize it had to be done. You're too chicken-hearted, so it was up to me." His voice swelled angrily. "The goddam snoopin' cow dick got what he deserved. I hate the whole tribe of 'em. Now, come on and —"

"But — but," the other man stammered, "you told me we'd let him go if he kept his mouth shut —"

"You heard him refuse your offer," Lantern-jaw snarled. "What else was there to do?"

His companion mopped a wet brow with a blue bandanna. "But — but, hell's bells, this is murder —"

"You getting an attack of conscience at this late date?"

"You're mighty right I am." The words sounded worried, fearful. "Stealing a few cows is one thing. Killing is another. Besides, you promised me Wyatt wouldn't be harmed."

"I had to do that to keep you in line, cowman. You were getting too shaky to suit me. Where's your guts? It was him or us —"

"I'm damned if I'll ever trust you again," the light-complexioned man commenced angrily. "I don't ever want —"

"You'll trust me more than ever," Lantern-jaw sneered. "There ain't nothing else for you to do now. You're in this as deep as me —"

"I've never yet killed —"

"You will, brother, you will," Lantern-jaw stated coolly. "Trouble with you, you just ain't

15

been pushed to the wall yet. Getting rid of Wyatt makes things a mite easier for us."

The other just stared horrified at the dead man in the chair, without saying anything beyond, "But it's murder — just plain murder. I won't — I won't —"

"Damn it! Pull yourself together," Lantern-jaw snapped. "What's done is done. I'll cut Wyatt's ropes and we'll get him out of here. Some of his blood has already trickled down to the floor. You get busy mopping that up while I take care of his carcass. We don't want to leave any sign behind —"

"I won't — I won't have anything more to do with this business," the other commenced defiantly. "You and me are through —"

He paused suddenly when he found himself looking into the round black muzzle of Lantern-jaw's six-shooter.

"What were you saying?" Lantern-jaw asked sarcastically. "Mebbe you'd like to join Wyatt, instead of co-operating with me." His voice turned steely hard. "Make up your mind. I'm getting damn' sick of your palaverin'. You with me or against me?"

The reluctant words when they came carried tones of defeat. "I still don't like it, but — but I'm with you, I guess. There don't seem nothing else for me — now."

Lantern-jaw lowered his gun, grinned triumphantly. "You show good sense, pard. Don't worry, you'll get over being squeamish about a little killing. You just got to figure we acted in self-defense, and you'll see things my way. And now, let's get busy. We got to get this stiff away from here."

A few days later, some hundreds of miles away, Jim Ryland, head of the Artexico Cattlemen's Association, sat frowning at his desk as he studied a telegram that had been brought in to him but a few minutes before. Ryland ran gnarled fingers through his gray hair and lifted his head to gaze, unseeing, at the busy street beyond his office window. Horses and wagons lined the thoroughfare on either side. A cowhand walked his pony past Ryland's line of vision. A horse-drawn streetcar jangled by. Spurs clanked on the sidewalk below the window.

A step sounded at the open doorway of Ryland's office. Ryland jerked his head around to see Charlie Talman, the local county sheriff, filling the opening. He said, "Oh, hello, Charlie. What's on your mind?"

Talman, a middle-aged man in shirt sleeves and a vest bearing his badge of office, shoved his black sombrero to the back of his bald head and said, "We-ell, it's a hot day. I figured you might be in the mood to slip down to the Owl's Head for a couple of beers. If it's the heat that gives you that worried look, some beer might help. On the other hand, if you've got something on your mind, we'll forget it. I don't want to intrude on

17

your business hours."

"Come in and sit a minute." Ryland indicated a chair near the desk, then continued, "Yeah, I am sort of bothered. Maybe I'm just imagining trouble where it doesn't exist, though." Talman asked a question. Ryland went on, "A spell back we got a call from one of our members over in the Holster Basin country. I sent Steve Wyatt to investigate."

"And now," Talman broke in, "I suppose Steve has stopped sending in reports, or somethin' of the sort."

Ryland shook his head. "Reports have been coming through regular, but now I'm commencing to wonder if Steve is sending them. He hasn't even mentioned whether the sage is green, or —"

"Whether the sage is green?" Talman frowned. "You making your operatives report on plant growth and give weather reports nowadays, Jim?"

"You don't understand, Charlie," Ryland explained. "A few years back one of our men was captured by a rustler gang. They got his credentials and continued to forward reports to headquarters as our man had been doing. We got wind of that and settled things before they'd gone too far, but since then I've always had our operatives close their reports with some mention of whatever plants happen to grow in the section they're operating in. That's supposed to be secret, of course. It gives me an additional iden-

18

tification on a report so I know who is actually sending it. Sage grows pretty widely through the Southwest. Before Steve left we agreed he'd end his messages with some mention of the sagebrush. This time of year the sage should be coming in green, and he should mention it, so I'll know things are going along all right."

"And Steve ain't mentioned the sage this week?" Talman asked.

Ryland swore irritably. "This is the third week he hasn't mentioned it, Charlie. I don't like it. Suppose something's happened to Steve Wyatt? I've got a hunch something is dead wrong."

"Maybe not," Talman said. "Steve could be mighty careless sometimes on anything like that. I know he always hated writing letters. Maybe it just slipped his mind. Why don't you telegraph him and find out what's doing?"

"I don't like to do that either," Ryland scowled. "I don't know whether he entered the Holster Basin openly, or if he kept his business secret. I've always let Steve work in his own way. If I sent him a telegram, it might upset his plans in some manner. Last time he mentioned the sage in a report, he said that he thought business was looking up. That meant, to me, that he was on the track of something. Then came a message saying he'd made a mistake. That message didn't mention sage. The next message the same, and it added there was nothing new to report. Now today I get a telegram stating his trail leads down into Mexico. Nothing in it about sage, either."

"Maybe he just forgot."

"That's what I'm hoping. Like you say, he always hated writing letters. That's why I let him report by telegraph." The lines in Ryland's face deepened. "I keep thinking that this was Steve Wyatt's last job. He was aiming to retire to that acreage he's got out in the country and raise garden truck and smoke his pipe. It will be tough on his wife and youngster, too, if —"

"Hell, don't let yourself think things like that," the sheriff interrupted. "Steve has taken care of himself in some mighty tough spots before. He's likely all right."

"I hope you're correct, Charlie. Just the same if I had another operative handy I'd shoot him to the Holster Basin in a hurry to see what's what. Trouble is, every one of our men is busy right now." He rose from his chair. "Shucks! Maybe I'm just imagining things. But if I don't get a report on the sage right soon, I'm going to look into things — even if I have to toss this desk job out of the window and head for the Holster Basin myself. Come on, we'll go get that beer you mentioned. I reckon I'm just behaving like an old woman. Likely there isn't a thing for me to worry about."

Nevertheless, his features were still clouded with concern as he followed the sheriff from the office.

Sundown Mallare Arrives

It was bordering on the hour of nine in the evening when Sundown Mallare rode into the town of Holster City. Holster City — so named in its earlier, wilder days because of its capacity for carrying plenty of action — lay in almost the exact center of an expansive basin which, in its turn, owing to a geological formation that followed roughly the contour of a huge six-shooter holster, was known as the Holster Country.

Here was practically everything that goes to make up a cattleman's paradise: lush grass, plenty of water, and a convenient shipping service furnished by the T.N. & A.S. railroad which had its cattle pens built at the eastern end of town at the end of a rusty-railed spur whose tracks quickly became bright during the cattle-shipping season. Also, until recently the Holster Country, or Holster Basin, as many chose to call it, had been remarkably free of that bane of the stock raiser — cattle thieves.

Holster Basin lay along the edge of the Mexican border, in United States territory. A rider leaving the southern side of the basin worked his horse gradually and with considerable climbing up the steep, rocky slopes that bordered it on all

21

sides, passed through piñon and mesquite, with a scattering of tall pines on the lower levels, eventually crossed the crown of the range, then descended on the opposite side to find himself in Old Mexico. Such proximity to the Land of the Dons had led some cowmen to suspect Mexicans of running off stock, but when the wiseacres paused a moment to consider the matter, they pointed out that driving cattle up those steep slopes and getting them across the saw-toothed Terrera Bruta Range wouldn't be the simple matter some had cracked it up to be.

To Sundown Mallare, forking his pony into Holster City, those sharp peaks, etched against the star-studded night sky, seemed to go straight up. It was the same to the west, where the Terrera Brutas swung sharply in a northerly direction to form the top of the holster-shaped valley. Back of Mallare and to the north and northeast the curve of the "holster" was formed by rolling hill country and the terrain was lower. These hills were tree-and-brush studded and were known as the Chaparra Hills.

Holster City wasn't much of a town, though during cattle-shipping season it assumed a teeming activity. It was typical of most cowtowns of its size in the Southwest of that day. There was a single, winding, unpaved main street, dusty in summer and muddy during rains. Parallel to it was a second street, given over to residences, and bearing the name of Fremont. There were three cross streets: Houston, Tonto, and Santa

Fe. Main Street held a number of saloons, a bank of brick construction, a two-story frame hotel, and various other establishments of commercial enterprise.

"Holster City," Sundown Mallare commented mentally, as he rode past the first straggling adobe huts that dotted the approach to town, "doesn't look overly exciting. Probably sort of isolated down here in this basin."

Rectangles of yellow light shone across the dusty road here and there where buildings were still occupied. Mostly the stores were dark, though. A few ponies waited at hitch racks in front of saloons. There were no wagons in sight. Some place, farther on, booted heels clumped along the plank sidewalks.

"Still," Sundown continued his musing, "I shouldn't judge this town too soon. Maybe it just *looks* half asleep. Come to think of it" — he laughed softly — "I've never seen much activity from a box of dynamite, either, until somebody exploded it. We'll see what we'll see."

Mallare's attire proclaimed him to be a cowhand. A close observer noting his humorous gray eyes, red hair, and roughly hewn features might have been smart enough to have seen in him something more than an ordinary cowhand — the sort that moved fast in an emergency, used his head, and knew how to emerge from a ruckus topside up. But little of this showed on the surface. Mallare's sombrero was a battered gray, his shirt was a faded denim. There was a bandanna about his neck, and his bibless overalls were cuffed at the ankles of his well-worn, high-heeled boots. A Colt's six-shooter was swung in a holster at his right hip, and in the boot under one leg he carried on his saddle a Winchester repeating rifle. There was a bedroll at the back of the saddle.

To offset the belligerent appearance of six-shooter and rifle was a brand-new thirty-five-foot throw rope, one end of which was fastened to Mallare's saddle, its remaining length being allowed to trail behind him over the earth as he traveled. Sundown had been trying to get the kinks out of that lariat all day. So, after all, he looked peaceful enough, and he was seeking a job, somewhere in the Holster Basin, he hoped.

In build Mallare was lean and angular, almost loose-jointed. Shortly after his birth fond parents had bestowed on him the Christian names of Stephen Douglas. By the time he was old enough to ride, rope, and brand he endorsed his pay checks, S. D. Mallare. Someone mentioned one day that Mallare's flaming thatch of sorrel hair resembled to no small extent the hues sent forth by a setting sun. Someone else pointed out that the initials, S. D., doubtless stood for Sundown. And the name Sundown stuck to Mallare from then on.

So there's a picture of Mallare as he rode into Holster City: a lean, muscular cowhand with laughing gray eyes and features chiseled out of granite with a none-too-sharp chisel, forking a

24

roan pony named Coffee-Pot, with a new throw rope trailing behind. Just looking for a job, too, and not expecting any trouble of any sort. Not immediate trouble. On the other hand, not running away from a mix-up either, should he become involved in one.

One thing Sundown had never learned well was running. Walking in cowboots was bad enough, locomotion by horse was always preferable. Sundown's parents had heard somewhere (this was about twenty-five years back —) that too much walking is inclined to make a child bowlegged, so they had lifted him into a saddle as soon as he was old enough to hang on. Something must have gone wrong with the parents' theory, because it was the riding, not walking, that gave Sundown's long legs their slightly warped appearance.

Near the center of town Mallare drew rein before the Royal Flush Saloon, eased himself down from the saddle, and waited while his pony drank from the watering trough at the edge of the sidewalk. Meanwhile, Sundown had recoiled his lariat over his saddle horn. Then, loosening his saddle girth, he flipped over the hitch rack, rounded the end of the tie rail, and approached the swinging doors of the saloon.

He paused just within the entrance as the batwing doors at his back slowly swung to a stop, to adjust his eyes to the light. There were a number of men at the long mahogany bar to the right which was presided over by one Ton-and-a-Half

Jenkins, owner and bartender, a drink dispenser of no mean ability who weighed close to the neighborhood of three hundred pounds. At the other side of the room were a couple of round-topped tables where a scattering of men idly played seven-up with packs of dingy cards.

Sundown nodded to a few who had glanced up at his entrance, crossed to the bar, and put down a half dollar. "Bottle of suds," he informed the fat barkeep. Ton-and-a-Half set out a bottle of beer and a glass. Mallare filled the tumbler and allowed some of the foamy amber fluid to slide down his parched throat. Then he refilled the glass.

Ton-and-a-Half mopped at the bar with a damp cloth. "Riding far, cowboy?" he inquired genially.

"That depends," Sundown replied. "No farther tonight, leastwise. It's a long way between towns out this way. I'm hoping one of your local liverymen will let me bunk in his hay tonight."

The fat barkeep chuckled. "You're flattering Holster City, son. There's only *one* livery, the Lone Star. I reckon Zed Danvers will let you sleep in his loft so long's you don't go to sleep with a live butt in your mouth. Zed don't like fires in his livery."

"I can understand that," Sundown said. "I understand fires are bad for the hay. Very drying, they tell me. I'd be careful." He changed the subject. "Anybody around here doing any hiring?"

"Damned if I know for certain," Ton-and-a-Half replied. "I don't think so, though. There's only three outfits in the Holster Basin — what you could really call outfits — the Window-Sash, Flying-Box-9, and the Lazy-E. There's a few piddlin' outfits scattered around the edge of the basin, but they're not what you'd call real spreads. If I'm not bad mistook the ranches mentioned is full up right now —" He broke off as a voice at the far end of the bar demanded some service, then nodded and turned back to Sundown. "You sort of stall along with your beer and I'll make some inquiries when business lets up a little."

"I'll do that, thanks." Sundown's eyes followed the fat bartender as he moved along the length of bar. Ton-and-a-Half moved surprisingly easy for a man of such poundage. Sundown poured some more beer in his glass and rolled and lighted a brown-paper cigarette. He took a few sips from his tumbler and let his gaze roam along the bar. Two men about midway of the long counter caught his attention.

Both were cowmen, to judge from appearances. One was clad in the usual cattleman's togs and had light sandy hair, sharp blue eyes under bushy brows, and straight, tight lips. A rather hard, ruthless face, Sundown decided. "I can't say," he mused, "that I'd care to tangle with that hombre unless I knew what I was doing." Sundown's gaze went to the man's companion who was, undoubtedly, a Mexican. A

27

tall, steeple-crowned sombrero topped the man's shiny black hair. A small mustache adorned his upper lip. He was taller than the average Mexican, with wide shoulders and slim hips. The holster at his hip looked well worn. The two had their heads close together and were talking in low tones.

Ton-and-a-Half was suddenly back in front of Sundown. "You wondering about that pair too?" the barkeep said genially, jerking his head toward the men Sundown had been watching.

"Not particularly." Sundown shrugged. "I've got to admit they do sort of stand out, though."

The bartender nodded. "The whole basin is conjecturin' about those two."

"Why? Who are they?"

"The sandy-complected gent calls himself Jake Munson. The Mex goes by the name of Luis Montaldo. There's a rumor they're looking around the country for cattle properties, though I'm damned if know who started the rumor. Them two don't say. They just sort of appear in Holster City now and then, stay a day or so, and then drift out."

"Make any trouble?"

"Not that anybody can lay a finger on. They mind their own business and are plumb close-mouthed. They don't make friends with anybody, but they don't make enemies either. . . . But you were looking for information about a job. Drink up your beer and the house will buy one for you while I see what I can do." He placed a second bottle, opened, before Sundown, then raised his voice. "Hey, Nort, how you fixed for hands?"

A big, bulky-shouldered man with bluish-gray eyes and straw-colored hair disengaged himself from a small knot of men to whom he'd been talking, and demanded, "Why you asking?" He wore chaps over his levis, a gray shirt, and a stiff-brimmed sombrero. A week's growth of whiskers covered his muscular jaw. "Why you asking?" he said again as he approached Sundown and the bartender.

"This feller —" Ton-and-a-Half commenced.

"My name's Mallare," the cowboy introduced himself. "I'm looking for a job."

The barkeep again broke in, completed the introduction, "This is Nort Windsor, Mallare. He owns the Window-Sash outfit."

The two men shook hands. Windsor surveyed Sundown from head to foot. "Well, you look like a cowhand, anyway." He smiled. "Looking for work, eh? I don't know, though, whether you'll find any or not. My payroll is full up. Might be the Lazy-E could use a bronc-snapper. Echardt, of that outfit, was saying yesterday he had a bunch of broom-tails that needed gentling. You could try Echardt. The Lazy-E lays about twenty miles northwest of Holster City —"

"If Echardt ain't closed out his ranch and gone fishing," the bartender interrupted, chuckling fatly.

29

"Fishing?" Sundown looked surprised. "Around here?"

Nort Windsor shook his head. "That's just a standing joke hereabouts, Mallare. Echardt was out to the coast one time, and now he's always saying he'd like to sell out and go to California and fish in the ocean. He could sure afford it too. I'll bet he's made a million out of cattle in his day. Whether he's got that million, I couldn't say. He's too damn' generous for his own good. He'd be a good man to work for if you could get on." He paused, pondering. "Whether or not the Flying-Box-9 needs any help, couldn't say. That's Zane Balter, their foreman, I was talking to just before Ton-and-a-Half called me. I'll ask him for you, if you like." Without waiting for Sundown's assent, he turned and called, "Hey, Zane, c'mere a minute!"

Zane Balter rocked up to Sundown and Nort Windsor. He was about Sundown's age, with greasy black hair and a swarthy dark skin. He wore overalls cuffed at the ankles, a flat-topped sombrero, and a cerise-colored shirt. The holster at his right thigh was scuffed and scratched. He had probably not shaved for the two past weeks. There was something sharply belligerent in the glance Balter threw Sundown as Windsor introduced the two men. Balter didn't offer to shake hands, just nodded shortly. Sundown returned the nod, drew deeply on his cigarette, and dropped the butt on the floor to be ground beneath his boot toe. Then he said to Balter,

"I'm looking for a job. Windsor, here, allowed you might know whether your outfit is taking on anybody."

"I do," Balter said shortly. "We ain't."

Sundown smiled thinly. "Brief and to the point. Thanks. I'm obliged for the news. It's plumb enlightening." There was just a touch of sarcasm in the tones that got under Balter's skin.

Windsor spoke quickly, sensing the hint of trouble brewing between the two. "That puts the matter strictly up to Echardt's Lazy-E then, Mallare, if Balter says the Flying-Box-9 is full up —"

"Yeah," Balter sneered. "It does. And if the Lazy-E is wise, they won't do any hiring of strangers neither."

"That so?" Sundown asked quietly. "You got any particular reason for talking that way, Balter?"

"I got plenty of reason," Balter flared, "the same being we don't want strangers in the Holster Basin." He cast a quick glance over his shoulder toward Jake Munson and Luis Montaldo who, drawn by Balter's loud voice, were listening to his words.

Jake Munson spoke, the words even-toned but carrying an edge, "You talking about anybody in particular, Balter?"

Some of the belligerency died from Balter's manner. "I wasn't talking about you, anyway, Jake."

"That's just fine," Munson said.

31

Luis Montaldo's teeth shone whitely in a smile. "Ees what you call 'eem superfine, Señor Balter. I'm theenk no one of us ees look for the trouble, no?"

"No!" Balter snapped.

"Ees vairy fine." Montaldo smiled again. He and Munson turned back to their drinks.

Sundown spoke to Balter: "I'm still asking your reason for objecting to strangers."

Balter glowered. "I'll give it to you, direct and to the point. We don't like strangers because there's too many cows being run off now as it is. Once strangers start pouring in, there's no telling where this thieving may stop. At present most everybody knows who his friends are" — again that quick glance toward Munson and Montaldo — "*most* everybody, I say. We'd like to keep it that way. So why don't you fork your bronc and try some other section, Mallare?"

"Maybe that's none of your business," Sundown said easily.

"Maybe I can make it my business," Balter half snarled.

By now others in the room were taking note of the angry conversation. Balter had, in a way, thrown down the gauntlet; he seemed bent on making trouble. A trifle too much liquor was back of that. Nort Windsor looked embarrassed and tried to quiet Balter.

"Look here, Zane," he protested, "you're just jumping to conclusions. Mallare came in here to inquire about work. He's done nothing to you.

Why not be a mite civil?"

"Aw, let him rave." Sundown grinned, shoving his sombrero to the back of his red hair. "When a man doesn't know how to carry his liquor, I'm never surprised when he starts running off at the mouth."

"You meaning me?" Balter bristled.

"If you feel like taking it that way," Sundown said quietly. He was trying to avoid trouble if possible. "I'd like to know just what you've got against me. I come here looking for work, and right off you commence to see red. Shucks, Balter, the kind of work I want hasn't a thing to do with a hidden running iron, if that's what's bothering you."

With an effort Balter curbed his temper. "Strangers in Holster Basin mean just one thing to me," he rasped. "Cow thieves, or sneaks. And by sneaks I mean cattle dicks. Never saw a one yet that was worth his salt."

A soft laugh parted Sundown's lips. "So you've got it into your head I'm a cattle detective, eh?" He threw back his head and laughed as though at something extremely humorous. "Jeepers, Balter! That's the last thing I expected to be accused of being. Think again, cowman. Now do I look like a cow dick?"

Balter swept him with a glance, realizing now he had said too much. "To tell the truth, you don't," he admitted grudgingly.

"And if I was," Sundown persisted, "would it annoy you much, Balter? You should know that no honest man fears the law."

Balter's eyes blazed hotly. "You hinting I'm not honest. Why, you —" He called Sundown a name.

Sundown stiffened. "How would you like to have your face knocked out from under your hat?" he snapped.

Nort Windsor intervened before Balter could make answer. "Look here, Zane," he said angrily, "you're going too far. There's no call for you to act this way. You'd best go on back to the Flying-Box-9 and sleep it off. Tomorrow, if you got any sense a-tall, you'll apologize to Mallare. You fool, can't you see he's trying to avoid trouble? Now go on, slope for home."

Balter stood glaring at Sundown a moment, then shrugged his shoulders and turned toward the doorway, muttering something to the effect that they could all go to hell. A second later the swinging doors closed at his back.

Nort Windsor turned back to the bar. He sighed deeply and ordered a whisky from the barkeeper. When the drink was served he downed it at a gulp, replaced the glass on the bar, and spoke to Sundown again. "Damn' it to hell! I don't know what we're going to do with Zane Balter. He's getting edgy as all hell. It's worry causes it, of course. His outfit, the Flying-Box-9, has lost more beef stock than any of us. Zane feels responsible, being he's foreman. He gets to frettin', then drinks a mite too much, and his temper grows plumb ornery. Just the sight of

34

a stranger in the basin starts him off. He suspects everybody he hasn't known for several years."

"Even cattle dicks, apparently," Sundown put in.

Again Windsor drew a deep sigh. "We brought an Association man down here some weeks back. We didn't know who he was when he came in, of course, but most of us suspected. The feller got to snooping into everybody's business in an effort to learn things. Most people didn't mind, but Zane resented it. Said it was an insult to his honor, or something of the sort. That's crazy, of course, but you know the way some men are built."

Sundown nodded, adding, "Didn't the detective do any good?"

Windsor shook his head. "He did a lot of riding. Even Zane settled down and became friendly with him, and commenced looking for miracles from the dick. When the dick didn't catch the thieves right off, Zane got disgusted and allowed as how cow detectives weren't much good."

"Did the Association man give up?" Sundown asked.

"I reckon he did," Windsor said moodily, "but it was forced on him. We found his dead body five days back. He'd been shot twice. Once through the head and through the body. From close up."

Sundown took a sip from his beer glass. "Just like that, eh? Shot to death out on the range?"

"He'd been buried, but not deep. The coyotes had dug him up. A cowhand from the Slash-Y was out looking for a horse that had run off, and had a dog with him. The dog ran across the body and set up a howling. Lucky the coyotes hadn't got around to doing much harm yet." Windsor drew another deep breath. "I don't know as it makes much difference, except to the feller's family, at that. Anyway, we shipped the body back to his home, after we'd notified the Association and got the address."

Sundown asked a question, and Windsor explained: "Sure, we knew who he was. His credentials were in his pocket. Feller name of Steve Wyatt."

Sundown said quietly, "This Wyatt must have run onto something and got caught at it."

"That's how it looks to me." Windsor frowned. "But it's got everybody in the basin plumb edgy. No telling when some cow thief is going to ambush a man —"

He broke off at a sudden voice from the vicinity of the entrance. Zane Balter stood there, just within the swinging doors, his features contorted to a scowling black mask.

"You, Mallare," he spat in ugly tones, "whose face were you threatening to knock from under his hat?"

Sundown swung around to face the angry man. He said easily, "Yours, if I recollect correctly, Balter."

"I'd advise you to change your mind, Mallare," Balter jerked out. "Either that, or get to work damn' sudden. I'm waiting for you!"

Balter already had his fist wrapped around the gun butt in his holster. He'd been ready to draw even before he pushed into the saloon, assuring himself of that much advantage should Sundown elect to go for his gun.

Strange Doings

Silence had fallen over the Royal Flush Saloon. The eyes of every man in the place were fixed on the ominous form of Zane Balter halted just within the entrance, face flushed with drink and anger, eyes hard, legs widespread. The man's right hand tightened on the butt of his Colt's forty-five, instantly ready to draw at Sundown Mallare's slightest movement.

Sundown forced a slow smile, though as yet he didn't say anything. His eyes slid sidewise, taking in Jake Munson and Luis Montaldo, and saw that both men were watching Balter. A couple of men standing at the bar near Sundown moved suddenly out of gunshot range and crossed the room to the opposite wall, their hurried steps scuffing loudly in the quiet of the bar-room.

"Look here, Zane," Ton-and-a-Half commenced in worried tones, "I don't figure to have —"

"Keep your mouth out of this, Fat," Balter snapped, "or you'll be next, when I've finished with Mallare."

"And when will that be?" Sundown asked quietly, stalling for time.

"Just the instant you raise nerve enough to make a fight out of this," Balter sneered. "What's the matter? Lost your guts?"

Sundown laughed softly. "You know," he said, "I haven't quite decided that point yet. I'm just thinking things over." He leaned back against the bar, resting his weight on his elbows. One boot heel was hooked on the brass rail near his feet. Various thoughts coursed swiftly through his mind: perhaps he could talk Balter out of his intentions; maybe it might be worth while to try jumping to one side, drawing and shooting as he moved — or he could draw without moving and — Balter's tones again intruded on his abstractions.

"Better make up your mind fast, Mallare," Balter was growling. "I ain't got all night." He fidgeted impatiently. "I'll give you just one chance. If you got sense enough to apologize to me and then fork your horse and get out of Holster City pronto —"

"Apologize for what?" Sundown queried.

Balter opened his mouth to speak, then hesitated, scowling. "You — you said something about knocking my face from under my hat. You want to take that back?"

Sundown said, and there was a certain touch of humor in his tones, "How could I take your face back when I never had it? And looking at it right now, I don't think I'd ever want it. I've sure as hell seen better-looking faces in my time, Balter — and anything that might happen to it

39

sure wouldn't improve it none —"

"Damn you, Mallare! I'm sick of this palavering! Either you pull your iron and go to work, or, by Gawd, I'll —"

"Look here, Balter," Sundown interposed. "My hand is nowhere near my gun butt. You've already got a grip on yours, ready to yank it clear of leather. How about you and me making an even break of this? Take your hand off your gun, then we'll both start our draw at the same time —"

"No, by Gawd! You're trying to trick me into something. Either you make up your mind —"

Jake Munson's voice interrupted Balter. Munson said sharply, "Balter, take your hand off that gun butt. If there's going to be any lead-throwing in here, Mallare is going to have an even chance."

Balter's jaw dropped. He glanced quickly toward Munson and saw that Munson had already filled his fist with the butt of his six-shooter. "Look here, Jake, this is none of your business —" he started a protest.

"I'm making it my business," Munson half-snarled. "I don't like to see a stranger come in here and get stepped on by any damn' fool who don't know enough to hold his liquor and then starts throwing challenges — after he's got his own draw half made. That sort of proposition smells, Balter, and so do you. If you like fighting, that's your business. If Mallare wants a ruckus, that's his. But you'd both better start off even.

You ain't took your hand off that gun yet, Balter. I don't want to have to tell you again."

Balter released the grip on his gun butt, glanced nervously at Sundown, then back to Munson. "I don't get the idea," he said.

"But you 'ave act wisely, Señor Balter," Luis Montaldo put in. "My frien' Jake he like to see the fighteeng 'andle' on the square basis. I'm theenk I'm feel he is correc'."

"Much obliged, gents." Sundown nodded toward Munson and Montaldo.

"Por nada," Montaldo said. "For notheeng. We like only to see the square deal, señor."

Munson didn't say anything, but turned back to his drink on the bar as though bored with the whole subject.

Sundown nodded again and swung his attention back to Balter. "You still feeling the same way, Balter? I could still knock your face from under your hat — or we can both go for our guns now. There's a new deal been made, hombre. Now it's up to you to call the turn."

Balter's eyes bored into Mallare's a moment, but before he could speak, Ton-and-a-Half took a hand in the game. He came puffing up from behind the bar, a sawed-off shotgun clutched in his beefy paws. The sawed-off weapon was swung in a short arc to cover both Mallare and Zane Balter.

"I don't figure," he panted heavily, "that neither of you two fellers are going to pull any guns in the Royal Flush. If you crave to sling lead, go

41

on outside and sling it in the street. My saloon ain't any Roman arena, so you two gladiators can tote your troubles into the open air. I don't aim to have my mirrors and glasses shot up — not if I can prevent it. But you two got an alternative — you can cool down and step to the bar and drink on the house. But if you start any shootin' in here, I swear I'll blow you both to hell."

Sundown swung around to face the bar, turning his back on Balter. "Jeepers!" He grinned. "We can throw lead any time, but free drinks come mighty infrequent."

Ton-and-a-Half nodded grimly, kept his shotgun leveled at Balter. "Come on, Zane, get up to this bar. This was all your fault in the first place. If you want to crook your elbow, do it with a shot of bourbon in front of you."

Nort Windsor got into the conversation. "Come on, Zane, forget it. Mallare isn't looking for any scrap. Let's have a drink and be friends all around."

Balter backed another step toward the doorway. "I'm not drinking," he growled sulkily. "This matter can be settled some other time when outsiders don't butt in" — at this point Jake Munson emitted a sarcastic laugh — "and when I ain't got a scatter-gun leveled at my head. Mallare, I'll square things with you another time."

"Any time you feel conditions are to your satisfaction" — Sundown spoke over one shoulder

42

— "just say the word — so long's it's outside the Royal Flush, and we'll meet with Colts, Winchesters, or fists. Take your pick. It's up to you!"

But Balter was already halfway to the door, and only a muttered curse drifted back. Sundown watched him until the man had barged through the swinging doors, then turned back to the bar, a quiet smile twitching his lips.

"Now that's settled," Ton-and-a-Half resumed in more placid tones, "we can resume the festivities." He stooped below the bar and replaced his shotgun, then straightened up. "If you waddies will float up to the bar I'd like to set 'em up for you. Things has certain reached a purty pass when an honest drink dispenser has to supply his stock free gratis in order to keep his joint from being wrecked. Men, name your reinforcements."

The patrons of the Royal Flush lined up at the bar while the ponderous barkeep set out glasses and bottles. For the next few moments little was heard except the clinking of glasses and some noisy gurglings. Ton-and-a-Half said to Sundown, "Sorry I had to throw my twin barrels on you, Mallare, but I couldn't show any favors."

"It's all right." Sundown laughed. "I understand how it is." He poured some more beer into his glass.

"Don't you pay Zane Balter's threats any attention, Mallare," Nort Windsor put in. "He's a good hombre at heart, but, like said, his tem-

43

per's been mighty hair-triggered of late. On top of that, he had one or two drinks too many tonight. He'll have forgotten it by tomorrow, and I hope you will have too."

"He didn't bother me to any extent. I've seen men get mad before. It just struck me sort of curious, though, him suspecting I was a range dick."

"Maybe not so funny if you think things out a mite," Windsor said. "I told you about that other dick, Wyatt, being found dead. Well, I suppose that it's more or less natural that Zane would think the Artexico Association would send another man into the basin to replace Wyatt."

"I suppose you could look at it that way," Sundown conceded. "But I don't see why the subject of range detectives would rile Balter so much."

"It's a touchy subject with him right now," Windsor explained. "Zane had been so upset when Wyatt didn't catch the thieves right off that he sort of shot off his mouth two or three times and what he said wasn't complimentary to Wyatt. Some folks got to thinking that maybe it was Zane had killed him. The upshot was that Dave Beadle — Beadle's our local deputy sheriff — rode out to the Flying-Box-9 and asked Zane a heap of questions. That riled Zane some more. Fortunately, he had an alibi."

"The alibi being?" Sundown asked.

"The fact that Zane was over to my place the day the detective was killed," Windsor explained. "That is, so far as the doctor could determine the time of death, after the body was found, which same wasn't too accurate, of course. A body can't be dead and buried and then have some medic put his finger smack dab on the instant he breathed his last. But, anyway, there was no proof could be found against Zane. Just the same, he nigh hits the ceiling every time a cattle dick is mentioned."

Windsor produced a sack of Durham and papers and rolled a cigarette. Sundown produced his own tobacco and followed suit. After lighting up, Windsor went on, "Trouble with Zane is, he's got a right good opinion of himself and the hot temper on top of that. But every man has some fault or other. Me, I've always maintained that a hot temper was a bad thing to have but a good thing to keep. And when you mingle a temper with a touch of swell head —"

"What's Balter got to be swell-headed about?" Sundown queried.

Windsor frowned. "Not too much, to tell the truth, except his gun work. He's fast — that is, shooting at targets, tin cans, and such. And accurate. I don't believe there's a hombre in Holster Basin to match him. He and I always got on all right, after one or two little arguments when we first met. But that was years and years ago. You'll like him when you get better acquainted."

Sundown was disinclined to agree, though he answered carelessly, "You're probably right, providing I'm around here long enough to get acquainted with Balter. I've got to get me a job some place. Just where did you say this Lazy-E outfit is located?"

"You'll find the ranch buildings out about twenty miles northwest of town," Windsor gave information, "not far from the Verde River — which ain't very wide, but furnishes good water. It sort of laces around the edge of the basin. My Window-Sash lies in the opposite direction, fifteen miles from here. The T.N. & A.S. railroad divides my holdings from Echardt's. On my west is the Flying-Box-9, owned by Chris Newland, with Zane Balter as foreman. Newland is sort of easy-going and a right white hombre. You see this whole basin is shaped like a gun holster. My spread occupies the part of the 'holster' where the gun barrel fits, and is second largest of the three main spreads hereabouts. The Lazy-E is the biggest, and lays in the part of the holster where you find the trigger guard and cylinder of a six-shooter. Newland's ranch, the Flying-Box-9, has the portion of the holster taken up by the gun hammer. His outfit is the smallest of us three —"

"No other outfits around here?" Sundown asked.

"Not in the basin, and such ranches as you'll find scattered on the rim of the basin, here and there, don't scarcely deserve the name of ranches. Just small stuff. As there's just the three of us owners in the basin, we don't bother

46

stringing any wire to amount to anything. In spite of our separate holdings, we consider it the same as open range, and us three owners run our stock together. Always hold calf-branding and beef roundup at the same time, of course."

"That's natural," Sundown nodded. "Well, I'm obliged for the information. I reckon I'll drift out to the Lazy-E tomorrow morning and see if Echardt has a job to offer."

"Good luck to you," Windsor said genially. "I'd like to see you land something and stay. We're a pretty good bunch here, at least we think we are. Except for the rustling I've mentioned, Holster City and the basin is kind of slow now, but she was sure a ripsnorter in the old days. Lots of history written in lead then. Well, I've got to be sloping along toward home. I'll see you some more, I hope. S'long."

"Adiós," Sundown replied.

Gradually men kept drifting from the saloon. Ton-and-a-Half moved along the bar, extinguishing two of the three lights swinging from the ceiling. Jake Munson and Luis Montaldo prepared to leave. They started past Sundown, then Munson halted, looking at the cowboy.

"I'll say much obliged to you again." Sundown smiled.

Munson said in his hard voice, "Forget it. I just never taken much to that Balter hombre, and if you was in for a scrap I wanted to see you get a square break."

Sundown said, "Why you interested in me?"

47

"It wasn't you in particular." Munson frowned. "I might have done the same for any man in the same fix."

Luis Montaldo put in, "Eef you do not get a job in theese parts, do not be in the hurree to leeve."

"Any particular reason?" Sundown asked.

"Might be we could give you a job," Munson supplied the answer. "You look like a rider to me."

"I can ride." Sundown nodded.

"You didn't lose your nerve when trouble came," Munson said. "You stacked up good. Might be we could use you."

Ton-and-a-Half was at the far end of the bar now. Sundown said, "What sort of job did you have in mind?"

"Does it make any difference if the pay is right?" Munson asked.

"Yeah, reckon it does," Sundown replied. "I like to know what a job is before I sign on the payroll."

Munson's hard face grew still harder. "Maybe you're too damn' particular," he rasped.

"Maybe I am," Sundown said easily.

Surprisingly enough, Munson didn't take offense. "Sometimes it pays to be particular," he conceded. "C'mon, Luis, let's get out of here."

He strode toward the swinging doors with no further word. Montaldo lingered but a moment, saying to Sundown, "Eef you do not get the job, steeckaround theese parts. We weel see you

48

again. Maybee then you take a job weeth us. *Adiós,* Señor Mallare."

"*Adiós,*" Sundown repeated. A small frown gathered on his forehead as he watched the two men depart.

Ton-and-a-Half came down the bar. Sundown shook his head to indicate he needed no further service. He said good night a few minutes later and headed for the street. The swinging doors banged at his rear.

He was about to step toward the hitch rack when he heard his name called. Turning, he saw the weighty bartender standing on the saloon porch.

"You'll find the Lone Star Livery just across the street," the big man said as he moved out to the sidewalk. "Thought I'd better tell you, in case you didn't know. Zed Danvers owns it, but there'll likely be a nightman on now. Tell him I sent you across, should he kick up any fuss about your bunkin' in his hay."

"Thanks, Ton-and-a-Half," Sundown said, and waited, feeling sure the big barkeep hadn't come out just to give him the location of the livery stable. "And thanks for what you did for me tonight."

"Don't mention it, son." He paused awkwardly. "A spell back did I hear Jake Munson offer you a job?"

"You've got sharp ears."

"Sometimes I need 'em," the big man grunted. "I'd go slow if I was you. We don't know much

49

hereabouts regardin' Jake Munson and Luis Montaldo. They come and go, and they're right close-mouthed — but sometimes those sharp ears you mentioned hear things."

"What sort of things?" Sundown squinted through the gloom trying to make out the big man's features against the background of lighted doorway.

"Nothing much," Ton-and-a-Half grunted reluctantly, "but one morning there was nobody but them two in the Royal Flush. Between serving drinks I'd been out back stacking some beer cases. They didn't notice when I came back in. Montaldo was talkin' at the time — no, he wasn't saying anythin' in particular — and here's the point: he was talkin' as good English, or American, whatever you like to call it, as you and me, without the least trace of that Mex accent he uses when folks are around."

"The accent is a fake, then?" Sundown asked.

"As phony as the snow tinsel on a kid's Christmas tree," Ton-and-a-Half said earnestly. "The instant he sees me come into the saloon, he starts talkin' that broken Mex palaver."

"What does it prove?" Sundown wanted to know.

The fat man scratched his head. "Damn' if I know," he admitted, "except there's sort of strange doings on the prowl is my guess. Otherwise, why should Montaldo be puttin' on an act?"

"You tell me and I'll tell you. And you don't

50

know anything about 'em, eh?"

"No more than I've already told you, son. So you think twice before you take any job with 'em. Whatever they're up to, I'd say Montaldo was the leader. He talks the most and smiles a lot — though I can't say he ever says much. Jake Munson — well, Munson is one hard customer to buck, if you ask me. I ain't sayin' he's a crook, mind you, but I'd hate like the devil to cross his trail and not be ridin' his way, if you know what I mean."

"I get you. What about Zane Balter?"

"Aw-w, reckon Zane's all right, if he don't drink too much. Then he gets proddy. And he's got an idea he's a fast gun."

"Is he?" Sundown asked.

"I never knew of him beatin' anybody to the draw. But neither did I ever see him draw against anybody. But he can sure shoot hell outten tin cans and a mite faster than anybody else I've watched doin' it."

Sundown nodded. "Thanks again. I'll bear in mind what you say."

"Forget it." The big man turned and moved ponderously back into his saloon. The bat-wing doors swung at his back.

Sundown glanced both ways along the darkened street. There were but a few dim lights to be seen. Overhead the stars were low and sharper than a coyote's tooth in the indigo sky. There didn't seem to be any movement on either side of the roadway. "I guess," Sundown told himself, "Balter isn't the kind that lies in wait to ambush a man. Or maybe tonight isn't his night for ambushing."

He strode around the end of the hitch rack, picked up Coffee-Pot's reins and led the pony across the street to the Lone Star Livery. Arriving, he was forced to awaken the nightman, who was fast asleep in an armchair. The man rose, rubbing his eyes, put up Sundown's horse, then gave the cowboy permission to sleep in the hayloft.

Sundown climbed to the loft and for a time lay stretched out in the fragrant hay, mulling over the events of the past few hours. Balter might be all right, when strictly sober; that was for time to decide. Nort Windsor seemed a likable enough cuss. Ton-and-a-Half looked like solid gold, a man to tie to in a pinch. Montaldo? Munson? Mentally, Sundown shrugged his shoulders. Again, time might tell. *Quién sabe?* He dismissed the pair from his mind and his thoughts turned to the Lazy-E outfit. He wondered if Curry Echardt would have a job for him. Oh, well, if he didn't, something else would turn up. *Mañana* was another day. . . .

Sundown Goes Down

It was broad daylight when Sundown opened his eyes. He reached for his sombrero, thrust it to the back of his flaming thatch of hair, then drew on his boots. He rolled a brown paper cigarette but didn't light it until he had climbed down the ladder from the loft. On the lower floor, after paying the proprietor of the livery, he saddled his roan pony and rode into the street. The morning sunshine angled down hotly on Holster City's main thoroughfare; there were but few people abroad. Here and there a pony stood before a hitch rack. Sundown glanced across the street toward the Royal Flush Saloon, but it hadn't yet opened. Farther east along Main he saw a sign on a false-fronted frame building that proclaimed it to be the Kansas City Chop House. Here he dismounted, entered, and enjoyed a breakfast of ham and eggs, coffee, hot biscuits, and pie.

It was shortly after eight-thirty when Sundown stepped up to his saddle again. There were more people on the street now. Ton-and-a-Half was busily engaged with a broom on the porch of the Royal Flush. He glanced up as Sundown momentarily drew rein to say "Good morning," set his broom carefully to one side, then moved heavily out to the hitch rail.

"I was wonderin' if you'd left town yet," he said. "Now to get to the Lazy-E you turn northwest at the end of town. You'll see the trail, and you won't have any trouble —"

Sundown cut in, "Nort Windsor gave me directions last night."

"That's good. Hope you land on with Curry Echardt. He's a white man, and if he took a liking to you, he might put you on his payroll even if there wasn't much to do. He's right well fixed with cash. He could retire right now if he wanted to. Like we told you last night, he's always threatenin' to sell out and go to California and fish. I reckon it's just Virginia — that's his daughter — keeps him here. She likes the Holster Basin country —"

"What's she like?"

Ton-and-a-Half chuckled fatly. "A looker if you ask me — or any other man 'round here. Lots of fellers tried sparkin' her, but they never seemed to get any place. Her maw died years ago, and Virginia sort of runs the house for Curry. Somethin' else, if Curry Echardt takes you on, you'd best tell him about Munson and Montaldo takin' your part in that ruckus with Zane Balter last night. It would be best if Curry hears that from your own lips before anybody else gets to tellin' it."

Sundown studied the fat man for a moment. "Why?"

54

The barkeep explained: "Them two bein' under suspicion around here like they are, some folks might think it queer them sidin' you that way. It might be thought you just pretended not to know them."

"That's an idea at that," Sundown conceded.

They talked a few minutes longer, then Sundown kicked Coffee-Pot in the ribs and continued on his way. Within a short time the roan pony was loping off across country, and Holster City grew rapidly smaller at its rear.

The trail to the Lazy-E was wheel-rutted and well worn, and Sundown had no trouble following it, as it led up gradual slopes only to descend in the same leisurely fashion on the opposite side. All rolling country along here. Occasionally the rider passed through small forests of scrub pine, mesquite, and chaparral when he struck high ground. The lower levels were carpeted with lush waving grass. At times, in ascending a slope, Sundown passed rocky ridges, upflung in rather grotesque formations. Now and then the trail led through narrow gulches and across dry washes.

The sun was hot and bright. A few fleecy clouds chased each other lazily across the cerulean sky. Sundown whistled as he rode. Suddenly, as he urged the pony up a rather steep rise of ground, he ceased whistling and checked the pony's gait just as he reached the crest of the incline. Only a short distance below him he saw a standing horse. A rope's length away from the animal was a calf, sprawled on its side and with three of its feet tied together. Beyond was another rise of land, covered thickly with greasewood and manzanita.

Sundown came to a complete stop. Except for the horse and calf, there wasn't a living thing in view. The rider was evidently back in the brush, gathering fuel for a branding fire, Sundown guessed. His guess proved to be correct. Within a few minutes a man emerged from the thicket, carrying an armload of twigs and dry branches. His back was turned to Sundown, and he apparently didn't dream there was another human being within miles of him.

A few feet to Sundown's left a great outcropping of sandstone rose from the earth. Moving slowly, he reined Coffee-Pot behind the big rock, out of sight, where he could view what followed. Within a few minutes a thin column of greasy smoke was ascending from the briskly burning heap of twigs. Sundown was near enough to hear the crackling of the fire now and then when the wind lifted the sounds to his ears. He reached down and placed one hand about Coffee-Pot's nose, that the horse might not whinny its proximity to the unknown man's mount.

"Dang funny," was the thought that coursed through Sundown's mind. "Both Balter and Windsor mentioned rustlers last night and this sure *looks* suspicious. At the same time, that hombre down there, below, might be on the level. Maybe he just picked up a stray that was missed during roundup."

The man bending over the fire finally rose, a short length of iron rod, one end glowing hot, in his hand, and approached the helpless calf. Instantly Sundown reined his pony out from behind the sheltering rock and spurred down the slope, at the same time muttering, "If that hombre's on the square, there'll be no objections to me saying 'hello' to him. If he's not — well, we'll see what we'll see."

He descended the incline at an easy running walk. The man was bending low over the calf, just about to apply the hot iron to its hide, when he heard Sundown's approach. Like a flash he came erect, dropping the iron and swinging about to face the approaching horse, one hand reaching toward the holster at his right hip.

Sundown had been prepared for that. Even before the man's fingers had touched gun butt, Sundown's gun had flashed into view. "Don't draw, waddy!" he yelled warningly.

By this time he had caught sight of the mother cow, also hog-tied and sprawled on her side, behind a clump of mesquite farther down the slope.

The rustler, if rustler he was, raised both arms high in the air. Six-shooter still leveled, Sundown reined his pony to a stop at the side of the crackling fire. The man with the upraised arms glowered at him, but maintained a sulky silence.

"Nice morning for branding," Sundown

observed dryly. "I figured calf roundup was finished long ago in this basin."

"It was," the man growled. "Me, I'm just pickin' up strays here and there. What in hell's the idea of throwin' down on me like this?"

"Saw you reaching for your gun," Sundown said cheerfully. "I just didn't want to take chances. What was your idea?"

"I don't take any chances, neither," the fellow replied, forcing a smile. "I reckon we're both mistaken. But there's too many cow thieves around for me to get careless."

Sundown nodded. "That being the case, you can lower your arms. You and I haven't any fight — yet." He replaced his gun in holster. "I note you got the cow tied down too."

"Yeah," the fellow replied. "She objected right strenuously to me ropin' her dogie, so I had to tie her down while I worked."

That was reasonable enough too. Still, Sundown wasn't quite convinced. He turned away a moment, reining his horse to get a better look at the calf's side — at least that was the idea he endeavored to give the other man.

Instantly the man reached for his gun, but Sundown was too fast for him. A streak of light flashed along his blued-steel barrel as his weapon leaped out — up — the movement halting in a burst of black powder smoke and white flame.

The two reports blended almost as one, the rustler's shot missing its mark, while Sundown's didn't. The rustler staggered back, weaved about a moment on weakening legs, then crashed forward and lay still.

Sundown looked grimly down on the silent figure a moment, then reholstered his gun and stepped down from the saddle. Stooping, he carefully turned the body on its back. The man was dead.

"Damn it all," Sundown growled, "I didn't want it this way. I'd figured to just wound him, then learn what's what. But he was too fast to trifle with, and — well, it was him or me. His very actions proved him guilty, but still, I just don't like killing."

He stood a moment longer, considering, then moved away from the body and over to the prone calf which struggled a little as he approached. The small animal showed plainly on one side a Lazy-E brand. A short distance away lay the cow. Investigation proved that it, too, carried the Lazy-E marking. Sundown came back to the fire, noting the small section of wet blanket and the canteen standing near.

"Just ready to do a mite of blotting on that brand," Sundown said soberly. "Yep, his actions proved him guilty all right. Picking up strays, he said. I never did quite believe that. Figured to burn a new brand on both animals. Wonder what brand he had in mind?"

He looked from the dead cow thief to the calf, then at the cow thief's horse, as though to find some marking that would give him the information he wanted. "Let's see," Sundown mused, "there's only two other big outfits hereabouts, the Flying-Box-9 and the Window-Sash." His eyes widened a trifle as they took in the Lazy-E design on the calf's brown hide. "Jeepers! It wouldn't require much burning to change this into either of those other two markings. Course, maybe this rustler was figuring to burn something entirely different." Sundown shook his head and heaved a long sigh. "Well, I reckon there's not much else to do except go through this hombre's pockets for some identification, then load him on his pony and take him in to the deputy at Holster City."

He had just started to stoop toward the dead rustler when something struck his head a terrific blow. Simultaneously, from the crest of the next rise of ground, came the sharp crack of a repeating rifle. With his final bit of waning strength Sundown turned toward the sound, then his legs buckled and he pitched to earth, his right hand already closing, automatically, about the butt of his six-shooter, as he went down. As he struck the ground his sombrero fell off and rolled a couple of feet away.

Silence descended on the scene. Sundown's pony turned its head inquisitively toward the prone figure huddled on the sandy earth. The bound calf started to struggle slightly, but gave up after a feeble effort. Flies droned near, drawn by the freshly spilled blood.

Abruptly a pair of horsemen appeared over the

top of the rise. Loping quickly down to the branding fire, they pulled to a halt and dismounted. One went to look at the dead rustler, while the other approached Sundown. He eyed the blood matting Sundown's red hair, then turned him on his back. One glance at the bloodless features convinced the man. "I got him dead to rights," he announced triumphantly. "Thought as much. I don't often miss at that distance."

The other man scowled. "Sid's dead too. This hombre must have surprised Sid right in the middle of the job. Sid tried though — his gun's out." He came over and stood looking down at Sundown, then moved across and examined the Winchester on the cowboy's saddle. "I can't say I like the looks of this," he said soberly.

His companion cursed. "I hate to lose Sid, but, dammit, it served him right! More than once I've warned him not to do any branding along this trail here. You never know who might be coming from the Lazy-E."

"It's too late to fret about that now. The thing for us to do is let these cow animals loose and clear out pronto before anybody comes along. We can take Sid's body with us. This other hombre we should bury, or hide some place, but we ain't got time. We'll just have to leave him for the coyotes and buzzards. You pick up Sid's things. I'll release the calf and cow. We can't take time to brand 'em now. I suppose they were convenient, and Sid always was too lazy to pop his animals out of the brush."

He turned away and quickly loosened the ropes binding cow and calf. The animals lumbered away from the scene as fast as their legs could carry them. The dead Sid was placed across the saddle of his horse and lashed with a lariat into place. Meanwhile, the man's pardner was engaged in stamping out the now-smoldering branding fire. Stooping, he retrieved the running iron the dead rustler had dropped and started for his horse. On the way he once more passed Sundown's silent form. At sight of the motionless figure, a sudden rage possessed the man. "Damn you and all your sneaking breed," he cursed. "Always sticking your nose in where it ain't wanted. For a plugged peso I'd take time to heat this iron and brand you, as a warning to show folks what happens to hombres who snoop into things that ain't none of their business."

By this time the other man was in his saddle, leading behind him the dead rustler's horse with its lifeless burden. "Come on," he urged impatiently, looking fearfully about, "we got to get out of here. Don't you be getting any crazy ideas. I want to slope mighty pronto. The law's awful tough on murderers —"

"The law be damned and you too," the other sneered, though he realized the truth that lay in his pardner's words. "You're just plain chicken-hearted. All right, all right, hold your hawses. I'm coming."

Suddenly, in an abrupt display of temper he raised the running iron and swung it savagely at Sundown's defenseless forehead. A scarlet gash appeared instantly along the unconscious cowboy's eyebrows. "Take that, you goddam' cow nurse! I wish you was alive to feel it!"

Still cursing, he turned and ran toward his waiting horse. Neither man spoke, though in the eyes of the one who had been urging his companion to hurry there was something of contemptuous disgust, almost horror, for the other's mad action. Within a few minutes they had led the dead rustler's horse, with its former owner's arms and legs dangling limply on either side of the saddle, out of sight over a rise of land.

But Sundown Mallare wasn't dead. Warned by some inner sense, he had doubtless moved a trifle at the moment his murderous assailant had fired, and the rifle bullet had cut through his thick mop of reddish hair and furrowed an ugly wound along the top of his head. The blow from the running iron was by far more serious than the wound made by the rifle.

For hours Sundown lay out under the broiling Southwest sun. Buzzards circled and floated on sluggish wings overhead but made no attempt to draw near. Perhaps they sensed he wasn't dead. Perhaps it was the presence of the faithful Coffee-Pot, standing patiently near, that kept the scavengers at a distance.

Eventually Sundown's eyelids lifted on darkness. For a moment he couldn't comprehend what had happened. His head ached as though it would split. He struggled to a sitting position, shaking his head as though to dispel the cobwebs that clouded his brain. Shaking his head only made the pain worse, but it did succeed in clearing his mind.

"That cow thief must have had a friend — or friends — close by," Sundown muttered, "and they let me have it as soon as they saw me intruding on their little job. Maybe it serves me right." The words came bitterly. "I must be getting dim-witted not to have thought he might have pards near. I should have been on the lookout." He swore softly under his breath, then, "Good cripes, it's dark. No moon, no stars. Can't even see my pony."

With an effort he struggled erect. A wave of dizziness passed over him, then he got his balance again. "Coffee-Pot, you good-for-nothing, flea-bitten bag of skin and bones, where you at?"

A whinny reached him through the darkness. Sundown's heart leaped. "Still here, are you?" he said affectionately. "I'll be right with you. Don't go to shyin' away from me now. This is no time for foolishness."

He groped about on the ground and, luckily, located his sombrero. A wry laugh parted his lips as he fingered the bullet holes in the crown. "Let this be a lesson to me," he said, "never to lower my guard again." Then, led by further sounds from his horse, he staggered through darkness until he could touch the animal.

"Hold still, now, Coffee-Pot, until I get my canteen. My head aches like a thousand devils was inside, pounding with sledge hammers, and I got a thirst on me that needs a heap of moisture. Reckon you have too. I'll save you a drink out of my canteen, if you don't mind me pouring it down your throat. My hat won't hold water any more." He forced another bitter laugh. "Sometimes wonder if it ever held brains."

He tilted the canteen and drank long of its contents. As the lukewarm water trickled down his parched throat and laved his swollen mouth, he commenced to feel a trifle better. Quite suddenly something else occurred to him. Coffee-Pot's saddle, when he had felt it, was hot to the touch! Sundown's aching brow furrowed as he listened to the whirring of insects. Why — why, these weren't night sounds. There were no night birds, either. It was still daylight. The sun was warm on his face.

Tragic comprehension swept over him in a rush. "Coffee-Pot," he exclaimed, choking, "it's not night at all. It's — daylight — and I can't see! My God, I've gone blind!"

"My Light's Disappeared!"

Virginia Echardt, daughter of the owner of the Lazy-E Ranch, was traveling at an easy lope, the following morning, on her way to Holster City to pick up the mail. At her side rode Rawhide Lacey, one of her father's cowpunchers. Since rustling had become prevalent in the Holster Basin, and particularly after the murder of Steve Wyatt, Curry Echardt felt it would be safer if someone from the Lazy-E always accompanied his pretty twenty-year-old daughter on her rides about the country. That morning, it happened, the task fell to Rawhide Lacey. Rawhide was all that the name implies — lean, lengthy, sinewy, and tanned — and fully as toughly built as the material from which he derived his nickname. He wore the usual cow-puncher togs and was somewhere in the vicinity of thirty years of age.

The girl and the man urged their ponies across a shallow dry wash, then started up an incline to the level once more, Virginia's mount in the lead. As she gained the crest of the slope, the girl sharply drew rein, an involuntary exclamation of surprise parting her lips.

"What's up, Miss 'Ginny?" Rawhide called sharply. "See a rattler or something?"

He spurred quickly to the girl's side, then he, too, saw what she was looking at. Fifty yards ahead of them on the trail a tall cowboy was stumbling along, leading behind him a roan cow pony. He, too, appeared to be headed for Holster City, though something seemed definitely lacking in the cowboy's sense of direction.

Rawhide and Virginia drew rein and watched his maneuvers for a few moments. The progress the cowboy was making was certainly a stumbling one. At times he would wander from the trail, then stagger back again. Twice he fell to his knees, only to climb erect with some difficulty and continue doggedly on.

"Drunk!" Rawhide announced enviously. "The lucky stiff. I wonder where he got it."

"Drunk?" Virginia asked dubiously. "Do you think he is? He looks as though he had been hurt. His clothing is all dust, and that last time he got up after his fall I thought I saw blood on his face, though I couldn't be sure. His sombrero shadows his features."

"Sure." Rawhide laughed. "Blood, dust. Aces to tens he's been fighting. What a ripsnortin' brannigan he's been on! Danged if some hombres don't have all the luck!"

Virginia gave a small sniffing sound and her nose wrinkled. "Rawhide, do you think getting drunk is anything to be proud of?"

Rawhide shifted uneasily in his saddle under the girl's steady glance. "We-ell, maybe not, now that I give the matter due consideration. A man should be able to handle his load without staggerin'. Now that you mention it, I'm commencing to feel that waddy up ahead there is a plumb disgrace to the whole Holster Basin. Nothin' like that has ever happened hereabouts before." A grin tugged at his wide mouth. "Want I should ride ahead and reprimand him, Miss 'Ginny? Or maybe I could persuade him to sign the pledge. It's times like this a feller is most amenable to pledge-signin'." He sighed. "I should know."

The girl smiled slightly. "Oh, Rawhide, be sensible."

"It's being sensible that makes me talk like this. Boy howdy! I'll bet that feller's head is achin' like boilermakers is at work inside of it."

"Well, I don't think he's drunk at all," Virginia stated. "Let's go see."

"Whatever you say, but remember I warned you, Miss 'Ginny."

"Warned me, fiddlesticks!" Virginia retorted. "Come on."

They urged their horses into movement, Rawhide trying to persuade the girl to let him investigate first. But Virginia refused to listen.

By this time the object of their attentions had caught sound of their voices. He had come to a halt, swinging around to face their approach, and stood there, listening intently and swaying uncertainly on his legs.

"Rawhide, he's not drunk!" Virginia cried.

"He's been injured." She quickened the movements of her mount. "I knew I was right!"

In a moment she and Rawhide had come abreast of Sundown Mallare. His face was turned in the direction of their voices. Rawhide, too, now realized the cowboy had been hurt. Blood had dried across his nose and down one cheek.

"Somethin' wrong, cow poke?" Rawhide asked.

"We-ell, sort of." Sundown spoke hesitantly. "I seem to have lost my way. I'd be obliged to you folks if you'd put me right on the road to Holster City." The words came with difficulty.

"Why, you're on the right trail now," Virginia answered. "All you have to do is just keep straight ahead." She was eying the ugly red welt that ran across Sundown's eyebrows.

At sound of the girl's voice Sundown put up one hand to remove his sombrero. Virginia and Rawhide noted his red hair was matted with coagulated blood. "That's just the trouble," Sundown was saying, "I seem to have trouble keeping 'straight ahead.' " He forced a slight smile. "I keep getting tangled in my directions."

"What happened to you, cowboy?" Rawhide asked, gazing into Sundown's gray eyes. There was something vague about those eyes. Rawhide considered: they didn't meet a man's look squarely.

"I was headed for the Lazy-E, to see if I could

69

get on as a hand," Sundown explained. He was finding it more difficult to remain erect now, and it was necessary to exert every ounce of his will to overcome that dizziness that kept overtaking his senses. "I ran into a feller getting ready to draw funny pictures with a hot iron. We had a ruckus, but managed to down him. Then somebody threw a chunk of lead at me from a rifle and connected —"

Rawhide slipped from his saddle with some haste, and just in time to catch Sundown as the wounded man's legs wilted beneath him. "Take it easy, waddy. I'm just plumb dumb not to have noticed before that you needed some help."

Virginia passed down her canteen. Sundown took a long draught and then straightened sheepishly. "I reckon I must have lost a heap of blood or something. My head feels like it had connected with a bronc's hoof too . . ." He continued talking, but his words were rambling, unsteady, and lacked continuity.

"We'll take him with us at once," Virginia informed Rawhide. "The sooner we get him to the Lazy-E, the better. He was headed that way in the beginning. Besides, it's nearer than Holster City."

Sundown caught the words. "No use taking me to the Lazy-E now," he protested thickly. "I was after a job there, but under the circumstances, I couldn't hold one —"

"Nonsense," Virginia cut in crisply. "You'll be all right when your wounds heal. I'm Virginia

Echardt. My father owns the Lazy-E." She, too, was noticing that his eyes failed to focus on the person to whom he was talking. There was a queer, indefinite look about them. They were rather nice eyes too.

"Pleased to know you, Miss Echardt," Sundown said, holding to consciousness with an effort. "You don't understand. I'm thanking you for the offer — but — but — you see, my name's Sundown Mallare — only maybe the name should be Sun*out* — because my light's sure disappeared. I can't see anything —"

"Are you trying to say you're blind?" Virginia exclaimed, puzzled by the confused explanation.

"That's it," Sundown said. "Yep, I can't see one solitary thing. I'd get on my horse, but I keep slipping out of the saddle. Never did remember going down — just the times I got up. Figured I'd better walk — not have so far to fall —"

He sagged suddenly in Rawhide's arms, and the sightless gray eyes closed. He was a dead weight in the other man's grasp.

"I'll be damned," Rawhide said grimly, endeavoring to hold Sundown upright. "I'm beggin' your pardon, Miss 'Ginny, but I couldn't help it. The murdering skunks that did this should be made to stretch a rope —"

"Never mind the apologies, or any other kind of talk, Rawhide," Virginia broke in swiftly. "Under certain circumstances a few 'damns' can be excused. You just said what was in my mind. I'm going to get this man home as soon as pos-

71

sible. You get him up into his saddle, then tie him securely so he can't fall off. There's a lariat hanging on his horn — it looks almost new too."

Spurred to action by the girl's words, Rawhide did as ordered. Within a few minutes Sundown's limp form was tightly trussed on Coffee-Pot's back. He slumped down over the saddlehorn, but the lashed rope prevented his falling from the saddle.

"There you are." Rawhide was panting slightly from his efforts. "What next? Want I should lead Mallare's pony?"

Virginia shook her head. "You climb on your pony and get to Holster City as fast as it'll take you," Virginia said. "Find Dr. Pearson and bring him back with you. I'll take this man home and have him comfortable by the time you arrive —"

"But, Miss 'Ginny," Rawhide protested earnestly, "we can't do that. Curry ordered you should never be left to ride alone. He —"

"Do as I say." The girl's tones were commanding. "I know what Dad's orders were, but this is a different matter —"

"Curry ain't going to like it," Rawhide persisted in troubled tones. "He's like to skin the hide off'n me if —"

"I'll fix it with Dad," Virginia said impatiently. "Now go on, get going. Make it clear to Dr. Pearson that this is an emergency. And don't worry about me; I'll be all right." She patted the holstered six-shooter suspended at one side of her deerskin riding skirt. "Get started, Rawhide."

With no further word of protest Rawhide nodded and leaped into his saddle. An instant later his pony was raising clouds of dust along the trail that led to Holster City. Then Virginia turned her mount and, gathering up Coffee-Pot's reins, led the roan pony and its unconscious burden along the way that ran to the Lazy-E Ranch.

"You've Got a Job!"

Sundown regained consciousness to find himself bound into his saddle. Coffee-Pot had been stopped just within the white-washed gateway fronting Curry Echardt's big rambling ranch house. Virginia had dismounted and stood some feet away. Echardt himself, a tall, lean, kindly man with iron-gray hair and weathered features, helped Sundown to the ground after releasing the rope which had held the cowboy in his saddle.

"Seems like we — we arrived some place," Sundown mumbled. His head cleared a trifle after a moment, and he tried his best to smile.

"I'm Curry Echardt — Virginia's father." The hearty voice reached Sundown's ears. "You're at my place — the Lazy-E."

Sundown felt a hand grasp his own. Already the cowboy was learning the feel of things. Echardt's hand was big, vigorous, with long, strong fingers that felt good to the touch. It needed just that to make Sundown take to the man.

Echardt said something to Virginia about preparing a bed for Sundown. Sundown protested that, trying to make it clear he didn't want to be put to bed. He insisted he felt all right, except for his eyes and a little dizziness. Maybe some food would help that; he hadn't eaten for a spell. Echardt still thought he'd be better off un-dressed and between blankets, but after a quick glance and shaking of the head from Virginia, Sundown had his way.

They helped him into the big main room of the house and placed him in a chair. Then Virginia went to get food. At the first swallow Sundown commenced to feel better. He sat straighter in his chair. Once food and coffee — the coffee was cold but strong — had been put away, Virginia proceeded to care for his wounds. She cleansed and dressed the bullet-made furrow at the top of Sundown's head, then gave her attention to the ugly bruise across the cowboy's eyebrows. By now this had turned purple, though the skin wasn't badly broken, nor had there been a great deal of bleeding at this point.

Once Sundown broke in on the proceedings with a request that Coffee-Pot be taken care of. "That little pony hasn't had —"

"Don't fret about your horse," Echardt said. "I've already had one of my hands see to him. I gave orders for food, water, and a good rub-down."

"I'm obliged to you," Sundown said, and Virginia went on with her bandaging.

With food in his stomach and washed and cleaned up, Sundown was feeling much better. Echardt suggested that he stretch out for a spell and get some rest. Sundown declined. "I'm feeling right chipper now. If I could only see, everything would be fine as silk. I'll be drifting on after a little."

Immediately he sensed the touch of injury in Echardt's make-up. "Most folks," the big man complained, "don't turn down my hospitality that way. Not only that, you can't go yet. I want to hear your story when you feel like talkin'. Besides, 'Ginny sent to Holster City for Doc Pearson. You can't leave until he's seen you."

"That wasn't necessary —" Sundown commenced.

"I happen to think it is," Virginia said quietly. She laughed softly. "If not on your account, on mine. I don't want the responsibility of your healing, not if I can get the doctor to take it. For all I know, I may have treated your wounds the wrong way or something."

Sundown said at once that he doubted that, and Echardt put in a remark to the effect that he figured to keep Sundown at the Lazy-E for a day or two, anyway.

Sundown thanked them and automatically reached for his Durham and papers. There'd been certain difficulties when he'd eaten: occasionally he had spilled bits of food down his shirt front. Now he was having trouble with his tobacco. A large quantity of the grains from the Durham sack spilled to the floor before reaching the cigarette paper.

Echardt said considerately, "Better let me roll

that smoke for you." He avoided reference to Sundown's blindness. "Your hands are kind of shaky yet."

Sundown was grateful for that. Echardt rolled half-a-dozen cigarettes and placed them near Sundown's hand where it rested on a table beside his chair. Then he placed one of the cigarettes in Sundown's mouth and held a lighted match until the end of the tobacco was glowing.

After the first two or three mouthfuls of gray smoke had drifted from Sundown's lips, a puzzled expression crept into his features. "Tobacco doesn't seem the same when you can't see the smoke," he announced. "Lots of times when I've smoked at night, out on the range, I've noticed that you've got to see the smoke or the red end of the cigarette to really enjoy it. Well, suppose I'll just have to get used to not seeing my smoke for a spell. It's a funny feeling, having your lights put out all at once like this. My eyes don't hurt any either."

Virginia and Echardt exchanged quick glances. Ordinary men would have found it difficult not to give way in the face of such tragedy. They could see Sundown was holding his will with a steel rein now — accepting this unexpected affliction like a man. Echardt gazed at the wide-open gray eyes, finding it extremely hard, even now, to realize they were sightless. He sensed the struggle that was taking place within the cowboy. To occupy Sundown's mind, he suggested that Sundown tell him all that had happened.

"Of course," Echardt said, " 'Ginny has told me what you related to her, but I reckon it wasn't all — or I might have lost some of it in the excitement of your arrival."

Sundown launched into a recital of his story from the time he had reached Holster City. At mention of Zane Balter, Echardt frowned. "Yeah, Zane does get a mite quarrelsome at times," Echardt said, "but I don't think he had any call to jump you in such fashion. He needs speakin' to."

Sundown continued with his story until he had reached the part played by Jake Munson and Luis Montaldo. "I don't see," Echardt said sharply, "why those two should jump in and take your part. Did you know them from some place else?"

"Never saw them before in my life," Sundown said earnestly.

"What kind of a job did they offer you?" Echardt frowned.

"I can't tell you that either," Sundown said.

"I figure you was smart not to take it," Echardt growled. "Us folks in the basin would give a heap to know what those two are doing. But so long as they mind their business, there's not much we can do about it. And with all the cow stealing going on nowadays —" He broke off and swore under his breath.

"Now, Dad," Virginia interposed, "there's no

use you getting into a temper. Wait until you've lost as many cows as the Flying-Box-9, then you'll have something to really get mad about."

"I'd be blasted if I'd stay around here that long," Echardt snorted. "I'd sell the Lazy-E first, and then go out to California where I could sit on the beaches and fish. Damn! I never did get enough of fishing in my life — But I'm interrupting, Sundown. Get on with your story."

Echardt had lighted a big black cigar by this time. Virginia was seated at his side, listening. Echardt didn't speak again until Sundown had nearly finished.

". . . and it was just a couple of minutes after that brand artist and I had our lead-throwing party," Sundown concluded, "that I heard the rifle crack. At the same moment the slug struck me. Then my lights went out. I don't know how long I was unconscious, but as I come to figure it now, I must have laid there the rest of that day and all night and then woke up this morning sometime. After a spell I got myself straightened out a mite and I climbed into the saddle. I think I was headed for Holster City, but I can't be certain. After a time I got sort of faint in the head, and I felt myself slipping. When I woke up again I was on the ground, still clutching my pony's reins. I got back into the saddle, and the same thing happened again. Eventually I figured it might be better to walk. I passed out a heap of times then too."

He couldn't see the sympathetic glance that

passed between Echardt and his daughter. Echardt cleared his throat and said awkwardly, "You was sure enough having a rough time."

Sundown shrugged his shoulders. "I reckon I was, but I didn't think much about that part of it just then. Mostly I was trying to stay on my feet and forget that my head was aching like blue blazes. And I was right thirsty too. Those things sort of kept my mind off what a rough time I was having." He gave a short laugh. "It seemed like every time I woke up I was just getting up from laying on the ground. The queer thing about it was that I never remembered going down, either."

Echardt realized the fighting spirit of the man in those few words, the spirit of a man who could keep putting one foot before the other long after his consciousness had blanked out. It must have been a terrific struggle for Mallare to keep going in such fashion. A man of less indomitable will would have given up long before.

". . . and so," Sundown was saying, "I just kept on going that way. You see, there was really nothing else to do. I had to try and get some place."

There was a lump in Echardt's throat. Nothing else to do? Cripes A'mighty! The average man would have just laid down and died.

"And then, a little time after, Miss Virginia and your man caught up with me." Sundown fumbled for another cigarette.

Echardt struck and held a match for Sundown. "Did you get a chance to look at the cow and calf that brand man had hawg-tied before you were shot? I've been wondering whose brand they carried, being this close to the Lazy-E. Course, Flying-Box-9s and Window-Sash critters often graze over this way —"

"I saw 'em," Sundown replied, "saw both cow and dogie. They were Lazy-E stock."

"T'hell you say!" Echardt burst out. "My stock, eh? If they were left on the trail, Rawhide will spot 'em on his way to Holster City. I don't suppose the cow thief you shot will be there though. Likely the feller, or fellers, who laid you out released the stock pronto and took the dead man's body away with 'em as soon as possible. You didn't know him, of course?"

Sundown shook his head. "Nope, he was a complete stranger to me. I'm right certain he wasn't among the men in the Royal Flush when I was there, though I could be mistaken. Of course, after my run-in with Balter, I didn't pay much attention to anybody else. For all I know this cow thief could have been a friend of Balter. Probably I shouldn't say that, but I must admit I don't care much for that hombre."

Virginia interposed a question: "You don't think it was Zane Balter who shot you, do you, Sundown?"

Sundown considered the matter. "Er — no — can't say I do. It could have been Balter, maybe. I hadn't thought of that before."

Echardt frowned. "I don't hardly think it was Zane. He's right proddy at times, but I'd hate to think of him dry gulching a man. He's got a temper, I'll admit, and is inclined to be quarrelsome. If Chris Newland wa'n't so danged easy-going, I imagine he'd got rid of Zane long ago. But Chris always maintained Zane was a good foreman, in spite of his faults, and Chris should know. He's all right. I've known him and Nort Windsor for years, and I couldn't ask for better neighbors in this basin. This cow thief you shot, what sort of a looking hombre was he?"

"About what I'd call medium build," Sundown replied, "dark hair, blue eyes. Nothing much there to identify him. His togs were about the same as any cow poke might wear. He was riding a chestnut gelding."

Echardt considered what Sundown had said, searching his memory for some man who might fit the description. Finally he sighed and shook his head. Virginia said, "There's any number of men in the Holster Basin who could fit that description, and more of the same who come to Holster City from time to time. Some other clue to the rustlers will have to be turned up."

Her father nodded agreement, then turned back to Sundown. " 'Ginny tells me you were on your way here to see if you could get a job. That right?"

Sundown forced a smile. "Seems plumb foolish now, doesn't it, but that's what I was aiming to ask you about when I started from

82

Holster City — just a job, that's all."

"You got it," Echardt said. "You're on the Lazy-E payroll right now."

The cowboy raised one hand in protest. "Don't you go to ribbing me, Mr. Echardt," he said, and the words were coming hard. "I know you can't really mean that. I don't want your pity. I couldn't stand *that*. I know as well as you I wouldn't be of any use around a ranch in this condition —"

"Damn it," Echardt said irritably, "I said you was hired and I mean it."

"But, Mr. Echardt —"

"And I don't want any 'mistering,' neither," Echardt snapped. "I'm 'Curry' to all my hands, and you're one of my hands. Now, no more arguing, please. You got into this trouble protecting Lazy-E stock, and from that moment on, even if you didn't know it, you were on the Lazy-E payroll. We'll talk no more about it. The matter's settled."

"But can't you see," Sundown said earnestly, "that I'll be worthless to you? A cowhand is no good without eyes. No telling how long this trouble will last. If my sight comes back soon, I'll be glad to sign up with you, but meanwhile — well, I'd best get me a tin cup and go to begging on some street corner." Despite the laugh that accompanied the words, his tones held a trace of bitterness.

At this point Echardt exploded. "Great Jehoshaphat and the Seven Bald Mountains!" he burst out impatiently. "Have I got to rope and hawg-tie you to keep you on the Lazy-E? By all the tarnation devils in hell — !"

Virginia interrupted with some haste, "You'd better do as Dad says, Sundown Mallare. He generally gets what he wants."

"Certain he'll do as I say," Echardt snapped. "Like's not I'll need him as a witness against cow thieves one of these days. Look here, Sundown, I've got plenty of influence in Holster City. If necessary, I'll get a court order to restrain you from leaving my property." Then, in more kindly tones, "Why, man alive! There'll be plenty of things you can do around here. I've seen hombres handicapped worse than you working around outfits. You know cows and horses. Just because you can't see is no sign that knowledge has left your head. Anyway, this trouble with your eyes ain't going to last."

Sundown was having trouble with his eyes right then; a suspicious moisture kept entering them, and he was forced to do some rapid blinking. Virginia may have had something to do with the matter, when he finally consented to stay.

"The doctor must be on his way here now," she stated. "As a matter of fact, he could be due any minute, providing he wasn't busy when Rawhide got there. I haven't the least doubt Dr. Pearson can get you fixed up in no time. One thing the Holster Basin can boast of is a mighty good doctor. Now you quit worrying, Sundown; things are going to come all right for you."

There was something sustaining, almost a healing, in the girl's words and in her manner as she leaned across and lightly touched his hand. There was friendship in her touch, and perhaps something more than mere friendship.

The blind man suddenly found himself surrendering. "Well, thanks a heap," he said awkwardly. "If you put it that way, I'll be pleased to stick around — for a few days, anyway."

"Now you're talking sensible," Echardt growled. "And what's more, cowboy, I'm aiming to see you make it more'n a few days too. Now that's settled, we can —"

He paused as hoofbeats were heard outside. Virginia rose and went to a window. "Here's Dr. Pearson now," she announced. "Rawhide made even better time than I'd hoped."

Beyond Help

Dr. Pearson, when he entered the house, proved to be a dapper, fastidious, abrupt little man of about forty years of age, with hair graying at his temples and shrewd brown eyes. He had the reputation of being considerably more up-to-date in his manner and methods than were the usual practitioners found in frontier towns of the Southwest. Doubtless in a large city he would have gone far in his chosen profession, but he preferred, actually loved, the western cow country and its people, even though he had been born in the East and had taken his medical degree there. As he himself had put it, people in the Holster Basin were healthier, their ailments were more ordinary, aside from the treatment of gunshot wounds now and then, and he could lead a more leisurely existence; and, after all, no man should be expected to work himself to death — not if he wanted to keep his patients alive.

He came briskly into the room where Sundown awaited him, set down his small black bag, and stripped riding gloves from his thin, long-fingered hands. Curry Echardt started to tell what had happened, but Pearson cut him short. "No need to go into details, Curry," the doctor said abruptly. "Rawhide Lacey's already told me what happened. Fact is, on our way here we stopped a second where Sundown had his trouble. Nothing to see, though, except some ashes from a brand fire and some footprints." He crossed over and took Sundown's hand. "You're Mallare, eh? And you got shot up some. Well, I don't believe you're in any danger of dying — not for fifty or sixty years yet, anyway, and providing I don't lose my head and start dosing you with medicine."

He turned and opened his bag, producing dressing gauze, bandaging, and one or two other objects. By this time Virginia had appeared with a basin of water. Pearson examined first the wound on Sundown's head. "Humph!" he grunted. "Not much for me to do here. 'Ginny, you seem to have handled this in first-chop fashion. Any time you want to turn nurse, let me know. I could use you."

His deft fingers quickly washed and rebandaged the wound, then he turned his attention to the ugly-looking welt that ran across Sundown's eyebrows. He bathed the wound, then pressed various points with light fingertips. "That hurt?" he'd say, or "A little tender here, I imagine."

"It's a mite sore," Sundown admitted, "but it doesn't hurt much."

A slight frown scored Pearson's forehead. He considered the matter, prodded a little more. His frown deepened. "Well," he said finally, "this swelling should go down within a few days. The skin's not broken to a large extent. You're lucky, Mallare; you won't even have a scar there." As though reluctant to leave off, he pressed Sundown's forehead at another point. "Did that hurt much?"

"None to speak of," Sundown replied. "No more than any similar bump would, I reckon."

Pearson looked a trifle puzzled. "Any idea what those buzzards hit you with?"

Sundown shook his head. "Not the slightest — unless it was the running iron that hombre had intended to burn the calf with."

"That's probably it." Pearson nodded. "This is just such a mark as would have been left by a blow from a length of three-eighths or half-inch iron rod. If the end of the iron had caught you, it would have ripped open the skin. It looks to me as if that fellow had struck you a sort of glancing blow — for which you can thank your lucky stars. As it is, you've just received a rather severe bump that you'll not even feel within a few days."

"But my eyes, Doc," Sundown reminded Pearson a trifle impatiently. "When will I be able to see?"

"Don't rush me, young fellow," Pearson replied. "I'm getting to that part of the job. Come over here near the window where I can get a good look at those eyes." Taking Sundown's arm, he led him across the room. Here Pearson studied the gray eyes intently, turned back the lids, and peered diligently at the eyeballs, had Sundown turn them to left and right and up and down. Then he led Sundown back to his chair.

Sundown said, "Well?"

"I asked you not to rush me. I'm not through yet," Pearson said brusquely. He struck a match and waved the flame before Sundown's face in an effort to determine whether or not the cowboy's eyes would of their own accord follow the moving light. They wouldn't. The doctor commenced to look concerned. "Ever have any trouble with your eyes before?" he asked.

"Not a bit," Sundown replied. "Look here, how long will this last?"

"I can't tell you," Pearson said evasively. "Remember, please, I'm not through examining you yet. 'Ginny, will you please lower the window shades?"

The girl moved to carry out the order; in a minute the room was shrouded in gloom.

"Close your eyes until I tell you to open them," Pearson told Sundown. Echardt and Virginia came nearer now. After a minute Pearson said, "All right, open your eyes. Now what can you see?"

"Just black — like it was before," Sundown replied.

"I see," the doctor responded. "I thought, in the present state of your vision, the strong light might have been too much for you. Apparently that's not it." Again he scratched a match and held the flame very close to Sundown's wide-open eyes. "Now, tell me what you see."

"Not a solitary thing," Sundown answered. "Just blackness." There was a hopeless note in the cowboy's voice. His sharp ears heard the sound of Pearson's breath as the doctor blew out the match, and he realized what Pearson had been trying to do. "If my eyes had been right I'd have seen the fire of that match, wouldn't I?"

"We've already decided your eyes aren't right," Pearson said quietly. "That's one reason I'm giving you these tests. But don't tell me you couldn't see anything. I know you can." Something of pleading crept into his voice. "I don't mean you're to define objects clearly: Couldn't you even see a faint circle of light when I held that match close to your eyes? It was mighty close, Sundown. You must have —"

"I know how close it was," Sundown cut in. "I could even feel the warmth, but I couldn't see one thing —"

"Can't you even see a faint grayish light now?" the doctor persisted. "You know, sort of like looking through a fog?"

There was a moment's pause, then Sundown's answer: "Nope. Not a thing. It's all pitch-dark."

Pearson gnawed perplexedly at his gray mustache a moment. "Well, if that's the case, this blindness will take a little while to wear off, Sundown. But don't worry. Your eyes will come all right after a time —"

Sundown asked quickly, "You're certain of that?"

Pearson's reply was evasive. "How can a man be *absolutely* certain of anything in this day and age? But I know what I know. I'm certain you'll be alive tomorrow, but I can't be absolutely certain. You might be hit by a bullet. It happens occasionally in the basin. You might have a heart attack, though I doubt it." Shrewdly he shifted the conversation slightly. "I'll tell you what I would do though, in your place. I advise you to wear dark glasses — smoked glasses, y'know — until your sight returns. With your eyes wide open the way they are, the sun's light might be too strong for them. So long as you can't see anything for a while you'll have less tendency to blink in a bright light. No use weakening your eyes, y'know. You'll be needing them one of these fine days. I've got an old pair of dark glasses at my office I'll send out to you. They may not fit your nose and ears accurately, but they'll do until I can order you another pair. First chance you get to come to Holster City, stop in and I'll take some measurements — width of your head, placement of ears, and so on."

Sundown said thanks, and Virginia again raised the window shades. Pearson closed his black bag after giving the girl a few simple directions for the care of Sundown's wounds. He shook hands with the cowboy, saying, "I'll drop out and see you from time to time. We'll hope you'll regain your sight before too many days pass, but don't get impatient. I'll be frank with

91

you. This thing may require a couple of months or more before it clears up to our satisfaction."

Sundown reflected as the doctor left the room: A couple of months or more. That was going to be tough. Still, he reckoned he could stand it. He shrugged his muscular shoulders. Cripes! He'd have to stand it. There wasn't anything else to do. He heard Virginia at his shoulder, then felt her place a cigarette between his lips. There came the striking of a match and the girl's quiet tones: "Well, if you can't see the flame for a few days, you can still make use of it, Sundown. Light up. I understand smoking is good at a time like this."

Curry Echardt had followed Pearson outside to the doctor's waiting horse. "Well, what's the real verdict, Doc?" Echardt asked when the two were alone. "I've got a hunch you didn't tell Sundown everything that was in your mind."

Pearson climbed up and settled into his saddle. He looked down at Echardt, and a rueful smile twisted his lips beneath the gray mustache. "Curry, I just couldn't see any use telling him — maybe I lacked the requisite nerve to break that sort of news. Anyway, by the time he's waited two-three months, some of the shock will be gone, and he'll have learned — somewhat — to do without eyes. It won't do any harm to let him go on hoping, y'know."

"Do you mean his sight is gone altogether?" Echardt exclaimed.

Pearson nodded curtly. "So far as I know. I

can't do a thing for him —"

"Hell's bells!" Echardt said. "With all your knowledge of medicine and surgery, you can surely —"

"Look here, Curry, I'm not God and I'm not Jehovah or any other divine creator. In short, I can't work miracles. Briefly, he's beyond the help of mere man. There's nothing known to the medical profession that can help Sundown Mallare."

Echardt winced at the words. "But what's to be done? Couldn't an operation — ?"

Pearson snorted violently. "An operation? Doesn't it ever occur to you, Curry, that eyes are damned delicate organs and aren't supposed to be monkeyed with? Someday doctors may know how to deal with such problems, but we haven't yet — not that I've heard of, and I keep up mighty well with medical progress, even if I am a small cow town doctor."

"But I don't see why —"

Pearson said, "Oh hell," impatiently, and launched into a long technical explanation of Sundown's visual problem and why it couldn't be solved.

Finally Echardt raised one protesting hand. "Whoa up, Doc! You're leaving me behind with the drags. You should know I can't savvy that sort of *habla*. For cripes' sake, speak American. Are you insisting Sundown is blind for good?"

"No, for bad," Pearson snapped. "That's the only way to put it. You see, that blow Sundown received has brought about some sort of pressure on the optic nerves. It may be due to a swelling that will reduce after a time — hell, no, I can't say how long a time — but I'm more inclined to believe it is some slight fracture of the frontal bone. If it is a fracture, there is little to fear *on that particular point.* A fracture in a man of Sundown's age will heal quickly, but doubtless the pressure on the optic nerves will remain. To put it another way, there exists a certain paralysis of those nerves. Sundown's vision is gone."

Echardt nodded his comprehension of the explanation, but stubbornly again spoke of an operation.

"Good Lord, Curry," Pearson said testily. "Where are you going to start operating? A doctor wouldn't know exactly where to start looking for trouble. It's too delicate a matter for blundering around. A doctor can make mistakes on broken legs or arms or ribs and still not cause too much trouble — always. But a man's head — his eyes and brain — isn't a watch that can be turned over to a jeweler to take apart, readjust, and then assemble again. If we knew the precise points the blow had affected, and could give a similar blow a second time, there's one or two chances in a hundred the bone might be jarred back into place, and thus relieve the pressure on the nerves — but of course that's impossible. We don't know, that's all, and there's no way of finding out. Science hasn't traveled that far yet."

"Would an optic specialist be any use?"

Echardt commenced, then broke off in some confusion. "Not that I doubt your ability, Doc, but I was thinking if some specialist —"

"You should doubt my ability," Pearson said gruffly. "Don't ever trust one doctor too far. The best of us make mistakes. We're only human. Perhaps an eye specialist could help Sundown. I couldn't say. Oh, I don't think I'm giving up. I'm going to write letters to a couple of men who know more about eyes than I ever dreamed of knowing, but in this particular case I'm 100 per cent sure they'll only confirm my diagnosis. I've seen two other cases very similar to Sundown's, and in each instance the patient remained totally blind all his life. Nothing could be done for them."

"There isn't a bit of hope then?" Echardt asked dismally as though he hated facing the truth.

Pearson didn't answer this question directly. For a time he sat lost in thought, it seemed, gazing off across the range country and the distant mountains. A rather queer look came into his face. "Curry, do you believe in miracles?"

"Huh?" The owner of the Lazy-E glanced up in some surprise. "Miracles? We-ell, it — er — that is, it tells of miracles in the Bible — about fishes and loaves and such and dead men being raised —"

"Yes," the doctor agreed, "the Bible does tell of such doings." He gathered up his horse's reins. "That's what I'm talking about. When a miracle of that sort takes place in the Holster Basin, then Sundown will have regained his sight."

Without another word he nodded curtly to Echardt, kicked his mount in the ribs, and loped off along the trail to Holster City.

Echardt trudged back into the house, his forehead furrowed with mingled thought and sympathy for the unfortunate Mallare. Within the house he found Virginia talking to the cowboy and trying to bolster up his hopes. Sundown caught the sounds of Echardt's steps as the man entered the room. "Did the doctor have anything else to say about my eyes?"

"Your eyes?" Echardt stalled. "Oh, nothing, nothing much. You heard him say everything there was to say. Just said they'd be all right after a spell. We weren't talking about you. I wanted to ask him about — about some other business. Nothing that concerned you a-tall."

Sundown sensed the untruth of the statement. "Look here, Mr. Echardt —"

"My name's Curry, dammit, and you'd better learn that, Sundown."

"All right, Curry, but I want to point out something if you'll listen. I'm no kid; I can't stand being pampered, but I can stand bad news when I have to hear it. I know you're trying to put me off. Let's hear the worst. Are my lights out for good?"

Echardt realized he couldn't stall forever. He looked at Sundown's square jaw and decided that here was one man who could come back strong, regardless what sort of punishment was meted out to him. The ranch owner after a moment slowly, reluctantly nodded his head, then remembering that Sundown couldn't see, answered, "I reckon your eyes are going to be plumb useless, son. But don't you worry. Pearson's verdict isn't final."

Virginia appeared to take the news harder than Sundown. A sort of gasping sound left her lips, then she was speechless. The corners of Sundown's mouth tightened slightly, then he gave a short mirthless laugh. "Thanks for telling me." He nodded briefly, and reached for his sack of Durham and brown papers.

"We're not going to take one man's word for it," Echardt persisted stubbornly after a short pause in which he'd been admiring the game way in which Sundown had accepted the news. "I'm going to get some big optic specialist here who'll like's not fix you up in less time than it takes to tell about. It's just a matter of paralyzed optic nerves, or something simple like that. It can all be taken care of easy, I'm betting."

Sundown had to smile at the man's awkward kindness, though there was a touch of grimness in his tones when he said, "Sure, it's just a matter of time, I reckon. Meanwhile, would you mind leading me outside? I'm craving a smoke, and I don't want to be spilling tobacco all over the floor. If I'm due to go through a spell without seeing things, I might's well learn as soon as possible to roll a cigarette neat."

Echardt swallowed hard. He and Virginia exchanged pitying glances. Then the big ranchman moved across the room and took Sundown's arm. "Come on, I'll take you down to the bunkhouse and you can get acquainted with the boys when they come in. You already know Rawhide Lacey, and the rest of my crew are white men too. You'll find us all back of you, Sundown, and just as soon's you get your bearin's a mite and can make to get back in a saddle, we'll go after the skunks who're responsible for this business and spray 'em with hot lead. From now on your fight is my fight, and we're not through yet by a damn' sight. We're just starting!"

Smart Shooting

Nearly four months drifted by — four months which brought no change to Sundown Mallare's eyes. He was, he was reconciled to this fact now, hopelessly blind. True to his word, Curry Echardt had had a noted eye specialist from the East visit the Lazy-E Ranch, but this specialist had accomplished no more than to verify Dr. Pearson's original diagnosis. Pearson himself spent long hours poring through many medical tomes, in hope of finding something to help Sundown's condition, but all to no avail. From time to time the doctor appeared at the Lazy-E to put Sundown through fresh examinations and to prescribe various medicaments, but nothing attempted brought back the cowboy's sight. There was, apparently, nothing more to be done.

The men about the ranch were quick to take to Sundown. His unfailingly cheerful attitude in the face of his affliction won the admiration of everyone in the outfit. As Tom Leslie, the spare grizzled foreman of the Lazy-E, put it, "If Sundown can keep up his spirits under these conditions, he sure must have been one *muy buen hombre* before he lost his sight."

And Rawhide Lacey had added, "Cripes A'mighty, yes! Right now, if it wa'n't for them smoked glasses he wears, you'd think there wa'n't a thing wrong with his eyes. Even when he takes the glasses off, his eyes *look* all right — to other folks. You'd never figure he can't see things. And handy! Say, you ought to see that Sundown waddie weave a rawhide catch rope. You'd swear he had eyes in the ends of his fingers."

It was true. Sundown had noticed that when his vision vanished his senses of feeling and hearing became much more acute. It had been no time at all before he was able to repair bits of harness that were brought to him, and he plaited rawhide lariats for every man on the Lazy-E. He cleaned guns, too, when the weapons required it; saddling a horse was no trouble at all for him, if someone first roped the beast. When necessary, he helped gentle new broncs that arrived at the Lazy-E. Once in the saddle, there wasn't a horse on the ranch that could unseat him, regardless of how the animal pitched, sunfished, or swapped ends. No doubt about it, Sundown Mallare was a rider!

His usefulness didn't end there, either. Curry Echardt was interested in breeding fine cattle, and Sundown produced from his experience and memory an invaluable fund of information relating to the raising of both Angus and Hereford strains, more than once saving money for the owner of the Lazy-E with his treatment of stock ailments. Considering this advisory capacity, which Echardt fully appreciated, Sundown was earning every cent of the money which each payday brought to him.

By this time Sundown and Virginia Echardt had become firm friends. Often, when not engaged with other duties, Sundown accompanied the girl on rides, sometimes to town to pick up the mail and sometimes just out on the range. The word of Sundown's adaptability became known throughout the Holster Basin, and he made many friends. Nort Windsor had, in fact, once told Sundown that any time he felt an inclination to leave the Lazy-E there was always a job awaiting him on the Window-Sash spread.

Only Zane Balter remained aloof, refusing to recognize Sundown when the two met. This, of course, bothered Sundown not at all, though he continually wished for his eyesight that he might get on the trail of the cow thieves who were still devastating the country. The more he considered the matter, the more Sundown commenced to suspect that Zane Balter knew more than a little about the stealing. However, having nothing solid upon which to pin his suspicions, Sundown kept his beliefs to himself.

Sometimes the men wondered why Sundown still carried the holstered forty-five at his hip. Without sight the gun was useless. Sundown, rather sheepishly, had once said he had carried the weapon so long that nowadays he felt undressed without it. He kept it clean and from time to time inserted fresh loads in the cylinder. And then there came a day when Sundown discovered he could still handle a six-shooter.

Virginia Echardt had had "Biscuits" Benmore, the Lazy-E cook, pack a lunch and asked Sundown to accompany her on a ride into the Chaparra Hills. She made some vague mention of some cows Curry had seen over that way, from a distance, and had wondered whose stock they were. Horses were saddled and the two rode off, Virginia carrying a book with her. Once into the hills, the cows in question were quickly discovered to be Lazy-E stock.

"I could probably have told you that in the first place, if I'd known exactly where you were going to bring me," Sundown commented.

"You know this range pretty well, don't you, Sundown?" Virginia said.

"Jeepers, 'Ginny, I should. I asked everybody I met about the lay of the land and so on, so I could be sure to have it set in my memory. Talking to your Dad and the Lazy-E hands has given me a pretty good idea of where our cows graze and so on. Well, shall we turn back?"

"Not on your life," Virginia said instantly. "It's too nice a day to stay home. Besides, I have some letters to write, and I hate writing letters; if I were home I'd feel duty bound to get at it. And something else, we've not eaten our lunch yet and I brought along a copy of Scott's *Ivanhoe* to read to you awhile before we return. This is a sort of picnic for us."

"Sounds good," he replied. They rode a few miles higher into the hills, not talking a great deal, and eventually dismounted in the shade of some tall pines to consume the lunch. Sundown was unusually quiet. He was thinking about Virginia Echardt a great deal these days, caring for her more than he wished to admit even to himself. If it hadn't been for his eyes . . . An involuntary exclamation parted his lips, but when Virginia glanced at his sober features and the smoked glasses over his eyes, he made no attempt to explain, nor did she pursue the subject.

They had finished with the food and were comfortably seated on blankets spread on the earth when Sundown spoke abruptly. "I'd give a heap to be able to see you — just once."

Something in his tone startled the girl. "Why?" she asked.

"Isn't it reasonable I'd want to know what you look like?" he countered. "I've done a lot of guessing, of course, but you can't call that satisfying."

Virginia's eyes sparkled. "Shucks," she said, "that's easy. I'll tell you. I'm close to forty years old, skinny as a beanpole, my eyes are something between brown and gray — sort of mud-colored, I imagine, and my mouth is too wide. I've got a nose that looks like a baked bean; I'm close to six feet tall, and my hair is a sort of faded brown —"

Sundown's sudden chuckle interrupted the

girl's words. "There should be a law against it," he said dryly.

"Law against what?" Virginia asked.

"Against telling lies of that sort — self-perjury —"

"But, Sundown —"

"Let me take over a minute," he said firmly. "In the first place, you're not near six feet tall. I can tell by the sound of your voice that you're around five foot seven. And no voice like yours ever came out of a forty-year-old beanpole —"

"I think I'd better commence reading to you," Virginia interposed rather hastily, and opened the book in her lap. "We don't want to waste the whole afternoon talking about me."

"Who doesn't?" Sundown said, and continued, "Your hair is soft and thick and black and has got a sort of wave in it. You've got dark brown eyes and a clear complexion that's sort of like an ivory with a lot of tanning on it and a sort of healthy flush in the cheeks. And I must mention a *muy elegante* smile with very white teeth. You're just a mite past twenty and as graceful as — as —" He hesitated and groped for an appropriate simile. Not finding one, he continued, "And your eyelashes are real long —"

"Sundown!" Virginia exclaimed. "Where did you learn things like that?"

"When a man can't see, he has to ask questions," Sundown replied. "I've asked everybody on the Lazy-E, from Curry down, and a heap of folks in town too. Oh, I didn't ask openly what you looked like, but I sort of weasled information out of folks, with a question here and a hint there. Then I sort of put the pieces together, until I commenced to get an idea of what you looked like —"

"Look here, Sundown Mallare, it seems to me —"

"— but it can't be as good as actually seeing you. You tell me a lot of things yourself, when I hear your voice. Sometimes when you'd briefly touch my hand it taught me something. I think mostly, though, your voice has taught me the most about you, things that" — the words were coming a bit unsteadily now — "that even you didn't know you were telling me —"

"I think," Virginia interrupted in mock sternness as she quickly flipped over the pages of her book, "that you'd better be quiet for a time. I'm going to read to you."

"Just a moment," Sundown said. "I'd sooner hear you talk right now, instead of hearing other men's writings. Sometimes, listening to your voice, it's almost as good as seeing you." He broke off. " 'Ginny, I know I shouldn't be saying this, but I'm not quite so blind as you think I am — where you're concerned. I can see — sense is the word I should use — a lot of things that you —"

He checked himself, realizing he was voicing thoughts he had never intended to utter. For a moment or so his emotions had gone beyond control. He shook himself impatiently, muttering something under his breath that had to do with being a "damn' idiot," and then continued in curiously flat ones, "Go ahead with the reading, 'Ginny. I didn't intend to interrupt by running off at the head thataway."

But Virginia had closed the book and was gazing down the hill slopes, out across the range, a faraway look in her dark eyes. She turned, after a moment, with sudden decision. Sundown heard her movements, then felt her soft lips brush his own.

For a moment he couldn't speak, and when he did find his voice it held a sort of gasping quality. "Why, why, 'Ginny, you — Well, I've got to admit I'm plumb enthusiastic about — Say, look here, what's the idea?"

Virginia settled back on the blanket at his side. "Sundown," she said, and her words were very steady, "there's no longer any use of trying to fool ourselves. I know how you feel about me. I know it is only your blindness that has prevented you from telling me. I've known all this for weeks. And so long as *you* wouldn't speak, it put the matter squarely up to *me*. And I wanted you to know exactly how I felt —"

The words were never finished. There ensued various periods of silence, broken now and then with conversation. Mostly, on Sundown's part, the conversation consisted largely of protestations, but after all he was in love, and his protestations were, at best, rather feeble. Not only feeble, but easy to overcome, within limits. He would not, however, commit himself to anything definite. Virginia was finding him very stubborn. "There's no sense of us arguing this now," he pointed out, and his tones sounded very happy, "but I just won't have you marrying a blind man. It wouldn't be right."

"Sundown! Don't be silly. To me it makes no difference."

"I know that now," he said earnestly, "and it makes me feel — well, I haven't the words to make you understand just how I feel. But we're going to forget this has happened — for a long time, anyway. Someday, if I feel I can support a wife, why, then —"

And so they argued while the sun slipped lower in the west, until the time came for departure. "I'm going to tell Dad about this just the moment we get home," Virginia stated firmly as they arose and started to fold their blankets.

Sundown grinned. "Exactly what I want you to do. He'll have sense enough to put his foot down and keep you from doing anything foolish. I aim to speak to him myself." With that, he turned and made his way toward the waiting horses where he tightened the cinches.

Virginia had stooped to pick up the blankets, when the sudden dry, wispy rattling sound reached her ears. She stiffened and backed a step, gaze searching the earth. She saw first the light glistening on the two beady eyes, and then the rest of the thick, sinuous form but a few feet away. How long the reptile had been there was uncertain. Perhaps it had just arrived.

At any rate, the snake was full of fight, its triangular head lifted a trifle from the earth. Its tail agitated the rattles to a gray-yellow blur; the red forked tongue was darting rapidly in and out.

Sundown was several yards distant. Virginia had commenced to back farther off when the sound of the snake's rattling reached his ears. He tensed, one hand reaching to his six-shooter.

"Stand very still," he warned the girl in a low, steady voice. "Don't make a move."

The snake was preparing to strike. Again came the dry *whirr-rr-r-ing* of its rattles. Sundown had the sound located now. He got his gun aimed in the direction of the snake, then started waving the muzzle slowly back and forth in a short arc. With Virginia standing like something hewn from granite, the moving gun caught the reptile's attention. In a moment the snake's ovate head was swaying in unison with the moving gun muzzle.

Suddenly Sundown released the hammer. Fire and smoke and lead spurted from the barrel of the six-shooter.

Through the drifting powder smoke Virginia saw the headless, squirming coils writhing frantically about the earth, whipping old leaves and dust to a miniature cyclone. Slowly the anguished movements died away, a convulsive shudder ran through the snaky length, and except for a spasmodic twitching of the buttoned tail, it lay still.

For a second neither the girl nor the man spoke. Then Virginia said weakly, "Why — why, Sundown, you hit him!"

At the sound of her voice the blind man relaxed. "Thank the Lord he didn't strike you. I was afraid I might have missed, and then he'd reached you —"

"Missed?" Virginia laughed shakily, not through fear, but incredulously at the thing she had witnessed. "Sundown, you shot its head clean off! I don't see how you did it. Was it luck, or — or can you see again? Are your eyes all right?"

Sundown smiled slightly. "No, my eyes are just the same, so I guess we'll have to call it luck. Luck and a trick. A trick in which I had the snake's help. You see, I didn't shoot at once when I pulled my gun. When you held perfectly quiet, the swaying muzzle of my six-shooter was the only thing to attract the snake's attention. With everything else motionless, that gun barrel had Mr. Snake watching close. When I moved the muzzle, he moved his head. After a few moments the dang fool snake was keeping his head right in line with the gun barrel every second. So when I figured he was ripe for a target I let go with my shot —"

"That *is* a trick!" Virginia exclaimed.

"I've done it before, when I could see the snake, but not always. Some snakes just won't bite on such bait. I don't know if they're wiser or just too stupid to watch close."

Virginia exhaled a long breath. "Well, I'm certainly glad your trick worked this time." She moved nearer to the dead reptile, bending down to examine it. "It's a Tiger rattlesnake, Sundown. We don't often see that species around these parts. Mostly we get diamondbacks and in the more arid parts of the basin sidewinders. Golly! I'll bet this brute is nearly three feet long."

"Might be," Sundown said dubiously, "but he sounded less when I heard him thrashing around."

Virginia looked rather queerly at him but didn't say anything. Truly his ears had become a pair of eyes for the cowboy.

Later, when they were mounting the horses, Virginia said, "I don't see yet just how you knew where to aim. Did your hearing tell you that too? That snake might have been several yards away from where he was when you aimed your gun."

"Credit my hearing," Sundown laughed. "There wasn't much to it. I heard him rattling. That was practically as good as seeing him. I've noticed my ears are a heap more accurate since my eyes kicked out on me."

Virginia shook her head, still unbelieving. "All I say is, you did some mighty smart shooting."

Preparation

The man and the girl had almost reached the Lazy-E when Virginia again commented on Sundown's shooting. "I should think, Sundown, if your hearing is so sharp that you could learn to shoot again with a little practice."

The cowboy grinned. "You aiming to make a gun fighter out of me?" And at the girl's denial he went on, "At that, it seemed sort of good to feel that old Colt gun jump in my hand again. That's the first shot I've fired since I had the trouble with that cow thief. Lord! that's over four months back."

"It would likely require some time," Virginia continued, "but it wouldn't do any harm to learn over again how to shoot. You already know that, but you'll have to learn to depend on your ears instead of your sight. At least it would give you something to do when there's no work to occupy your mind."

Sundown looked thoughtful. "Yeah. Maybe you're right, 'Ginny. I reckon I'll have to give it a try. Now that I can saddle and ride again, it'd make me feel more like my old self if could get back the feel of a six-shooter. I might even learn to handle a rope again too."

"I don't think it would be too hard." She paused, and her cheeks colored slightly. "You seem able to write and address letters."

"Uh-huh, when a letter is necessary, I make out," he said carelessly.

"It seems necessary at least once a week," Virginia pointed out, and her color deepened. She suddenly caught herself. "I'm sorry I said that. It's no business of mine."

Sundown tensed slightly. "I don't exactly see —" he commenced, then paused. A certain awkwardness crept into his voice. "I know what you mean. Those letters I send off every week to Eloise Peters —"

"You don't have to explain," Virginia said loftily. "I shouldn't have mentioned it at all, I just didn't think —"

"Where'd you hear about Eloise?"

"One of the hands mentioned you wrote her regularly. I — I guess it was Rawhide Lacey saw the address on your envelopes. But it's none of my business." The girl's head was held high; her cheeks were crimson.

"Now, look here, 'Ginny. Eloise is nobody for you to fret about. What passed between you and me this afternoon is solid. Eloise hasn't anything to do with it."

"As I say, it is none of my business, Sundown. Was she somebody you planned to marry — ?"

"Aw, jeepers, 'Ginny! Nothing like that at all. Trouble is, I'd have a hard time making you understand. You see —"

"Just an old friend, I suppose, or a cousin or somebody like that."

"That's it" — eagerly — "you might say Eloise is an old friend. That's all there is to it, 'Ginny. It's like this —"

"Sundown! I'm behaving like an idiot." The girl was suddenly contrite, smiling. "You don't have to explain to me I — I guess I just had a twinge of jealousy. It's idiotic —"

"It sure is, everything considered," Sundown said, "but you got a right to know about Eloise Peters. You see, she doesn't —"

"Sundown! Please! Not another word about Miss Peters. I'll feel like a — a worm, if you start telling me. I'd rather not hear another word —"

"But, 'Ginny —"

"Not another word," Virginia stated firmly. "It's all making me feel very ridiculous, and the sooner we drop the subject, the better I'll feel."

"Well" — dubiously — "if you want it like that."

The matter was dropped, and they returned the conversation to other subjects.

That night Virginia had a long talk with her father in the big main room of the ranch house. She explained the happenings of the afternoon, but Curry Echardt was more impressed with her story of how Sundown had killed the snake than he was with the rest of her recital.

"He sure must have been a smart man with a six-gun when he had eyes to see with," Echardt commented when she had finished.

"Dad!" Virginia snapped with some exasperation. "Let's forget his shooting for a minute. What I want to know is how you feel about Sundown and me. That's the important thing, though I warn you that no matter how much you object —"

"Object?" Echardt removed his brier pipe from between his teeth. "Who said anything about objecting? On the other hand, you've got to realize, 'Ginny, that Sundown is hopelessly blind. Someday he might become something of a burden on you. You must realize that a cowhand's wages don't buy many luxuries. And we're not sure he could get a job as a cowhand. Sure, I'd just as soon keep him here from now on, but how would that set with Sundown? You know he wouldn't like that. He's mighty independent —"

"I could swing him to my way of thinking," Virginia said eagerly.

"I'm not so sure," Curry Echardt replied, "not in a case like that. But I don't aim to boss you. You're of age and can make your own decisions. What you decide is all right with me, and I'll do all I can to help. I'll say this for Sundown — he's white all through. And if he could take care of you, I'd be proud to call him son. I'll head down to the bunkhouse, after a spell, and have a talk with him."

An hour later Echardt appeared in the doorway of the bunkhouse where Sundown was talking with the rest of the Lazy-E hands, and

114

asked the cowboy to step outside a moment. Overhead a huge moon was sailing above the hills and the distant *yip-yip-yipping* of the coyotes could be heard. The two men sat down on a bench placed against one wall of the bunkhouse. Echardt stuffed tobacco into his pipe, scratched a match, and then held it for the cigarette Sundown had rolled, this last an accomplishment Sundown could handle now as well as any man with eyes. They puffed in silence a few minutes. Finally Echardt broke the quiet.

"You had a couple of visitors today, Sundown."

"That so? Who were they?"

"Luis Montaldo and Jake Munson."

"What were they doing here?"

"I was hoping you might be able to throw some light on it."

"I can't — not the slightest. So they're back again."

Echardt nodded, without thinking that Sundown couldn't see. "Yes, they seem to ride into Holster City about once a month. Nobody seems to know where they spend the time in between visits."

"So I understand. I've just never happened to be in town when they were there — not since that first night I saw them. I wonder what they're up to."

"You're not alone in your wondering," Echardt said dryly.

"You mentioned they were my visitors today.

Did they ask for me?" Sundown queried.

"Yes. I told them you weren't here. Course I could have directed them to the direction you and 'Ginny took, but I didn't feel like doing that, me not knowing much about them."

"I'm danged if I know why they should be calling here to see me," Sundown said, his brow furrowed with perplexed wrinkles.

"Maybe they didn't ride here just to see you," Echardt conceded. "They came in, watered their horses, and asked if you were here. Said they were just passing by and thought they'd say hello. Munson said he heard you'd been blinded and wondered if it was true. There's a hard-looking case for you, that Munson. Montaldo is pleasant enough. But I wish I knew more about those two. I offered to pass on any word they might have for you, but they said there was nothing special. Just happened to be over this way and dropped in. Maybe they were speaking truth, I don't know."

"*I* wouldn't know, Curry. What you say about Munson looking hard is mighty true, but maybe that's nothing against him. I've known some mighty tough-looking hombres who were gentle as a yearlin' calf. You can't always judge a man by his looks."

"That's true," Echardt agreed. "I do remember Munson saying something about it being right white of me to give you a job. I set him straight on that right pronto. Told him you earned every cent you drew down and there was nothing of charity in my actions."

"Thanks, Curry."

"For nothing," Echardt said gruffly. He cleared his throat. "There's another matter I want to take up with you."

"I know." Sundown smiled. "If you hadn't come down here tonight I'd have been up to the house to see you. I suppose 'Ginny has told you some things, but I wanted you to hear my side of it too. I wanted to talk to you and make certain things clear."

What came of the talk wasn't learned by other people for some time. Sundown explained he had no intention of marrying Virginia, despite the girl's wishes, until she had had ample time to consider the matter, and until he was certain he could earn a living sufficient to support both of them in comfortable fashion. He also told Echardt other things concerning his life. When he had concluded, Echardt reached over and took his hand. Sundown's fingers fairly tingled from the tight grip the ranch owner gave him.

"I'm wishing you luck, son," he said simply.

"I'll need it. Thanks."

"By the way, that was a smart bit of shooting you did this afternoon, Sundown."

"Lots of luck in it too. But I'm going to start practicing with my hawg-leg and see if I can learn to shoot without luck."

"That's not a bad idea. Any particular reason?"

"Preparation."

"Preparation for what?"

"Curry, someday I'm going to encounter the man who caused my blindness. I want to be ready. And I still hope to be able to run down the cow thieves in this basin. I feel that's a job I want a share in."

Echardt looked pityingly at Sundown's face, with the dark glasses before the eyes. Finally he said, "Well, a man never knows what he can do until he tries."

Sundown laughed softly. "And you never realize how hard you can try until you have to."

"I reckon you're right, son. Well, I've got to be getting back to the house. 'Ginny'll be thinking I got bogged down here."

He rose and strode up toward the Lazy-E ranch house, thoughtfully drawing on his brier pipe.

The following morning, when all hands except the ranch cook were out on the range going about their various duties, Sundown "broke out" a couple of boxes of forty-five-calibre cartridges and taking them out back of the corrals and buildings, commenced practicing with his six-shooter. The killing of the rattler the previous day had instilled in his mind a new confidence, and he felt that even now it wasn't too late to begin over again.

From a pile of rubbish near by he procured an armful of rusty peach and tomato cans. From this point on his procedure was to toss one of the cans to the ground, several yards away, draw his gun from holster, cock it, and fire, aiming in the direction from which came the sound of the rolling can.

It was a discouraging business at first. Chamber after chamber of his gun was emptied before he succeeded in scoring a hit. Then at the first metallic *plunk* that told of success, Sundown was ready to jump with joy. It was a slow business, though, finding and retrieving the cans after he had thrown them. Despite that, he warmed to his job with mounting enthusiasm.

It was sometime later in the morning that Virginia wandered out back of the buildings to see if it were Sundown doing the shooting. A wistful smile crossed her face as she drew near Sundown and saw him throwing bullet after bullet at a can that rolled over the earth some distance away, while flying lead kicked up spurts of dust all around it. Suddenly one of the leaden slugs found its mark. The rolling can spun sharply off at an angle, twisted violently around, and then came to a stop.

For a moment there was silence, then Sundown asked quietly without turning, "What do you think of that, 'Ginny?"

Startled, Virginia jumped at the sound of his voice. "Gracious, Sundown! How did you know I was watching you?" Even now she was standing several yards to his rear.

"Heard you when you arrived." He grinned, turning around. "I recognized your step."

That he had heard the sound of her footfalls, even through the rattle of gunfire, was even more remarkable. "Golly." She laughed. "Your ears *are* sharp. Just a moment, though. You couldn't have known it was *my* step. It might have been anybody's around here."

Light reflected from the lenses of his smoked glasses; his grin widened, "I knew it was your step, all right. It was softer than the *clump-clump* sounds of high-heeled boots these warp-legged cowhands around here make." He commenced to reload his gun. "Yep, I'm on the road to becoming a real gunfighter this morning."

He started searching around for his tin cans, but Virginia got them for him. Then the procedure was changed. Virginia stood near him and a little to the rear, then tossed the cans for him to shoot at. Once she made a trip to the house to get more ammunition. A great deal of powder and lead was consumed that morning.

From then on Sundown and Virginia were there nearly every day. Sundown's aim improved rapidly. His speed, too, increased, as occasionally he'd work on "fanning" his gun. Virginia would send a can rolling and bouncing over the uneven gravelly earth. As the first tinny sound reached his ears the cowboy's hand would swoop to the Colt six-shooter slung at his right hip. The weapon would come out and up in one smooth motion. At the same instant his open hand, palm at an angle and slightly down, would move in a blur across the gun hammer, and a steady stream of flame and smoke jumped from the muzzle, making the can leap and jump before the onslaught of hot lead.

Not a day went by that Sundown didn't practice. Sometimes two or three of the other punchers would be there to watch him and give advice or retrieve cans. Such days as Virginia wasn't on hand Rawhide Lacey helped out. One morning the lengthy, leathery-faced puncher produced a slablike object built from thick pine boards which had been crudely whittled and sawn to resemble the form of a man. This he propped up with a length of greasewood trunk some twelve or fifteen yards from Sundown.

While Sundown waited, Rawhide explained what he intended to do. Then Rawhide picked up a small chunk of rock and threw it at the wooden figure. The instant the rock struck the board, Sundown's gun was out, jumping in his hand, and belching fire.

When the gun was emptied, Rawhide hurried to examine the board. Something of awe came into his face as he announced the result. "You put three slugs through the middle, cowboy, and another slug nicked the edge about where the left shoulder would be. Sundown! That's shooting! Only one miss. Half the men on the range would be proud to do as well."

Sundown laughed. "I had a lot of luck there too. You see, I only heard your rock strike that board, but I didn't know what part of the board it struck. If you'd hit it high, or to one side, my shots might have been affected accordingly."

"Cripes! That's true." Rawhide frowned. "We've got to figure out something else. Look here, if you were shooting against a real man instead of a chunk of wood, you'd have to listen for the sound of his gun as it left his holster, wouldn't you, in order to get the correct bearings for your shot?"

"Correct," Sundown nodded.

"Got to figure out something else then — something that will make a softer sound on the right side of that figure, about where the holster sound would come from." His frown deepened, then his brow cleared. "You wait here a minute. I'll be right back."

He hurried away, but returned shortly with a fifteen-foot length of hempen rope. "Here's the idea," he explained. "I'll stand off to one side and swing this rope round my head. As I swing it, I'll let the end come nearer and nearer to the figure, until it just manages to touch in the vicinity a holster would be. When you hear the sound, you go into action —"

"Hey, nothing doing!" Sundown protested. "I want you off to the side or in back of me when I'm shooting. Your idea is too risky."

"Risky hell!" Rawhide exclaimed. "I'm more than willing to take the chance. Cripes! I'll be well away from the figure. I've seen you hit that wooden man, and I know I'll be safe."

"I couldn't chance it," Sundown said reluctantly; it was plain the idea appealed to him.

"Oh, so you're losing your nerve, eh?" Rawhide sneered. "Lost confidence in your shooting, eh? Dammit, Sundown, are you going to admit I've got more faith in your shooting than you have? What the hell! I only aim to live one life anyway. Come on, give it a try."

There ensued considerable more argument before Sundown surrendered. Then, to the accompaniment of swishing sounds made by the rope, there came further bursts of fast gunfire. At first it didn't go too well, Sundown being afraid of hitting Rawhide, but as time passed his marksmanship improved. This sort of practice went on for days, until at last Sundown was able to place all five bullets within the space that could be covered by Rawhide's two leathery hands. "Trouble is," Sundown chuckled, "I've been practicing on a right-handed man. Should I meet one who's left-handed, I'd sure miss far, wide, and handsome, unless I knew beforehand he was left-handed. But I'll work it out."

The two worked on other stunts. Rawhide would stand five cans on end, one atop the other. Then he'd stand off at a distance, swinging his rope. As the rope hissed through the air in a wide circle, he'd gradually allow it to approach nearer, moving but a fraction of an inch at a time, until the end of the rope eventually touched the bottom can. Sometimes the sound that issued forth was so faint that even Rawhide didn't hear it, but the slightest noise never escaped Sundown. He'd jerk his gun from holster, cocking as it came out, and start throwing lead. Down would tumble the tower of cans, rolling and jangling in all directions, while Sundown tried to hit as many cans as he could before the ammunition was gone from his cylinder.

It was Sundown's ambition to place a slug of lead through each can — one cartridge to topple the stack and the other four loads for the remaining cans. This was unusually difficult, as it became necessary to distinguish separately the various sounds made by a rolling can before and after it had been hit. Only twice did Sundown succeed in accomplishing this trick to his satisfaction, but as Tom Leslie, the foreman of the Lazy-E, expressed it, "You're shooting well enough now, ranny, to show up most of the gun throwers in this basin." Luckily the rubbish pile where Sundown procured his tin cans had been growing for years, so he never lacked for marks to shoot at, even though much of his wages went to buy Colt gun ammunition. In time his aiming and shooting became practically as accurate as they ever had been.

With the added confidence brought to him by his shooting, Sundown now turned his interest in another direction. One by one he had Rawhide Lacey turn the Lazy-E horses into an empty corral and run them around until he could memorize the sounds of their gaits. Eventually two horses were turned in at the same time, then three and four, and so on, until Sundown could say instantly which horse was which as it passed:

the gray, the chestnut, the pinto, and so forth, having already learned from Rawhide the color of the horse when it ran alone.

Roping brought not so many difficulties as Rawhide had expected. Shaking out his loop and the toss, he had never forgotten. All he had to do was judge by an animal's hoof sounds how fast it was traveling and how near it was before he made his cast. The day eventually came when under Rawhide's tutelage he roped a few cows out on the range.

Rawhide beamed. "Boy! You're as good as you ever were. You rope and ride and shoot! You can't ask much more of any man."

But what Rawhide and the others had forgotten was that Sundown always had to have some sound to shoot at when he drew his gun. Otherwise, he was hopelessly lost and as helpless as a blind man can be.

Challenge

The days were growing along toward autumn, and beef roundup time was approaching. Sundown was in the blacksmith shop one day, endeavoring to fit a new buckle to a bit of harness, when his ears caught the sound of Curry Echardt's wrathful tread. He could always tell when Curry was riled by the way he walked: each boot heel was set down with a sort of violence, as though he expected to drive it right into the earth. Echardt's face was clouded up like a thunderstorm as he approached the blacksmith shop. Sundown could hear the man swearing under his breath even before Echardt arrived at the open doorway of the building.

"Oh, that's you in there, eh, Sundown?" Echardt growled, peering through the doorway.

Sundown laid a buckle and strap on a nearby bench. "Sort of sounds like you were wrought up about something." He smiled.

"Wrought up!" Echardt raged. "Hell's bells on a tomcat! Who wouldn't be wrought up? Half of that herd of seventy-five Durham crosses I was breeding for a special market was run off last night. I had them cows wired in and nobody riding 'em. Figured 'em safe from cow thieves.

126

Those damn' rustlers took their time, cut out the best of that prime stock, and drove 'em off — cut my wire to do it too. Lucky I happened to be riding over that way, or the bustards would have like's not come back tonight for the other half of the bunch. Damn' 'em for a dirty crew of thieving coyotes, anyway!"

Sundown was expecting more. It came while he waited. "Where's Tom Leslie?" Echardt growled. "I guess there ain't much use of me hiring a foreman if he ain't around when he's wanted."

"Tom's out riding range with a couple of the boys," Sundown gave the information. "Seems to me like I heard you give him an order —" He broke off, then, "Anything I can do, Curry?"

Echardt said, "Oh, hell," and commenced to cool down. "That's right — I plumb forgot. Me, I'm always losing my temper over nothing. remember now —"

"You calling the loss of your stock 'nothing'?"

"Hell, no! But there wasn't no call for me to get mad at Tom like this. It ain't his fault he's not here. I remember now I sent Tom out myself to look over them Hereford yearlin's we're holding over near Verde River —" He broke off. "Them goddamned cow thieves! For two cents I'd sell this outfit and get shet of all such troubles. Then I could set out on the beach, or mebbe get me a boat, and spend my days fishin' in them California waters." He started to swear again. "When a man can't trust a friend —"

Sundown interrupted to ask again, "Is there anything I can do?"

The tirade ceased. Echardt said, "Huh! What? Oh yes, maybe there is something you can do, if you feel like keeping me company on a ride to the Flying-Box-9. Your ears are sharp. I'd like a witness to what's going to be said. By Gawd! I got something to go on at last. I'd like you to side me on the ride to —"

"What's the trouble with the Flying-Box-9?" Sundown inquired.

"What ain't?" Echardt exploded wrathfully. "Dirty crooks, the whole kit and kaboodle of 'em. There's the cow thieves!" His anger rose sharply, and for a few moments the air was purple-tinged with profanity.

Sundown waited a minute and then asked, "You sure you got proof, Curry? Chris Newland always struck me as being on the level. I sort of like him — though I never could understand his keeping Zane Balter on his payroll. Course if you've got actual proof —"

"Proof!" Echardt bellowed hotly. "You're damn' tootin' right I got proof." More swearing, and then he went on. "Rawhide rode in a spell ago driving one of my cows and a calf. The mother cow bears the Lazy-E marking, as should be, but the calf has been burned with the Flying-Box-9. Is that proof?"

"Sounds like something queer," Sundown admitted. "Did Rawhide pick 'em out of a herd? He might have made a mistake."

"No, they wa'n't with any herd. The two animals was just ambling across the range by themselves when Rawhide spotted 'em, the calf following the mother cow. He goes to investigate, sees 'em branded differently, and drives 'em in for me to see."

Sundown frowned. "I find it hard to believe that Chris Newland would be back of anything like this."

"He owns the Flying-Box-9," Echardt stated harshly. "I always figured him as being as good a neighbor as a man could find. I even" — aggrievedly — "invited him to come to California with me and go fishing someday. And this is the way he does me dirt. And here me and Nort Windsor have been thinking the rustlers had come working from outside the basin. And Newland pretended to agree with us. That dirty son of a bustard! Gawd, I'd never have believed it, neither, if I didn't have that cow and calf for proof. The thieves must have overlooked workin' over the mother cow's brand, or something, or maybe they got scared off before they got around to the cow. By geez! Newland and me are going to have this out. Right today! I'm aiming to drive the cow and calf over to his house and confront him with the evidence —"

"We're losing time talking," Sundown cut in. "I'll be right with you. Wait until I get my saddle and gun from the bunkhouse."

Five minutes later, the two men in saddles joined Rawhide Lacey a short distance from the ranch house, then, driving the cow and calf, branded Lazy-E and Flying-Box-9, before them, they started across the basin in the direction of Chris Newland's ranch. It was slow riding at times, as the cow objected to being driven, and Rawhide would have to urge her on her reluctant way with vigorous slappings of his throw rope across the animal's rump. Curry Echardt's anger increased with every yard of the journey, though it was a cold, more reasoning anger now.

As it was a pretty difficult matter to urge the cow and calf along at a gait faster than five miles an hour, Echardt's anger may well be imagined by the time the Flying-Box-9 ranch buildings were sighted. By now it was nearing five in the afternoon, and leaving the herding of cow and calf to Rawhide, Sundown and Echardt rode on ahead when they'd approached within a hundred yards of the ranch house.

They dismounted before the gallery to find Chris Newland seated in an easy chair, nursing along a bottle of warm beer. He put down the bottle and rose to his feet, his face stretched in a smile of welcome.

"H'are you, Curry! Good to see you, Sundown." He was a graying, heavy-paunched man with an indolent manner. "Rest your saddles and come set a spell. I'll get you some beer. No ice, though. Might be you'd sooner have whisky. Must be hot ridin' in this sun. How's tricks?"

"How's yours?" Echardt demanded curtly. He and Sundown paused at the foot of the flight of three steps leading to the gallery. "It's your tricks I come to see you about. How's your herds comin'? Increasing fast enough to suit you?"

Newland failed to notice Echardt's manner. "Increasin' in a hawg's eye," he chuckled jovially. "What with cow thieves runnin' 'em off right and left, I'm lucky to be holdin' my own. But come up and set —" He broke off as his gaze caught the moving figures a short distance from the house. "Ain't that Rawhide Lacey I see comin'? What's he doin' with the two critters? You fellers pick 'em up near the house or somethin'?"

"Yeah, near the house," Echardt said coldly. "*My* house. Rawhide ran across 'em this morning shortly after he'd started out. We drove those two animals over here to show you, Newland. It's *my* herds the rustlers been whittling on. And I'm wondering if you ain't got a bunch of Durham crosses that was run off on me last night."

The smile vanished from Newland's face. He bit into a plug of "eatin' tobacco" he drew from one pocket, chewed steadily a moment, then asked, "Curry, what's come over you? Is something wrong? Why should I have your damn' Durham crosses?" He spat a long brown stream that narrowly escaped striking Echardt's right boot.

Echardt said in a tense voice, "Newland, you and me have been friends for a good many years — leastwise I took it for granted we were — but that's no sign I aim to sit back and let you run your damn' Flying-Box-9 on my stock. Because we've been friends, I've said nothing yet to the law in Holster City. I'm going to give you a chance to square this business first. If you don't — Oh hell, Newland, your game's up and you might as well realize it."

A slow, bewildered flush crept over Newland's features, and for a moment he couldn't find his tongue. Then he descended the steps from the gallery and stood close to Echardt, eying him narrowly. Suddenly he laughed and spat a stream of tobacco juice toward a bit of sage growing near by. "Damned if you didn't have me fooled for a spell, Curry. Up to your old-time jokin', eh?" He chuckled. "For a minute there I was about set to get right mad. I thought you was intimatin' I was a cow thief —"

"I ain't intimatin' and I ain't jokin'," Echardt flared. "And you can't bluff me out of this, Newland. I've stated facts!"

Newland's Adam's apple made a convulsive jerk toward his chin. He turned to Sundown. "What's this all about? Has Curry gone crazy?"

"You won't get nowhere appealin' to Sundown, Newland," Echardt interrupted hotly. "I come here to make some *habla* with you, and by Gawd! you're going to explain a few things. I've stated it as plain as I know how and now I'll say it again — you've been stealing my cows."

Newland's feature turned crimson. "Ain't no man goin' to say that to my face and live to tell it." He choked. "You just wait right here until I

132

get my gun from the house." He turned and started back up the steps that led to the gallery.

"Hold it, Chris," Sundown said quickly. "This is no time to be shooting your facts from a gun. You'd better cool down and listen to what Curry says. The cow and calf Rawhide is driving in carry some mighty serious evidence. Before you go getting into deeper trouble, you'd better take a look at the critters. After that, you can talk, or go for your gun, as you see fit."

Newland darted an angry glance in Sundown's direction but swung around and stepped heavily back to the ground again. "So you've gone crazy too," he sputtered. "All's I got to say is, this business better be explained right quick."

Echardt hadn't waited to make a reply. He had gone out to meet Rawhide, who was just herding the cow and calf into the cleared space that fronted the Flying-Box-9 'dobe ranch house. Both animals were inclined to run, so Rawhide roped the cow and threw it on its side. While Echardt worked at the cow's feet with piggin' strings, Rawhide released his rope and quickly caught the calf and flopped it but a few yards from the other animal.

Echardt straightened from his task. "All right, Newland," he called. "Come and take a look at this, and then explain it — if you can."

Sundown had already started out to join Echardt and Rawhide, who was just dismounting. Muttering imprecations on his former friend, Newland made his way to the cow and glanced at the Lazy-E brand. Then he walked over to examine the calf. One look he gave at the freshly burned Flying-Box-9 brand, and his jaw suddenly sagged. "Gawd A'mighty!" he gasped. "And this dogie was following a Lazy-E cow! I saw that myself before you roped 'em down."

"If you'll admit that much," Echardt said grimly, "maybe you're ready to admit some more."

"Curry, you — you —" Newland turned to Echardt but was momentarily speechless. His arms waved helplessly in the air. Finally he found his voice. "Curry," he pleaded earnestly, "there's been some mistake. You've got to believe me. I know how it looks to you. I don't blame you a mite for talkin' as you did, but I swear I'm not to blame for this. My Gawd, you should know me better than that."

Curry Echardt didn't say anything for a moment, though the lines in his face softened a trifle. Newland again looked at the calf, his eyes bulging. "Why, dammit," Newland went on, again facing Echardt, "you've known me too long to think I'd do anythin' like this. I don't know who's responsible, but by the livin' —"

"All right, Chris," Echardt interrupted, convinced by Newland's confusion and evident sincerity that the man had had nothing to do with the rustling, "maybe there has been a mistake made. I'm asking your pardon for calling you a thief. I reckon I misspoke myself."

"Cripes A'mighty!" Newland exclaimed,

reaching to accept Echardt's proffered hand. "After seeing this, I can't say I blame you any. It sure looks like you had the goods on me. How do you suppose a thing like this happened?"

"Probably some cow thief had something to do with it," Rawhide put in dryly.

Sundown had detected the ring of truth in Newland's words and was gratified that Echardt realized the man was innocent of any wrong doing. About this time Sundown's memory returned to Zane Balter, foreman of the Flying-Box-9, and he began to wonder if Balter had had anything to do with the brand work carried by the calf.

"Do you suppose," Newland suggested after a time, "that this cow could have lost her own calf and then adopted one of mine?"

"In that case," Rawhide pointed out, "the calf would have had to lost its maw, too, otherwise there'd been two cows for one calf. And we know the calf was trailin' a Lazy-E cow."

"Chris's idea is possible, of course" — Echardt frowned — "but I don't think probable. Besides, that brand on the calf looks right fresh to me. I'd say there was a mite of blottin' been done over my Lazy-E marking."

"The more I think on it" — Newland scowled — "the more I think my idea is damn' improbable. There's something wrong here. Perhaps the brand wa'n't blotted a-tall. The dogie may have been branded by mistake. If it's a case of blottin', it's mighty smooth iron work." He stood looking down at the calf's brand.

"Sometimes," Sundown said quietly, "a feller's fingers can feel what his eyes can't see." He approached the calf, stooped down, and ran his sensitive fingers over the burned design. Then he rose to his feet.

Echardt said, "Know any more than we did before?"

Sundown nodded. "The brand's been blotted. I can feel where the new brand joins the old." It was the first time he'd ever examined a Flying-Box-9 brand. He went on, "The man who did this simply extended the middle leg of the Lazy-E — which lays on its back — and traced that leg into a figure nine. Next he extended the two outer legs and joined them with a straight line across the top. That made the box. To the two sides of the box he drew the two curved lines for wings."

Without waiting for comment, he again stooped down, this time near the calf's head, and felt of its ears. "These earmarkings are fresh, too, I'd say. The Lazy-E swallowforks right and left. Chris, your mark's an overslope right and underslope left, so the thief's marking simply chopped off our cuts." Again he straightened up.

"By Cripes!" Newland exclaimed. "There is something to the marvelous things I've been hearing about you, Sundown. You must have eyes in your fingers."

Sundown smiled. "I sure wish I had 'em some place, Chris."

At that moment Zane Balter rounded the corner of the ranch house, evidently on his way to confer with Newland about some ranch business. He stopped short upon seeing the four men standing near the fallen cow and calf, then slowly approached the group.

"H'are you, Echardt — Rawhide." He nodded greetings. For the moment he ignored Sundown, then noticing the cowboy's smoked glasses said, "So you're here, too, Four-Eyes. I'd expect to find you on some street corner, begging. Where's your tin cup?"

"If I had one" — and Sundown smiled thinly — "I'd carry it with me. I'd never think of leaving it out on the range, where I couldn't find it easy, if I did any nightwork."

Balter flushed. Sundown had been hinting that the man had business that took him night riding when honest men were in their bunks. A hot reply rose to Balter's lips, but Newland interrupted. "For cripes' sake, quit it, Zane," he said in a weary voice. "Do you always have to go around lookin' for quarrels? There's something more serious at hand."

Not having any ready retort with which to reply to Sundown, Balter glanced quickly at Rawhide and Echardt whose displeasure was plain in their faces, then turned to Newland, asking, "What's up?"

Newland told briefly what had happened, then went on, "You know, Zane, it looks mighty queer, this calf follerin' a Lazy-E cow. There's some crooked work here in the Holster Basin that I'd like to see cleared up."

Balter spat and shook his head. "Not necessarily, Chris. I figure that brand was burned on by mistake."

"Mistakes aren't blotted on," Echardt put in. "You know that much, Zane."

"Blotted or a mistake or whatever," Newland growled, "a thing like this looks bad for the Flying-Box-9, Zane —"

"Who says that's a piece of brand blotting?" Balter demanded belligerently. "Any damn fool can see that's a clean brand."

"I'll admit it looks that way," Echardt said, "but Sundown felt of them brands. We're taking his word for it."

"Furthermore," Sundown got into the conversation, "if there is anybody who doubts that brand was blotted, I think I can prove it."

"How?" Balter snapped.

"If you were as good a cowman as you claim," Sundown replied coldly, "I wouldn't have to tell you. But if you want to kill that calf and skin it, the underside of the hide will tell the story. It will show where the old brand joins the new."

Balter knew this to be the truth, as did the other men. He shrugged his shoulders. "Kill the damn' calf if you like, but that's an expensive way to try to prove your point." He was struggling to keep his temper. "It's no concern of mine what you do — and I still think that's a clean burn. But go ahead and kill it. It's no con-

138

cern of mine. It's Chris's calf, and if the mark didn't prove to be blotted, Chris would lose the price of one beef animal. But to hell with it, and you, too, Mallare. I don't give a damn what you decide. I ain't even interested."

"You're sure you're not?" Sundown asked sharply.

Balter tensed. "Why should I be?"

Sundown laughed softly. "You're the only one can answer that, Balter — at least right now."

Balter swore, then shrugged his shoulders and started off. He had progressed about ten or twelve yards when his evil temper gained the upper hand. Turning, he noted the four men had paid no attention to his departure. Their backs were to him while they considered and continued to talk over the matter of brand blotting. Balter's eyes narrowed as they fell on Sundown, and one hand went to his gun butt. Then Balter spoke in a loud voice.

"I'm still maintaining that the man who says that brand was blotted is a damn' liar!"

Three of the men near the calf turned to face Balter. Sundown alone retained his position, though he half turned his head toward the speaker, his ears strained for the slightest sound.

"If that remark was intended for me, Balter," Sundown called back in an even voice, "I'd advise you to take it back — or else fill your hand mighty pronto." There was no doubt about the challenge in Sundown's tones.

For a moment a tense silence settled over the

men. Sundown's hearing was alert for the first sound. Then it came — a soft, swift brushing of metal against leather, as Balter's six-shooter was jerked from its holster.

Sundown's weapon flashed up and out in one smooth motion as he started to turn, but he was still only half facing Balter as he thumbed his hammer, shooting by blind instinct and hearing. His six-shooter roared but an infinitesimal fraction of a second before Balter's shot, the reports of the heavy detonations blending into one crashing sound.

Balter staggered back, his aim disconcerted. The gun flew from his hand as he sat down violently on the earth, his sombrero tumbling to one side. A burning streak of fire ran across the bridge of Sundown's nose just where it joined his forehead as he felt Balter's lead crash through his smoked glasses, tearing them from his face. Even while he was experiencing these sensations, he felt himself falling, but continued, automatically, to thumb the hammer of his six-shooter in Balter's direction. But these last bullets passed harmlessly through the air, already filled with swirling powder smoke. By this time Balter was stretched full length, groaning, on the ground.

Abruptly Sundown realized his hammer was falling on empty cartridge shells. Still clinging to his weapon, the cowboy took quick, staggering steps in an effort to retain his balance, then dropped limply to the earth. Rawhide, Newland, and Echardt came to life then; they'd been standing as though dazed by the sudden action. Now they jumped to Sundown's side and stooped to examine him. After a moment Newland dashed into the house, to emerge almost instantly with a bucket of water. He handed it to Echardt, then strode over to the fallen groaning Balter.

A quick inspection of Balter's wound told Newland it wasn't serious. He commenced to swear, and seizing Balter by the collar of his woolen shirt, jerked him upright, employing not the least gentleness in the procedure. Balter's groaning increased; he started to sit down again. Newland shook him roughly. "Damn you, Balter, stay on your feet. You're not bad hurt, but you should be, you low-down coyote. You've took a slug in the fleshy part of your shoulder. I wish it had gone through your stinkin' heart. Nobody but a skunk would throw down on a blind man like you done."

"Damn it all, Chris," Balter whined, one hand pressed to his wounded shoulder, "he riled me. Maybe I shouldn't have —"

"Oh, shut your goddam mouth!" Newland snapped disgustedly. He turned and called to the others, "How bad is Sundown hit?"

"Deeper'n a scratch, but not so bad as a furrow," Rawhide called back. "He's going to be all right, I reckon."

Newland nodded and swung back on Balter. "And that's lucky for you, you lousy, two-bit, would-be gun fighter. Now you go on down to

141

the bunkhouse and wait for me. I'll bandage your shoulder, when I got time, good enough to get you to Doc Pearson in Holster City. I'll even saddle your bronc for you. I'll be glad to do that just to get you started on your way. I'm through with you! Ain't got no use for yellow-backed sneaks who'll throw down on a blind cowpuncher. You ain't such shucks as a foreman nohow. I should have fired you long ago. Never at the ranch when I need you —" He broke off, then, "Go on, get started! What in hell you waitin' for? Want I should put my boot to the seat of your britches? By Gawd, I got a notion to do just that!"

But he wasn't given time to carry out the threat. Hurriedly, on shaky legs, Balter made his way around the corner of the house and toward the bunkhouse.

Newland returned to the group around Sundown. "I can promise you I'll start that bustard on his way just as soon as he's fit to stay on a bronc's back. How's Sundown?"

"He's coming around now," Echardt replied, using his bandanna to mop blood from the cowboy's face.

Sundown regained consciousness within a few minutes. His wound wasn't severe, and Echardt soon checked the slight flow of blood that seeped into view where the bullet had cut across flesh.

"You sure had a narrow escape, son," Echardt said, as he helped Sundown to his feet. "You'll like's not have a little white scar to show what happened, but nothing else. Anyway, your glasses will cover the scar to some extent — make it less noticeable. But you're going to have to get some new glasses. Them you was wearin' was smashed all to hell. Lucky you didn't get glass in your eyes —"

Sundown interrupted to mumble something about having another pair of glasses at the Lazy-E bunkhouse. He was still dizzy, though his head cleared after a couple of minutes.

"Yeah, reckon I am lucky," he said. "What happened to Balter? Did I get him?"

"You plugged him in the shoulder," Newland said. "He ain't hurt bad — worse luck! I'm bootin' him out today."

Rawhide was chuckling. "I heard you givin' him hell, Chris. What was it you said about throwin' down on a poor blind cowpunch?" Rawhide snickered. "It's a dang good thing for Balter that Sundown is blind, or I'm afraid there wouldn't be any Balter to boot out."

Sundown was standing without aid now. Newland said, "No use us stayin' out here in the sun. Sundown will feel better if he rests in the shade of the gallery a few minutes. Something else, Curry, I want to settle with you for that calf —"

"Cripes! Forget the calf," Echardt snorted. "Whoever's responsible, it wa'n't you, Chris. I misjudged you by a mile."

"Just like Balter misjudged Sundown's shootin' ability," Rawhide grinned.

Just Curious

Dr. Pearson grunted as he finished examining Sundown's wound. "Damn' if you aren't a healthy customer. This is just about healed already, and it's only a week since Balter's slug hit you. Lucky you wasn't facing him, or that bullet would have taken you plumb between the eyes."

They were in the doctor's office in Holster City, where Sundown had come to get his wound dressed. It was his second trip to see Pearson. The office looked neat, containing only a desk, a couple of chairs, a long table, and a cabinet of surgical instruments. A shelf on one wall held jars and bottles of various drugs and medicines.

"I'm danged if know," Pearson said, "why you always have to take your punishment in the head. A man could get his head worn out that way — worn right down to the bone."

"I note you say 'bone' rather than brain," Sundown commented dryly.

"I'm not worrying about your brain any," Pearson said tartly. "To learn to shoot the way you have, with your handicap, requires brains. By God, I'd like to have refused my services to

144

Balter that day he come whining to me with the wound your bullet had made. The dirty scoundrel! I fixed him up as well's I could, but told him to get some other doctor thereafter."

"I understand he's left the Holster Basin."

"Must be. Nobody's seen him," Pearson replied, scowling. "Good riddance, I say." He continued to bathe Sundown's wound. Finally he stood back. "There, I've put court plaster on for you. Leave it on three or four days, then take it off gently. I don't think you'll require my services again — not on this job, though if you keep going the way you've started, Lord only knows when you'll be needing me again. That court plaster will be more comfortable than having the nosepiece of your glasses resting against a gauze pad, like it was before. Lucky you had a pair of extra glasses. I'll order you another pair right off, so if anything happens to those you're wearing —" He broke off; then, "This last jolt on the head you got hasn't made any difference to your sight, has it?"

Sundown shook his head. "I was hoping it might too. Practically the same place I got that first blow. But everything's just black, like it was before."

Pearson sighed. "Well, that's luck for you. All you can do is keep hoping. Your sight will come back someday."

Sundown laughed. "Now, Doc, you know you really don't believe that. You might just as well cut out the bluffing. I told you a long time ago I could take the truth. You don't have to pamper me along."

"I guess I don't," Pearson agreed. "Maybe you've got more courage than most men. I know most men, having gone through what you have, would have become embittered."

"Would that have helped them any?" Sundown asked quietly.

"Not one bit."

"There you are." Sundown shrugged his muscular shoulders. "I've just got to learn to make out with what I have."

"It's the only way to look at it, son." Pearson handed the smoked glasses to Sundown, who quickly slipped them on, then asked, "Who came in with you today?"

"Nobody."

"You mean you can find your way in without help?"

"Oh, I had help, if that's what you mean. My little Coffee-Pot horse. He just follows the trail in, and then back to the Lazy-E. When we're in town he knows just three stops, and I've come to recognize them — the Royal Flush Saloon, the post office, and Tim Foster's General Store. If I'm not sure which is which when he stops at a hitch rack, I get down from the saddle and feel of the tie rail. Each one has a sort of different feel, where broncs have chewed on 'em, and so on. And I count a certain number of steps for each place, from hitch rack to doorway. It's really plumb simple when you get used to it." Sundown chuckled. "Of course I lose my bearings now and then, in town. Then all I have to do is ask somebody the way. Having been in town before I went blind, I've got things located pretty much in my mind."

Pearson shook his head incredulously. "You beat anything I ever heard of. How did you get here today?"

"This is one of the times I had to ask questions. I knew approximately where your house is — you're on the next street, right back of the post office. I walked Coffee-Pot, turned a corner, counting his steps all the way. I could tell by the difference in the breeze when I'd reached the next street, then I turned my horse and counted the steps some more. Dismounted at what I thought was the right distance, fumbled around until my hand hit your picket fence, then I located the gate after a minute —"

"I'll be damned!" Pearson exploded.

"I likely will be too" — Sundown grinned — "if I don't get back to the ranch with the mail I picked up."

They talked a few minutes more, then Sundown left the house and got into his saddle. He swung Coffee-Pot back to the main thoroughfare, and after riding a short distance, stopped before the Royal Flush Saloon. Here he dismounted and entered.

There were a few men at the bar, among them Nort Windsor, who stood alone, a drink before him, talking to Ton-and-a-Half. At the far end of

147

the long counter Jake Munson and Luis Montaldo were conversing, their heads close together.

"Hi-yuh, Sundown!" Ton-and-a-Half greeted, as the cowboy pushed through the swinging doors.

"How's it going, Ton-and-a-Half? Hello, Nort," Sundown said.

"Glad to see you," Windsor replied. A frown creased his forehead.

"Wish I could say the same," Sundown chuckled.

"Dammit," Norton said, "how did you know it was me standing here?"

"Heard your voice, recognized it, before I came in."

Windsor's forehead cleared, and he chuckled. "You've sure got sharp ears. I'll buy you a drink on that one."

"Thanks. I was stopping for a bottle of beer. It's hot outside."

A glass of beer and a bottle were placed before Sundown. He poured his own, judging by the sound of the streaming liquid when the glass was full. Ton-and-a-Half asked, "How's that wound on your head, Sundown?"

"Practically healed. It didn't amount to much."

Nort Windsor cursed with some feeling. "That lousy bustard Balter. I wish you'd killed him, Sundown."

"I don't like killing if it can be avoided," Sundown said quietly, "even when a man has it coming."

"Balter had it coming all right. Taking advantage of you that way, figuring you couldn't see. Of course Rawhide Lacey has been telling us how you were learning to shoot again, but the tales he told sounded so wild, nobody believed him. Then, earlier in the week when he was telling about you and Balter, I had to admit he was throwing a straight rope right along."

"Has anybody seen or heard anything of Balter?" Sundown asked.

Windsor shook his head. "He's just dropped out of sight, so far's I know. I reckon he's left these parts."

"I wish he hadn't been in such a hurry. I didn't know until after I'd got over the shock of his bullet that Chris Newland had sacked him."

"I'm just as glad he's gone," Windsor growled. "What difference does it make to you? You want to reopen the fight?"

"I'd like to question him a mite."

"About what?"

"I've got a hunch," Sundown explained, "that Balter may know something about the rustling."

Windsor frowned, tugging thoughtfully at a lock of straw-colored hair. "That could be," he conceded at last. "Course, that business of somebody blotting a Flying-Box-9 over the Lazy-E on that calf could point to the Newland outfit, I suppose, but I don't just see Chris Newland as a rustler. In the first place he's too easy-going. In the second, I figure him honest. I've known all his crew for a long time, too, and I don't figure 'em as working with Balter —"

"I'm forced to agree with you, from what Curry Echardt has told me. Curry says you and your crew and Chris and all his hands can be trusted from here to hell and back — says he's known you all a long time —"

"That points to Balter working with somebody outside the basin, then?" Windsor asked quickly.

"It looks that way to me," Sundown nodded. He took a sip of his beer and asked, "You lost any more stock, Nort?"

Windsor swore bitterly. "Yeah. Night before last somebody ran off thirty-five head of Herefords on me. The lousy, stealin' bustards!"

Sundown said in a sympathetic voice, "That's tough."

"I'll tell a man it is," Windsor growled.

"How large a herd do you run?" Sundown asked.

"Just about eight thousand head at present," was the reply. Sundown put in a question. Windsor said, "What did you say?"

"I asked you," Sundown repeated in a low voice, "isn't that Luis Montaldo and Jake Munson down to the far end of the bar?"

Windsor said, "You hit the nail on the head. How did you know?"

"Recognized their voices."

"Damned if you ain't got the sharpest ears I ever heard of. They been standing there, talking mighty low to each other. Can you tell what they're saying?"

"No, damn it, can't," Sundown said ruefully. "I can just catch an inflection here and there, and that accent of Montaldo's."

Even as he spoke, Montaldo and Munson left their place at the bar and sauntered down to the point where Sundown stood talking to Windsor. Without waiting for their greeting, when they stopped, Sundown swung around and said without preliminaries, "Understand you men dropped out to see me at the Lazy-E sometime back."

Munson scowled. "Yeah, we did. We had heard you was blinded. We just happened to be riding by, and —"

"Why?" Sundown asked.

"Why was we ridin' by?" Munson asked. "Or why did we stop? I don't reckon we have to account for the reason we was riding over that way."

"Not yet you don't anyway" — Sundown smiled — "so guess I'm just curious as to why you came out to see me."

Montaldo got into the conversation. In his mind Sundown could see the white flash of toothy smile when the Mexican spoke. "Señor Sundown, eet was not jus' to see you we make thee stop. Eet had come to our ear' that you had suffer' the blindness total. Eet was to offer our sympathy that we make thee halt at the Lazy-E Ranch. We are both ver' sorry to see eet is true what we have heard."

Sundown said briefly, "Thanks. I had an idea it was something else you had in mind."

"No," Montaldo said, and added after a moment's pause, "No — not after we had learn' you had no eyesight."

Munson put in grudgingly, "From what we hear you done to Balter a week back, I reckon you don't need eyes, Mallare."

"Where'd you hear about it?" Sundown asked.

"Cripes!" Munson said harshly. "The word's carried all through the basin. That was good shooting, Mallare."

"It was good enough," Sundown replied shortly.

Jake Munson turned away with no further word except, "C'mon, Luis, let's get going."

The Mexican nodded, then turned back to Sundown. "At any rate," he said politely, "eet ees good to know you can once more — how I say eet? — handle yourself, Señor Sundown. I weel see you again, I hope. Keep thee good health."

"Thanks; same to you," Sundown answered. He turned back to the bar as the two men pushed through to the street.

"I'd sure as hell like to know where those two ride to all the time. And where they go," Nort Windsor said.

"I'm just as curious as you are," Sundown stated. "If I could only move about a mite freer, I'd be tempted to take up their trail."

Windsor didn't say anything for a minute, then, "I'd be glad to go with you, Sundown." He glanced quickly at the barkeep, farther down the bar.

Sundown considered a moment. "We couldn't follow 'em in plain sight."

Windsor, instead of replying, went to the entrance and peered out. Within a moment he returned. "Montaldo and Munson headed east out of town."

Sundown said again, "We couldn't follow them in plain sight. "

"Maybe we wouldn't have to," Windsor said. "I can read a trail."

"Go on."

"I noticed when I came in here," Windsor stated, "that Montaldo's and Munson's ponies were at the rack. A good-looking pair of ponies. I happened to pull in alongside of Montaldo's bronc. You know how a feller will happen to notice something. Well, Montaldo's chestnut was stampin' around in the dirt a mite, and I noticed the hoofprints." He paused.

"I'm still waiting," Sundown said.

"The chestnut's off hind shoe is wore off bad, on the outside. It would be an easy trail to follow."

Sundown nodded. "All right, we'll give them fifteen minutes' start."

"You're sure you want to do this?" Windsor suddenly looked worried.

"I've already said so."

"We don't know what they're doing around here, Sundown. They might object to being trailed. It could lead to shooting."

"I carry a gun and so do you," Sundown said, even-voiced.

"I reckon there's no use of further talk then," Windsor said.

Nearly twenty minutes passed, then, after calling their good-byes to Ton-and-a-Half, Sundown and Windsor left the Royal Flush Saloon and climbed into saddles. They, too, turned their ponies on the road that ran to the east out of Holster City.

Covered!

A short distance beyond the town Windsor and Sundown drew their ponies to a momentary halt, while Windsor dismounted to scrutinize the earth. After a time he straightened up, frowning. "In case you don't know it," he gave the information, "we've been following the road that runs to my ranch. Montaldo and Munson may branch off, farther on, but they're heading that way now."

"You picked up the trail quick," Sundown commented from his saddle.

"Nothing to it," Windsor replied. "That worn shoe on Montaldo's bronc stands out plain. Those hombres have been traveling fast, too, so I reckon we can step up our pace a mite." He mounted to his saddle once more, and the horses were urged on their way. "Now I got that hoof-print firm in my mind," Windsor continued, "I can spot it from the horse's back. I don't reckon I'll have to stop again, unless they veer off somewhere."

Five minutes passed, while Sundown and Windsor loped their ponies along at a steady clip, the trail swinging steadily to the southeast. "Sure as hell," Windsor called to Sundown against the rush of wind in their faces, "that pair is headin' toward my Window-Sash holdings. I wonder what they want over this way."

Sundown could tell by the man's tones he felt troubled. He asked, "Any particular reason they'd want to visit the Window-Sash while you're away?"

"None I can think of."

"You're sure they wouldn't be making contact with one of your hands?"

"I don't know why they should. I trust my hands. They've been with me a long time."

The horses increased their strides. Ten more minutes passed, and again a halt was made while Windsor stepped down from his horse. "I'm sure sorry," he said apologetically. "I figured I could see that hoofprint right along, but it suddenly seemed to disappear." He proceeded in a stooping position for several yards along the trail. "I've found it again." He spoke to Sundown. "We're still headed right." He returned to his horse and mounted.

Sundown said, "Feels like we're getting into rolling country."

"You're right. And it gets more up and down as it approaches the foothills of the Terrera Bruta Range. My house is sort of nestled between two hills."

Sundown could feel the sun hot on his shoulders as they rode. He judged that the sky was very blue as he remembered it. There might be a few clouds drifting easy overhead, and probably a buzzard soaring high up where it looked like speck size. Once he heard some distance to the right the sound of cattle.

"Your cows?" he called to Windsor.

Windsor shot him an incredulous glance. "Don't miss much, do you, Sundown? Yeah, reckon they're my stock, though they could be Flying-Box-9 or Lazy-E even. It's too far off for me to see brands or earmarks. Our herds sort of all mingle together at times. We never think of separatin' them until beef roundup."

The horses pounded on. Sometime later Windsor again called for a stop. "For a short spell," he explained, "we've got to slow down some. There's a stretch ahead where the dirt is worn down to hardpan and some flat out-croppings of rock. Hoofprints won't show up too plain." They pushed on again, holding the ponies down to a walk now. Sundown could detect the different sounds the hoofs made when they struck the harder footing. "Damn the luck," Windsor said at last.

"What's the matter?"

"I've lost the trail altogether on this going."

"You can't see the hoofprints?" Sundown asked.

"Not a trace."

The two pulled their mounts to a stop. Sundown said, "Let me try." He got down from Coffee-Pot and ran his finger over the rocky surface. Moving in a stooping position, he proceeded along the trail, sensitive hands feeling his way. Once he paused and glanced back. "Was it the off hind hoof on that bronc you were looking for?"

"That's correct."

"Worn off on the outside of the shoe?"

"You've called it right. Don't tell me you can feel that print!"

"I reckon. Come and look for yourself."

Windsor slid down from the saddle and stooped by Sundown's side. His gaze followed Sundown's fingers as they traced out a very faint scratching of a hoof. "By God," Windsor said in admiration, "I'd never seen that if you hadn't showed it to me."

"Those hombres are traveling a heap faster than we've been doing," Sundown commented.

"They sure are," Windsor agreed a few minutes later when Sundown had pointed out other tracks. He fell silent, then "I figured they might swing east or west at this point, but this settles it. They're heading straight for the Window-Sash. Nothing else to head for in this direction, unless they're just aiming to ride smack up against the Terrera Bruta Mountains. Well, that cuts down our problem some."

"In what way?"

"Now we know where they're headed, we don't have to bother looking for hoofmarks any longer. From now on we can make just as fast time as they've been making."

"You don't think it would be wise to go on as we've been doing?" Sundown asked dubiously.

"No reason for it," Windsor said. "There's no place else for 'em to ride in this direction, except my Window-Sash. Now we can pound our ponies right on in and ask Montaldo and Munson what in hell they want — Hey, wait a minute. I've got an idea."

"Spill it."

"Instead of us going on to the Window-Sash, we'll climb to the top of Center-fire Hill and from there —"

"Where's Center-fire Hill?" Sundown asked.

"It's a fairly high hill that stands just north of my place. There's a sort of hollow right at the top, like a firing pin makes in a ca'tridge. There was a scientist out here a few years back and he said he thought it was an extinct volcano, though the mouth of the old volcano had gradually filled up during the last several thousand years. Anyway, there's still a sort of hollow there, with a lot of brush and trees growing in it. I figure we can climb to the top, get to the rim of the hollow, and look right down on my ranch. If we hurry, we can get there in time to see Montaldo and Munson ride in, and see what they do around the place, or if they don't ride in, we might see them hiding some place near it to spy."

"Why should they spy on the Window-Sash?" Sundown asked.

Windsor paused. "I just don't know," he admitted. "Howsomever, they're heading for my place. If they'd wanted to talk to me, they had a chance back in the Royal Flush. Seems to me if we get up to the top of Center-fire Hill, we can at least watch their movements."

A trace of irritation crept into Sundown's tones. "Hang the luck! I wish I could see this country, and sort of get the layout in my mind." He smiled ruefully. "But I can't, so I guess it's up to me to follow your lead, Nort. Let's get going." He gave a sharp whistle and Coffee-Pot came trotting to his side.

The two men mounted. Now Windsor swung off the trail they'd been following and headed almost directly east. The going became softer under the ponies' hoofs, the hardpan and rock being left behind. Within a short time they reached mounting ground, then the horses were climbing even steeper grades, Sundown felt tall grass brush his stirrups, and a little later the waves of coolness striking his face indicated shadow, so he knew they were passing through trees. After a time he felt the sun hot against his body. Nort Windsor called for a halt and they stepped down, dropping reins over the ponies' heads.

"We're on the north rim of the hollow now," Windsor explained, "said hollow being about fifty yards across. It's filled with a tangle of brush and scrub oak and mesquite. Lots of catclaw too. We'd best go on foot from here on, until we get across. Look, it might be a good idea for you to hang on to my belt while I lead the way. I'll pick the easiest going, but you'd better guard your face as well as possible."

They started out. The earth was soft and crumbly underfoot as they pushed into the thicket of brush. Branches tore at arms and legs at spots; at others the way was more open and sunny. Then the passage was shadowed once more. A feeling of uneasiness had overtaken Sundown as the two men forced their way through the thick brush. More and more he was wishing he had his sight. Some sixth sense, instinct, call it what you will, was warning him that all was not well. His steps moved reluctantly forward behind Windsor's, but so long as he could think of no definite objection to voice, he continued to follow Windsor's lead. Eventually Windsor led the way once more into the open.

He was panting slightly when he spoke. "Something of a job getting through that hollow," he said.

"Wouldn't we have been smarter to ride our ponies around the rim?" Sundown asked.

"If it was just a matter of saving time, yes," Windsor replied promptly. "But I was afraid Montaldo and Munson might have spotted us from down below."

"You're probably correct, at that," Sundown conceded.

"Anyway," Windsor went on, "we're right on the south lip of the hollow now. You stay back. I'll go ahead and see if I can see anything of those two jaspers down below."

Sundown heard the man move forward several paces, then judged by the sounds that Windsor had dropped on his stomach to peer down the slope toward the Window-Sash buildings.

Sundown stood waiting, the sun hot on his body. Behind him rose the thicket of brush from which emerged the various chirping of birds and the tiny noises made by flies and other insects.

"What do you see?" Sundown asked at last.

"Not one solitary movement down there." Windsor sounded disappointed. "From here I can look down on the roofs of my buildings. I don't even see my cook, or any of the hands moving around. Course my punchers are still out on the range some place. Or they might be in the barn, getting the chuck wagon in order for beef roundup. I gave orders to re-tire the wheels this morning. But I can't see one damn' thing of Montaldo and Munson. Where do you suppose they disappeared to?"

"It's beyond my guessing," Sundown said.

Windsor grunted as he climbed erect and started to return to Sundown. He said something in a disappointed tone, but Sundown wasn't paying any attention now. The cowboy's interest was held in another direction. The chirping of birds in the thicket at his rear had suddenly ceased. There'd been a couple of frightened flutterings, and then silence. Windsor was still talking, but Sundown was ignoring the words. His ears were alert for other sounds, more ominous sounds. Somewhere in the brush, behind him, Sundown had caught what sounded like a man's hushed breathing. Yes, he was right.

There, again, was the sound. And Nort Windsor was in front of him. That meant someone was hidden at the rear. Carelessly Sundown allowed one hand to drop to the butt of his holstered forty-five, but the movement came too late.

"Don't jerk that hawg-leg, Mallare!" came the order in a harsh voice. "We've got you and your pard already covered."

Sundown stiffened and raised his arms in the air. Windsor swore and whirled around. "What the hell!" Windsor commenced. "Who in the devil — ?" He broke off, then, "Munson! Montaldo! How did you get up here?"

"Swung south of Center-fire Hill and climbed our ponies up," Munson snapped, "while you two were arriving from the north."

He and Montaldo had emerged from the brush, both holding leveled six-shooters. Windsor demanded angrily, "What's the idea you two holding guns on us?"

Montaldo said dryly, "Een thee interes' of — how you say heem? — self-preservation, no? We have hear' how fast weeth thee seex-gon is thee Señor Mallare. We do not dare to take thee chance. You have been cover' seence you have firs' arrive here."

"We left our broncs on the east side of this hill, so's you wouldn't hear them," Munson put in. "Now, if you hombres will promise to keep your guns in holsters, we can put ours away. Then maybe we can sit down and *habla* a mite. Mallare?"

Sundown nodded. "I promise. I know when I'm licked."

"Windsor?" Munson asked next.

"Hell, yes," Windsor said ruefully. "I'm willing to follow Sundown's lead for a change. He just got in a jam following mine."

"Ees good." Montaldo smiled. There was a rasping of metal against leather as he and Munson slipped their six-shooters back into holsters. Munson spoke further words, and the four men dropped to sitting positions on the ground. Durham sacks and papers were produced, and cigarettes were rolled. Matches were lighted, and blue smoke drifted in the sunny air, high above the rolling grasslands below.

Montaldo opened the conversation. "We are curious to learn jus' why you two have make thee follow of Jake and me?"

Windsor said stiffly, "Where in hell did you get the idea we followed you?"

Munson laughed harshly. "When you first got here, we heard you tell Mallare you couldn't see 'one damn' thing of us.' Besides, we spotted you from a rise of land a couple of times. Saw you dismount and examine the trail."

Windsor swore bitterly. "Damn it! I should have thought of that, but figured you were too far ahead of us."

"I should have thought of it too," Sundown said wryly.

Windsor shook his head. "It's not your fault, Sundown. You couldn't see the terrain the way I could. I should have been more careful. It's all my fault —"

"This self-condemnation," Munson sneered, "might be interestin' to you, but me, I don't give a damn about it. I'm still askin' why we were followed."

Sundown said quietly, "You should know, Munson, that you and Montaldo can't go riding around the country the way you do without raising folks' curiosity."

Montaldo said mildly, "Ees there a law what says a man can not ride where he wish', so long as he does no harm to annyone?"

"That's the question," Sundown pointed out, "whether you've done any harm or not."

"What sort of harm?" Munson growled.

"There's too much rustling going on in the Holster Basin," Sundown said directly.

"Oh, so we're suspected of rustling," Munson grunted. "What do you think of that, Luis?"

"Ees ver' fonny — ver' fonny indeed," the Mexican said, but he wasn't smiling now.

Munson sneered. "Yeah, I'm laughin' my head off about it. Whose cows are we supposed to have rustled, Mallare?"

"The Lazy-E, the Flying-Box-9, and the Window-Sash have all lost cows."

"Seems I've heard something to that effect," Munson said in a nasty tone, "but that's no proof me and Luis had anything to do with the runnin' off of the critters. I reckon you two jumped to conclusions."

"That's not been proved yet," Sundown said, even-voiced.

"So you've set yourself up to stop the rustling you say that's going on. Just how do you figure to do it?" Munson asked. "I'm plumb interested."

"I'm not stating that I can stop it. But I got an idea I could certainly slow the rustlers up for a spell."

"How?" Munson didn't appear over-impressed.

"In the first place I'd do away with running irons in the branding and have the stock raisers use stamp irons. It's too easy to blot a running-iron brand: it's generally drawn on in a hurry, the lines aren't always even nor the same size. A smart cow thief can take advantage of such carelessness and pick brands to blot that already fit in with his own ideas —"

"By God, that's right," Windsor put in. He seemed interested. "It's time us cattlemen in the basin took some steps to change things."

Sundown went on. "Take the Lazy-E — an E lying on its back. That can be changed to a Lazy-Box-9, if Chris Newland was a thief and inclined to do some stealing. Nort, here, uses the Window-Sash, which is even simpler to blot on an Echardt brand."

"That's true too," Windsor stated.

"Don't tell me you never thought of it before, Windsor," Munson said mockingly.

"Certainly I've thought of it," Windsor snapped, "but I'm no thief. Up until recently we didn't have rustlers in the basin and we all trusted each other."

"Another thing I'd do, if I had my way," Sundown continued, light flashing from his smoked glasses as he turned his head from Munson to Windsor, "is to change the earmarkings of the cattle in the basin. The Lazy-E swallow-forks right and left. The Flying-Box-9 overslopes the right ear and underslopes the left. That's a mark that could completely remove the Lazy-E marking. The Window-Sash, Nort, as you know, of course, crops right and left. Again, it's an earmarking that could remove the Lazy-E cuts completely."

"Ver', ver' interesteeng," Luis Montaldo murmured. "You are sayeeng then, Señor Sundown, that thee Flyeeng-Box-9 and thee Window-Sash are rustle of Lazee-E cows?"

"I didn't say that at all," Sundown denied swiftly. "I merely stated what could be done if Nort and Chris Newland were thieves. But what is to prevent some outsiders coming into the basin and blotting the Lazy-E cattle as I've explained could be done, and then running them off to sell elsewhere? Eventually, say, Echardt gets wise to what's going on. He accuses either Newland — and there's already been trouble in that line, as you remember — or Nort, here, of stealing his cattle. Hard feelings are set up, enemies made, a range war breaks out. That's what a big rustling ring would like. While Nort and Chris were busy fighting Curry Echardt, the rustlers could drop down and really make a big steal of stock. Do you hombres see what I mean?"

There was silence for a minute, then Munson said heavily, "Mallare, you're smart — mebbe too smart for your own good. A man in your condition — mebbe I should say position — shouldn't get too smart. If you get in a tight spot you might not be able to fight your way out. So long's you can't see, you'd be better off to stay out of things and mind your own business."

"Protecting Lazy-E interests is my own business."

"But you ain't said a single word yet to prove me and Luis are back of the rustling you mentioned," Munson reminded in his harsh tones.

"And you've said nothing to prove I'm wrong in my suspicions," Sundown snapped. "Exactly what is your business here, Munson?"

"That," Munson growled, "is none of your damn' business. But any time you think you can get anything on me'n Luis, you just go ahead."

Sundown smiled thinly. "You once offered me a job, Munson. Suppose I take you up on that offer now? Maybe I could learn more about you —"

"Offer's withdrawn," Munson said bluntly. "You're blind. You'd be of no use to us now."

Sundown nodded shortly. "All right. The next question is, what do you two intend to do with us? Should we disappear suddenly, this country might get right hot for you —"

"Who has said that you are to make thee disappear, Señor Sundown?" Montaldo affected surprise. "We have nozzeeng against you. You can make the leave when you like."

"You're letting us go?" Windsor sounded surprised.

"You can both go to hell for all of me," Munson growled. "Or any place else. I don't give a damn where you go. But just remember, I don't like to be trailed. Try anything like that again, and like's not you'll get your rear end in a sling. Go on now, make tracks. We'll leave after you've gone."

Sundown and Windsor got to their feet. Montaldo said politely, *"Adiós, señores."*

"Adiós," Sundown replied. He followed Windsor into the thicket.

"Look here, Mallare" — Munson spoke in weary tones — "why don't you just try mindin' your own business? Keep out of things that don't concern you."

"I've already given you my answer on that score," Sundown called back as he followed Windsor.

"On your own head be it, then," Munson said harshly.

Windsor heaved a long sigh of relief as he led the way across the hollow. "Maybe we're lucky to get off with a whole skin, Sundown."

"Could be," Sundown replied. He felt a loose branch whip across one shoulder and pushed it out of the way. "I reckon we don't know any more than we did, Nort."

"Except," Windsor said bitterly, "that I led you into a trap. I should have known better."

"No regrets, Nort. None of us can think right every time."

"God," Windsor said, "they could have bumped us off, easy as not."

"And when we disappeared the whole basin would be out looking for us," Sundown pointed out, "if they had killed us. I've a hunch that Montaldo and Munson aren't too keen on stirring up more interest in their movements."

"Maybe you're correct. This way, no harm's been done us. We stuck our noses into things and got caught at it. Then we had a talk. Can't anybody bring the law on those two for what they did, as I see it. Just the same, if they're not back of the rustling, I'll eat my Stet hat."

The two emerged from the thicket a short time later. Sundown gave a short whistle and in an instant Coffee-Pot was at his side, and he climbed into the saddle. Windsor mounted an instant later and they turned the horses down the slope.

At the bottom they drew rein a moment. Windsor said, "Want I should ride with you until we hit the Lazy-E trail?"

"Thanks, no. I'll make out. Coffee-Pot knows we're headed home by this time, I reckon. He knows the way."

"Good. I could probably have saved myself some time by riding around Center-fire Hill and descending on the side toward my place, but I just didn't feel like I wanted to run the chance of encountering Munson and that Mex again — not alone. Me, I'm going to be glad when I got my own four walls around me."

"I reckon I get the idea. Well, so long."

"Take care of yourself, cowboy. And I'm sorry as hell I led you into that trap."

"Forget it. We all make mistakes at times. And I feel it was my fault as much as yours. We just got too nosy at the wrong time, Nort."

"Yeah, I reckon." Windsor watched Sundown lope off in a northwesterly direction, and something of pity came into the man's eyes. "Blind as a bat," Windsor mused, "but, by God, he's as good a man as I am. All things considered, a heap better, I'd say."

Sundown Disappears

It was after dark when Sundown arrived at the Lazy-E, and the crew was at supper in the long mess shanty that adjoined the cookhouse. Biscuits Benmore stuck his head through the kitchen door. " 'Bout time you drifted in," he growled. "Does it take you all day just to pick up mail, Sundown?"

"Yeah, sometimes it does." Sundown grinned, as he found a seat at the long table and answered various greetings from the crew. Curry Echardt was there, having heard that Sundown was missing, and had grown somewhat worried.

"What took you so long?" Echardt wanted to know. "I was getting ready to send a couple of the boys to town to see if anything had happened to you."

"No, nothing happened — but it might have," Sundown said. "Let me get some of this beef and spuds under my belt, and I'll tell about it." The men rolled cigarettes and lighted pipes while they waited for Sundown to finish. He commenced to speak before he had completed his meal and told how he and Nort Windsor had followed Munson and Montaldo that day. Finally he drained the final ounce from his coffee cup

172

and reached for Durham and papers. "There," he stated, "you have the story. Now you hombres can go get the sack of mail in the bunkhouse and not let me take up any more of your precious time."

But for a while no one was interested in mail. A chorus of questions broke on Sundown's ears. Curry Echardt looked worried. He put a query to Sundown.

Sundown shook his head. "I've told you all I know. Nort and I just got overly eager and walked into a trap. And we're no wiser than we were before."

"Did they act awful mad at you?" Rawhide Lacey asked.

"Not particularly," Sundown said. "Peeved, maybe, at being followed, but I sort of gathered an impression they were having a good laugh inside at the way they'd turned the tables on us. There was a sort of sarcastic chuckle in Montaldo's voice when he talked."

"Damn' greaser," growled Cal Sawyer, a leathery-faced cowhand. "Could get my mitts on him —"

Ferd Calkins, young and belligerent, horse wrangler and blacksmith for the Lazy-E, stated belligerently, "What we ought to do is get a bunch of riders together and run that pair right outten the country."

"On what grounds?" Sundown asked. "We've no proof of any lawbreaking against them — yet."

"Grounds, hell!" Joe Saxon, short and muscular, snapped. "Just tell those bustards we don't want their kind in the basin and that they'd best move on."

"And suppose one of 'em — say, Jake Munson," Tom Leslie said, "refused to leave, Joe? Are you prepared to take on the job of running out Munson yourself?"

Joe Saxon fell silent. "Maybe I talk too much," he admitted at last. "Nope, I don't want to tangle with Munson alone. He looks like heap bad medicine to me."

"Anyway," Leslie pointed out, "they didn't do any harm to Sundown and Nort."

"Maybe they were too smart for that," Curry Echardt said. "Should Sundown and Nort suddenly drop out of sight, naturally our suspicions would fall on Munson and Montaldo. I've got a hunch they don't want too much attention pointed their way."

"But what are they doing around here, if they're not stealing cows?" Rawhide wanted to know.

Sundown commenced to roll a cigarette. "You tell me and I'll tell you," he said. "It's beyond my explaining."

"I just think," Curry Echardt said thoughtfully, "that I'll ride into Holster City, first thing in the morning, in the hope of finding those two and asking a few blunt questions. If they refuse to answer, then I figure it might be a good idea to write a letter to the U.S. marshal for this district and see what he can do."

"I'll ride in with you, if you don't mind," Sundown suggested.

"I'll be glad to have you siding me." Curry nodded.

But when they visited Holster City the following day there was no trace of Jake Munson and Luis Montaldo to be seen. In fact, a good many days were to pass before the pair again entered the town.

The following week beef roundup started. By the time that was completed and the cattle shipments east on the T.N. & A.S. railroad sent off, the days had grown shorter and the nights chillier. It wasn't until a count had been made at the close of the roundup that Nort Windsor, Chris Newland, and Curry Echardt knew exactly how many cows they had in their herds — rather how many they had lost to rustlers the preceding season. The exclamations of anger that rose on the air were extremely emphatic, and all three insisted that something would have to be done to stop the cow thieves before the stock-raising business in the basin was completely ruined. Of the three, Chris Newland proved to be the heaviest loser, though Windsor claimed to have missing nearly as many cows as Newland. The Lazy-E came off best, but that best was enough once more to stir threats of quitting stock-raising from Echardt.

"Don't know why I put up with it," he announced peevishly, "when I could just as well sell out and retire to California. Never yet heard of a cow thief gettin' tangled in a fishin' line. I'd like to go where I could get shet of the bustards for good and all."

"There's rustlers in California too," Sundown had pointed out.

"Yeah, but I wouldn't be raisin' cattle out there," Curry growled. "All's I would be doin' would be to sit with a fishin' pole in my hand and teach the worm to swim on his own hook."

"Sounds good," Sundown agreed, "but I've been thinking of something else." Echardt asked a question. Sundown went on, "Chris Newland is the heaviest loser to the rustlers. Also, his holdings are much nearer the Mexican border than yours."

"Does that prove anything?" Echardt asked.

"I don't know, but I think it does."

"I'm waiting to hear, Sundown."

Sundown explained. "There's been some talk that the little outfits to the north of us, outside the basin, have been doing the rustling. But I think it is someone nearer the border, for the simple reason that the outfit nearest the border has lost the most cows. No cow thief is going to come clear to here for his thieving when he can grab off Newland's cows without making a longer trip. Of course the herds of all three outfits sort of mingle at times, but mostly the cattle stay near their own outfits."

"Maybe you're right," Echardt shrugged. "At the same time, Windsor's stock is as near the border as Newland's Flying-Box-9. Why shouldn't Nort be as heavy a loser as Chris?"

"I'm not sure," Sundown admitted, "though from what I've heard the Window-Sash doesn't run quite as high-grade stock as the Flying-Box-9. That might have something to do with it."

"It might," Echardt conceded. "But can you tell me just how the rustlers get the cattle out of the basin? You can't convince me they drive 'em over those Terrera Bruta peaks."

"I somehow" — Sundown frowned — "don't think they do. But I haven't got the answer by a long shot. I just wish Newland hadn't sacked Zane Balter when he did. More and more I've come to feel that Balter had a great deal to do with the rustling. Newland was so easy-going that anything could be slipped over on him."

Echardt sighed. "Maybe you're right. It's beyond me. But what do you aim to do about it?"

"That" — Sundown smiled cryptically — "is something I've not yet quite figured out."

"Well, you'd best forget it for a spell. And if you don't drop up to the house more often and visit with 'Ginny, you're going to have that girl on my neck. She claims I'm keeping you too busy with cow business. I've tried to convince her otherwise but it's no go. It's going to be up to you to convince her I'm no slave driver."

"Tell 'Ginny to look for a visitor right after supper tonight." Sundown laughed. "I wouldn't want you to get the name of being a hard man to work for."

"Maybe 'Ginny has got a right to be concerned at that, son," Echardt said earnestly. "You've been spending an awful lot of time riding the range. You get in your saddle and we don't see you from morning until night. God only knows where you travel to day after day. What the devil are you looking for?"

"I'll tell you that when I find it," Sundown replied. "Fact is I've just been in hope of finding something, and I've had not one bit of luck so far."

"And meantime," Echardt grumbled, " 'Ginny blames me for it."

"I'll be up to the house to see her sure tonight," Sundown promised.

And that night he kept his promise. But the following morning, when Biscuits Benmore roused the punchers from their bunks, it was discovered that Sundown was missing.

"Well," Tom Leslie stated, "Sundown sure got an early start this time. Which one of you boys got up and roped his horse for him?"

Rawhide Lacey rubbed the sleep from his eyes. "Cripes! Sundown can do his own roping if he has to. Anyway, he doesn't have to rope that Coffee-Pot horse to saddle him. He just gives a sort of peculiar short whistle, and that pony untangles hisself from the rest of the broncs in the corral and comes trottin' to the gate. Don't worry about Sundown, he'll come ridin' in long about the time Biscuits gets the beans and those chunks of leather he's nicknamed steaks on the table —"

"I heard that," Biscuits Benmore paused to growl on his way to the kitchen. "What's wrong with my steaks?"

"What isn't?" Rawhide snapped, pulling on his boots.

"Put a name to it," Biscuits challenged.

"They ain't cooked right," Rawhide stated.

"You know a better way to cook 'em?" Biscuits bristled.

"Sure, just throw 'em in a brand fire."

Biscuits' eyes narrowed. "You think that would be good?"

"I didn't say it would be good" — Rawhide snickered — "I only maintained they'd be better than the way you burned 'em."

"Aw, you go to hell," Biscuits growled good-naturedly.

"Will you two quit wrangling?" Tom Leslie put in with some irritation. "I was talking about Sundown. I don't like the way he rides off alone, and him blind the way he is."

"But what could happen to him?" Joe Saxon asked.

"That I don't know, but should he run into Montaldo and Jake Munson again, he might not be so lucky," Leslie crabbed.

"Quit your worryin', Tom," Rawhide advised. "He'll be back by suppertime, you see if he ain't."

Ferd Calkins had an idea. "You know, he might be headed off on a trip to see that Eloise Peters he's always writing to."

"Who's Eloise Peters?" Leslie snapped, knotting a bandanna about his neck.

"I don't know who she is." Calkins shrugged his shoulders. "But I see him writin' a letter every week, and more than once I've read the address, when I saw the letter layin' on the table, or when it was my turn to take the mail in."

"Aw, I'm bettin' it's some old-maid aunt he writes to," Cal Sawyer said. "If you ask me, I figure Sundown's sweet on Miss 'Ginny."

"And I'd say his feelin's are reciprocated," Rawhide stated. "To tell the truth, though, I've seen that Eloise Peters's name on envelopes, too, and done some wonderin' about it. Not that it's any of my business —"

"Well, if it isn't your business, why spend so much time talking about her?" Tom Leslie broke in, "Come on, you waddies, finish your dressing. Biscuits will be callin' us to chow before you know it. It's already gettin' bright in the east."

"Tom's right, time's a-wastin'," Rawhide added. "And there's no sense of us wastin' more time worryin' about Sundown. Five bucks against two 'dobe pesos he'll be in by nightfall."

No one offered to take the bet, but that evening, when the men sat down to supper, Sundown's place at the long table was vacant.

Nor did the red-haired cowboy with the smoked glasses put in an appearance the following day. Curry Echardt's face commenced to take on a drawn appearance; the other men went about their work looking worried. Finally Curry rode in to see Deputy Sheriff Dave Beadle at Holster City. A group of riders was organized and the country scoured, but no trace of Sundown could be uncovered.

"All right," Echardt announced grimly, "we've fooled around long enough. First time Montaldo and Munson hit this country again I'm going to swear out a warrant against 'em. We've sat back like fools and let that pair ride the basin as they pleased. Now I'm going to learn what they're up to if it's the last thing I do. And if they haven't had a hand in Sundown's disappearance, I'll be mighty surprised."

But Munson and Montaldo had dropped from sight as well. No one could be found who had seen the Mexican and his harsh-mannered pardner. Nevertheless, the rustling went on as it had before. Every so often some puncher riding across country would find old branding fires and read signs proving that beef stock had been thrown and branded — but with what brand no one knew.

Range Detective

It was two weeks later that Sundown returned. The men were at supper when he arrived, and when Sundown appeared, grinning, at the mess-shanty doorway, punchers on either side of the table rose and gave yells of delight.

"Sundown!"

"Where've you been, you moss-eaten ol' long-horn?"

"The prodigal son returns — !"

"Whyn't you let us know — ?"

"Sundown's back!"

The men crowded around, shaking his hand and slapping him on the back. Sundown had lost some weight during his absence; his clothing looked dusty and worn.

"Damn' if I didn't think I heard someone ride down to the corral a spell back," Rawhide put in, "but I thought maybe it was Curry. He went to town today —"

"Curry got in about an hour ago," Joe Saxon said.

"Where in the name of the seven bald steers have you been?" Rawhide asked.

"It's a long story," Sundown laughed. "But give me a chance to eat first. I'm nigh starved.

Missed a lot of meals lately."

"Montaldo and Munson been holdin' you captive?" Rawhide growled.

"Who?" Sundown looked puzzled. "Why should they hold me captive?"

"We didn't know who else to blame it on," Tom Leslie said. "We had riders out scourin' the country, but couldn't find trace of neither you nor Munson and his Mex pard."

"Uh-huh." Sundown nodded. "I suppose it is likely they'd fall under suspicion. Nope, I've heard nothing of either of 'em."

There came the sound of fresh platters of food being banged down on the table, then Biscuit Benmore's voice, "If you waddies will shut up and let this prodigal son eat, mebbe he'll get some of his weight back. Sundown, you look plumb ganted up."

"I've had to do a hell of a lot of riding the past two weeks." Sundown smiled.

"Curry don't know you're back yet, does he?" Tom Leslie asked.

"No, I came straight here," Sundown returned.

"I'll go up and tell him, while you get started eating," Leslie proposed.

"I'll go up myself, then bring him back," Sundown said. He laughed a trifle self-consciously. "I want to see 'Ginny for a minute or so too. Biscuits, keep my chow hot, will you?"

"Gawd only knows what they'll ask next of a ranch cook," Biscuits grumbled, falling back into character. "Keep his chow hot, he says. Who in hell does he think he is, the owner?"

But Sundown had already passed out of the mess shanty and was on his way to the ranch house.

"And you'd better damn' well keep it hot, too, Biscuits," Rawhide threatened, "or we'll run one ranch cook named Benmore so far up into the Terrera Brutas that his hat will start floatin' in the clouds."

A half-hour passed before Sundown returned to the mess shanty with Curry Echardt. Echardt's features carried a look of relief and he was smiling broadly. "Well, boys, he's back," Curry stated, "and we're certainly glad to see him."

"Maybe now" — Biscuits Benmore stuck his head through the kitchen door — "his royal highness will deign to sit down to eat my food I've been keepin' hot."

"I wouldn't be surprised if you were right, Biscuits" — Sundown laughed — "though 'Ginny gave me a whole pie while I was at the house. Howsomever, that only filled out some of my hollow corners. Bring on your chow!"

He dropped down at the table where the others had long since finished eating. Echardt sat down beside him and commenced stuffing tobacco into his brier pipe.

"You ain't yet said where you've been," Rawhide reminded.

"Let me get some of this chow down first," Sundown said.

"And wait until you've heard his story," Echardt said. "Sundown's really done a job. And" — momentarily his face took on a grim look — "certain skunks are due to get their comeuppance right soon."

The men waited eagerly while Sundown put away steak, biscuits, potatoes, coffee, and pie. Finally he shoved back his plate, heaved a long sigh, and loosened his belt. He glanced at the ranch cook. "That," he stated, "was food fit for a king, Biscuits."

"I always knowed" — Benmore beamed — "that my talents was wasted on this outfit."

"My Gawd!" Cal Sawyer exclaimed. "*His* talents! Look, Sundown, it's all right to flatter Biscuits a mite — we got to keep him here until we can find another cook — but now you've plumb spoiled him."

"That's right appropriate," Ferd Calkins chuckled. "A spoiled cook spoils the food —"

"Now, you look here, Ferd," Biscuits commenced belligerently, "I'm not going to take —"

"You'll take something you don't like," Leslie interrupted, "unless you keep that big trap of yours shut, Biscuits. We're not interested in you. It's Sundown we're waitin' to hear from. After we been worryin' our heads off the past two weeks —"

"Jeepers!" Sundown laughed. "I'm mighty appreciative, but I didn't want you hombres worrying about me. Could I have done it, I'd have mailed you a letter, but where I was operating there wasn't any post office. But you shouldn't have worried."

"Exactly what I told these dumb cow nurses," Rawhide Lacey said. "I explained you were capable of getting around without your sight, and that you'd show up all right —"

"Yaah!" Joe Saxon scoffed. "You should have seen Rawhide, Sundown. He went around with a face so long that one misstep and he'd put his foot on his lower lip."

Curry Echardt spoke half humorously. "I never did see such an outfit. First you all wanted to hear where Sundown has been, but the past several minutes you've all been so busy talking you haven't give him a chance." His face sobered. "Sundown has uncovered something mighty important, boys, so I suggest you keep your mouths shut and give him a chance to tell his story. Go ahead, Sundown."

Sundown had been rolling a cigarette. He lighted it and drained the last drops from his coffee cup. Light from the oil lamps suspended overhead glinted on his smoked glasses as he directed his voice toward one end of the table and then the other.

"It's a sort of long story," Sundown began, "but I'll get through it as quickly as possible. To commence with, I'll own up to something you hombres didn't know about me. I came in to the Holster Basin as a representative of the Artexico

186

Cattlemen's Association —"

"What?" Rawhide blurted. "You! A range detective —"

"You mean you're a range dick?" from Tom Leslie.

Sundown nodded. "Correct. Anyway, I'm supposed to be. Howsomever, I've been sort of handicapped and couldn't do much until I got back on my feet again and got the feel of things. Curry has known it for quite sometime. I told him that night after I'd shot the snake — that day I was out riding with 'Ginny." He paused a moment to draw on his cigarette. "You'll remember, sometime back, there was one of our operatives came to the basin — a man named Steve Wyatt. And a darn good man he was too. But I think Steve must have got a little careless, and the rustling ring learned who he was. Anyway, Steve was found dead, if you'll remember."

"Shot twice, from close up," Tom Leslie said.

"That's right." Sundown nodded. "Steve had been sending in reports, weekly, to Jim Ryland. Ryland's at the head of our association. I suppose one of the rustling gang learned about those reports — it would be easy enough with Steve telegraphing them in to Ryland — and that was the end of Steve. However, Steve always closed his reports with a sort of identifying remark regarding the plant growth — in his case, he generally mentioned the sage was green. That told Ryland it was Steve actually sending the report, and not somebody else. But suddenly Steve's reports started arriving with no mention of the sage, so Ryland commenced to think the messages were being faked. He didn't have another operative to send into the basin at once, but the minute I finished a job I'd been working on, he sent me here to look into things. Well, you all know what happened to me, and if you think I haven't been nearly crazy at times, being so helpless when I should have been working, you've got another guess coming."

Sundown smiled a trifle grimly and continued. "Like I say, operatives weren't too plentiful, so there was nothing Jim Ryland could do except leave me here in the hope I'd be able to learn something, in spite of my blind condition. Then, as I became able to sort of take care of myself again, I prevailed upon Ryland to leave me here, though he was right reluctant to do it. Incidentally, I've been sending my reports to him to a post-office box number, rather than to Artexico headquarters, and I've been addressing them to the name of Miss Eloise Peters. So long as such reports came through, there was no need of me using the 'sage is green' identifying phrase."

Curry Echardt chuckled. "And learning who Eloise Peters was, was certainly a big relief to 'Ginny, Sundown."

Sundown smiled. "Cripes! I tried to tell her long ago that Eloise wasn't anybody in particular, but it was a rather difficult thing to talk about without revealing too much, and besides, she said she wasn't interested."

"In a pig's eye she wasn't." Echardt laughed.

"I'd just as soon have taken her into the secret," Sundown said earnestly, "only I was afraid to have her know too much. If any of the rustling ring had ever learned she knew something of an Artexico operative, no telling to what lengths they might have gone to get the information out of her. So it was best she didn't know what I was doing in the Holster Basin."

"But have you learned who's back of the rustling?" Rawhide asked.

Sundown nodded. "I've learned a hell of a lot about the bustards," he replied.

"Who are they?"

"Who's stealing the cows?"

Various questions ran quickly around the table, as the punchers clamored for information.

"Zane Balter and Nort Windsor," Sundown said tersely.

There was a sort of stunned silence at mention of Nort Windsor's name, then several angry, indignant remarks.

"Surely not Windsor," Tom Leslie protested. "Hell, I've known Nort for years. I ain't surprised at Balter. But, my Gawd, Sundown, not Nort Windsor. Why, I —" The words went unfinished, so great was Leslie's astonishment. His features expressed keen disappointment, as did those of several of the punchers at the table.

"I know how you feel," Curry Echardt said.

"It was a real body blow to me when Sundown told it."

Sundown said soberly, "I'd grown to like Nort Windsor pretty well myself. It's just another case of a good man gone wrong, I reckon. But there were a couple of things that made me suspect him. That day he and I ran into that trap Munson and Montaldo laid for us, I'd been talking to him in the Royal Flush Saloon. I asked him if he'd lost any cattle lately, and without hesitation he told me he'd had thirty-five head run off a couple of nights previously. Well, with cows scattered all over the range, from the foothills of the Terrera Brutas to the lower levels, it struck me sort of queer that Nort Windsor should be able to know so soon the exact number of cows he had missing. Particularly when he didn't say the cows had been stolen from some special herd he'd had fenced off, or anything of the sort. Of course he may have had some special way of knowing, but I doubted it, and put it down as a lie. With the Lazy-E and Flying-Box-9 losing cows, Windsor had to pretend to lose some too. Anyway, I tied that business up with something else I had in mind."

"What's that?" Tom Leslie asked.

Sundown drew a final inhale from his cigarette butt, then leaned down to extinguish the butt under the toe of his boot. He straightened up again and went on. "A short time before Steve Wyatt was killed, he sent into the Artexico headquarters a report on the size of each herd in the basin as well as of the smaller outfits scattered around. It likely took him a little time to gather these figures and I'm not sure exactly how he did it, but I believe they were accurate. At that time Nort Windsor's Window-Sash was reported as running eight thousand head of cows. I was talking to Nort one day in Holster City, and he told me at that time his herd numbered around eight thousand head. This was before beef roundup, mind you."

"Well" — Rawhide's forehead was furrowed with a puzzled frown — "those figures check. What's wrong with 'em?"

"I'll explain in a minute." Sundown smiled. "On the face of it, those figures sound all right, I'll admit, and meant that Windsor hadn't sold any stock since Wyatt had sent in his report. However, I've been down below the Mexican border since I last saw you. I've done a lot of riding, and I've found three different ranchers who have purchased from Windsor something close to twenty-five hundred head of stock the past year. These ranchers had bills of sale bearing Nort Windsor's signature. Now just where did those twenty-five hundred head come from if Windsor hadn't sold any stock since Wyatt made his report?"

"I'll be damned!" Tom Leslie exploded. "Why, that dirty, low-down bustard — !"

Curry Echardt interrupted with, "I meant to ask you when you told me this a spell back, Sundown, but it slipped my mind. These cows that

Windsor sold, were they in his own brand?"

"Some of them were," Sundown replied, nodding. "Branded with the Window-Sash marking, and it's my hunch those were Lazy-E cows whose brands had been blotted. The majority of the cattle, however, carried the Flying-Box-9 brand, which Windsor told the ranchers he had bought from Chris Newland. He also carried bills of sale for those, signed with Newland's name, but I figure he or Zane Balter forged Chris's moniker. Oh, it all looked genuine enough to those ranchers. Windsor had vented the Flying-Box-9 brand all proper."

"Just who are these ranchers he sold to?" Tom Leslie asked. "Doesn't look like they care much where they get their stock. Maybe they've got an arrangement with Windsor and Balter."

"I don't think so," Sundown said seriously. "Two of 'em are from Montana and the other one from Wyoming. They're stock raisers who were crowded out by sheepmen in those northern states and got right disgusted, so they headed for Mexico where they could get good grazing lands pretty cheap and made a fresh start. I learned there are quite a few cattlemen from the States who have moved to Mexico for the same reasons. And I think we're pretty safe in believing that it is to men like that Balter and Windsor are selling most of the rustled stock."

"You'd think," Tom Leslie growled, "those men would be a mite particular where they bought their cows."

"Would you be?" Sundown asked. "Put yourself in their place. Say you've come to Mexico and taken up grazing lands. You want to build up a big herd. When you hear of cattle to be had at a more than reasonable price, you'd be likely to jump at the chance to get them. Particularly if you're dealing with a man like Nort Windsor. Nort is damn' likable and nobody would ever take him for a crook. To those ranchers it all looked open and aboveboard."

"I guess you're right at that, Sundown," Leslie conceded.

"When you talked to those ranchers in Mexico," Echardt asked, "did you tell them you were trailing rustlers?"

Sundown shook his head. "No, so far as they knew I was just a cowhand riding through the country." He smiled sheepishly. "I guess I took advantage some of what they called 'my blind condition,' and I had to ask a terrific lot of questions. Those men couldn't do enough for me. They fed me, took care of my horse, and at night we sat and made *habla*. As I say, I asked a lot of questions and then pieced my information together. Oh, I ate well when I was visiting at those ranches. It was later, when I was camping out in open country, that I was forced to do without my meals on a good many occasions."

"It's still damn' hard for me to believe Nort Windsor is a rustler." Rawhide frowned. "I'd be ready to swear —"

"I don't think there's any doubt about it being Windsor," Sundown cut in. "These men told me they had bills of sale signed by Windsor, and what they told me about the man who'd sold them the stock certainly fitted Windsor's description."

Echardt nodded. "I reckon it's Nort all right, Rawhide." He turned back to Sundown. "How do you account for that Lazy-E cow and calf that caused your trouble with Zane Balter that day you and he crossed guns? That calf had certainly been blotted Flying-Box-9 — Chris Newland's brand."

"It's my opinion," Sundown replied, "that it was Zane Balter himself who probably did that blotting, and then turned the cow and calf loose near the house here so you'd come across it easy — you or one of the boys. It was Rawhide who drove 'em in."

"But why should Balter do that?" Echardt frowned.

"To throw suspicion on Newland," Sundown answered promptly. "If he could have got you and Newland to warring against each other, you'd have been so busy throwing lead at each other — and the crews of both outfits would have been in it too — that neither the Lazy-E nor the Flying-Box-9 would have had any time to watch its stock. And that would certainly have made things easy for cow thieves."

"I reckon you're right," Echardt said. "And also that action tended to take suspicion away from Windsor and Balter."

"Correct," Sundown agreed. "And the stunt of making bad feelings between you and Chris Newland nearly worked too. You were really primed to climb his frame that day we rode over there."

"Yeah, I was," Echardt admitted. "Only for you keeping a cool head I might have done something I'd have regretted all my life."

"I figured Chris was on the square," Sundown said. "He was so indignant and sincere and sorry when you accused him that I felt he was honest."

"Good thing one of us kept his head that day, anyway," Echardt said.

"Here's something else," Sundown continued. "At the time Steve Wyatt was shot suspicion fell on Zane Balter, I understand, and he was questioned by your deputy sheriff. However, as I understand it, Nort Windsor swore to an alibi for Balter at the time. Now that we know that Balter and Windsor are working together, I haven't the least doubt that Windsor lied to save Balter's skin."

"I figure you hit the nail on the head with that one, cowboy," Rawhide exclaimed.

The others nodded. Cigarette and pipe smoke swirled through the room. Biscuits Benmore had long since removed the dishes from the table and was engaged in washing them in his kitchen, though much of the time he was listening at the kitchen doorway. All the men were discussing at once the various things Sundown had related, and as they talked their faces took on a grimmer aspect.

Tom Leslie finally broke in with a question. "Look here, Sundown, you say that you know of some twenty-five hundred head those bustards run below the border and sold. Like's not there's been a lot more than that, since the thieves first started operating in the basin. All right, I'll take your word for it, but what I want to know is how they got them critters out of the basin in the first place. To drive a herd out of the basin, you have to pass Holster City. No man can drive that many cows past the town without being spotted by somebody. The only other way to get rustled stock into Mexico is to drive 'em straight over the Terrera Bruta Range, and I don't figure anybody did that either. Cows don't climb them ragged peaks that easy."

Sundown smiled. "I was wondering when one of you would get around to asking that question. It's a problem that bothered me for a long time too. I finally came to the conclusion that there must be a pass running through the Terrera Brutas some place that led into Mexico — a pass known only to the rustlers —"

Here Sundown was interrupted by Noisy Tanner, one of the oldest men on the Lazy-E crew. He was ironically called "Noisy" because of his extremely quiet ways and because he generally had nothing to offer in the way of conversation. "There's no pass through the Terrera

Bruta Range," he stated definitely. "I've been in Holster Basin a good many years now, and I've rid along every mile of that range, and I ain't never yet seen any pass."

"That's where you're wrong, Noisy." Sundown laughed. "I'll admit it's not easy to find. There's a lot of box canyons and draws over in the Terrera Brutas, and that's what this secret pass looks like, I imagine. It sort of goes in at an angle behind a big sandstone bluff, and it's pretty damn' narrow at the entrance. After a mile or so it widens out considerable. The entrance is hidden by scrub oak and high brush. I know. I had to push my way through —"

"Damned if I see how you do it," Rawhide said admiringly.

Sundown continued: "The opening to that pass lies just south of Nort Windsor's Window-Sash buildings. His holdings reach to the mountains at that point. You'd never notice that narrow opening in the rocks if you were just riding past. Once in the pass you find your course is a winding one, with high sandstone cliffs on either side. A horse's hoofbeats really echo in that twisting canyon. Eventually it gets wider and wider, and by the time you're through the pass, it widens out into a grassy valley. There's a sizable water hole there, and the grass grows tall. Lots of trees on either side of the valley. There's a small shack on one slope too. But it is in that valley that Windsor and Balter hold the stolen stock until brands can be changed and buyers found, and so on. To get out of the valley, there's another pass that opens into Mexico —"

"Well, may I be roped down for a polecat!" Leslie exclaimed in astonishment. "I've never heard of anything like it."

"I spent four days just feeling my way around that valley," Sundown went on.

"You worked at night, naturally," Echardt said.

"Naturally." Sundown nodded. "I didn't want to be seen, though, as you know, I had reached the point where day and night didn't make much difference to me. I lay in the brush and listened to voices and movements around me —"

"What did you do for food?" Rawhide asked.

"Sneaked into the shack when nobody was there and grabbed a can of tomatoes or peaches or something from a shelf. There'd be cold biscuits layin' on the table now and then, and sometimes cold coffee in a pot. At night I'd sneak down to the water hole."

"Cowboy! You sure ran chances," Echardt said.

"Not too many," Sundown replied modestly. "At night the rustlers stay pretty close to their fire. One night I crept up close and listened under a window while Balter and Windsor talked. Daytimes I stayed hidden in the brush and just listened to stray voices and the bawling of the cows. They're holding quite a sizable herd there at present."

"Well, if you heard Balter and Windsor

talkin',"" Tom Leslie said angrily, "I guess there's no further doubt of Nort's guilt. You're sure it was him?"

"Don't you think I'd recognize his voice?" Sundown asked.

"I reckon you would," Leslie conceded disappointedly. He heaved a long sigh. "Damn' the luck! I always liked Nort."

"A lot of us did," Sundown said quietly. He went on, "From what I heard of the talk between Balter and Windsor, I judge that Balter lives there all the time now. That's where he disappeared to when he left Holster Basin. Nort Windsor comes and goes, but generally never stays too long in the valley. I heard him tell Balter he didn't want his hands to get suspicious, so he shows up pretty regular at his ranch."

"So the Window-Sash hands aren't in on the rustling?" Echardt asked.

"Not from what I could gather. Aside from Balter and Windsor, there's a crew of around twenty-five or thirty men living in that valley and doing the rustling. When they figure to operate near the entrance of the pass, Windsor always sends his crew working in some other part of the basin and keeps 'em away from the vicinity of the pass. With just a small crew and him acting as his own foreman, he could get away with things like that."

"Do you reckon they're holding some of my cows in that valley right now?" Echardt asked.

"It wouldn't surprise me any — yours or Chris

Newland's. I didn't take time to make a close examination of brands, as you can understand, but I'd judge there were about three hundred animals in the valley right now. The night I heard Windsor and Balter talking, I gathered they'd just finished working over some brands, and they were ready to push the cows through into Mexico as soon as the brands healed. So I figure it's up to us to drop down on those bustards fast if we want to save those cows from being sold in Mexico. I got the information for you, but I don't just see how I can round up the rustlers without some help."

"I'll say you got the information," Rawhide exclaimed.

"And you'll get help too," Echardt promised. "There's not an honest man in this basin but will be glad to lend a hand in breaking up that rustler crew."

"And then" — Sundown smiled — "when that's done, I aim to crawl into a bunk and sleep for about a week. I've sure lost a heap of shut-eye the past —" He broke off as his sharp ears caught the sound of a soft footstep in the doorway.

The other men at the table were slower to react to the sound and for a moment noticed only that Sundown had ceased talking. Echardt said, "Go on, Sundown, what were you saying —" He, too, stopped suddenly and swung around on his seat, then, "What the hell," he burst out in an angry voice.

Jake Munson stood in the doorway, a drawn

gun in his hand, covering the group at the table. "Just take it easy, gents," Munson said in his harsh tones. "We've come to get Sundown Mallare."

"Don't Get Proddy!"

Silence descended around the table. Munson pushed farther into the mess shanty to make room for Luis Montaldo's entrance. Montaldo also held a leveled six-shooter in his hand. His teeth flashed whitely, but there was nothing of laughter in his voice when he spoke: "Eet ees bes' you follow the Señor Munson' order, gentlemen. Eef you jus' make to sit quiet, no harm weel come to you. Eet ees thee Señor Sundown we weesh to do the business weeth —"

"Now look here, Munson," Echardt protested. "You can't come sneaking in here and —"

"T'hell we can't!" Munson said roughly. "We've already done it. You take my advice, Echardt, and keep out of things that don't concern you. Just sit quiet and we'll take Mallare away and that's all there is to it."

"You'll take him over my dead body," Echardt snapped belligerently.

"That's possible too," Munson growled. "Come on, Mallare, up on your feet and don't start anything. You've fooled us long enough, coming here and pretending you were blinded —"

"I don't figure there was any pretense about it," Sundown said quietly. "You can check with Doc Pearson."

"You've fooled Pearson, or I miss my guess." Munson moved farther into the room and stood across the table from Sundown. "No man could outshoot Zane Balter the way you did — not when he was blind. Nor get around the country —"

"Damn it!" Rawhide put in earnestly, "I know Sundown was blinded. His shootin' — well, if you'd spent the hours I have with him, watchin' him practice, you'd know —"

"All that's neither here nor there," Echardt put in. "You try and take Mallare away from here and you're in for trouble, Munson — you and your Mex pard —"

"This isn't your time to start acting up, Echardt," Munson said heavily, "so don't you get proddy."

"What you planning to do with Sundown?" Echardt demanded.

"I already told you," Munson snapped, "not to inquire into things that are none of your business. You'll learn in good time what we're doing. And don't any of you hombres try to stop us."

"By Gawd," Rawhide swore, "you hombres must be fixin' to have a fight on your hands."

"You keep out of this, cow poke," Munson half snarled. "What you aiming to fight with? Cowhands generally take their guns off when they sit down to eat."

"Pairhaps," Montaldo said mockingly, "they plan to come at us weeth thee bare hand', Señor Jake."

"They won't come at us a-tall," Munson said heavily. "They got sense." All the time he'd been talking, his eyes had been steadily on Sundown. He went on, "You, Mallare, I told you once to get up from that table. I don't want to have to tell you a second time. Now, get up and move plenty pronto, unless you want to be bored with a lead slug."

Tom Leslie started an angry remark, but Sundown interrupted with, "Take it easy, Tom. It's me these two hombres want. Let me handle this."

"You're all through handling things," Munson said harshly. "You've already handled too much for my liking —"

"Now, you look here, Munson —" Echardt commenced.

"I'm warning you, Echardt, keep out of this." There was a dangerous undertone in Munson's words.

Feeling around the long table had grown tense. Three or four of the punchers sat stiffly, as though about to spring, just waiting for the order from Echardt or Sundown.

Luis Montaldo hadn't missed this attitude either. "I theenk eet bes'," Montaldo said in his cool, purring voice, "eef each man at theese table raise hees hand' and clasp them on hees head." His gun barrel swung along the table, and reluctantly the men raised their arms and did as they were told. Curry Echardt's face was apoplectic. He was almost choking on his wrath. Only Sundown had refused to obey Montaldo's orders. He sat as before, both hands below the table.

"You, Señor Mallare" — Montaldo's tones became sharp — "you hav' not raise your arm' in thee air. Ees bes' you do as I say."

Sundown smiled thinly. "Maybe I've got a reason for that too," he stated, "said reason being that I've got your pal Munson covered from under this table and have had ever since he came in. Oh, I know" — mockingly quoting Munson — " 'cowhands generally take their guns off when they sit down to eat,' but I got to the table late, and just happened to neglect that little dining convention —"

Munson swore, stiffened, but continued to hold his gun on Sundown. "Better surrender, Mallare. You haven't a dawg's chance."

"There's two of us then," Sundown said evenly. "My slug would have to pass upward through the table to reach your carcass, Munson, but that wouldn't be hard for a forty-five bullet. And if Montaldo shoots me, it might cause my trigger finger to jerk. Then you know what would happen. So the next move is up to you, Munson — you and Montaldo."

There was grudging admiration in Montaldo's voice when he spoke. "Eet seem' as eef thee table is turn', Señor Jake," he said philosophically. "Pairhaps eet ees bes' we make the explain to Señor Echardt —"

Sundown interrupted. "Montaldo, you might as well drop that imitation Mexican accent you're using. I'm not being fooled."

Startled expressions crept into Montaldo's and Munson's features. They exchanged quick glances, then stared hard at Sundown. Sundown laughed softly. "You hombres should know better than to get caught offguard that way. I had a prime opportunity to bore Munson then."

"Damn' smart you didn't try it." Munson grunted. "The shock of your slug might have set off *my* trigger finger."

"I'd already thought of that," Sundown said dryly.

Montaldo's smile was rueful, and when he spoke his accent had completely disappeared and his language was as good as any man's in the room, probably a great deal better than some. "It appears," he said evenly, "that I'm not as smart as I thought I was. I'd give a lot though, Mallare, to know just how you discovered my accent was faked."

"You don't have to give anything." Sundown laughed coolly, and he still held his gun on Munson under the table. "I'll tell you for nothing. Ton-and-a-half, at the Royal Flush, told me some time ago. He'd heard you talking to Munson once when you didn't know he was near."

Montaldo slowly shook his head in self-disapproval. "Pure carelessness, that's all it was. Jake, you'll have to watch me more closely after this."

"There's been enough palaver," Munson growled. "We've come for Mallare and one way or the other he's leaving here with us. And I'm warning the rest of you gents to keep out of this business. Mallare, you might get me, but Montaldo will get you. You've got a chance for a break if you'll come easy without trouble —"

"Why in the devil should he?" Curry Echardt again found his voice. "I'm warning you, Munson, that —"

Munson said in a weary voice, "Oh hell. I'll tell you why. I'm placing Mallare under arrest —"

"*You* are?" Echardt snapped. "Who the devil are you to be arresting anybody?"

"Deputy U.S. marshal for this district," Munson said bleakly. "Now you know, do you feel like messing up my job further, or do you listen to sense?"

"Deputy U.S. marshal?" Echardt exclaimed. A frown crossed his forehead and he gave a short skeptical laugh. "I'm afraid you can't push that one across on us, Munson. I happen to know the name of the deputy U.S. marshal for this district. His name's Matt Jackson."

"Ever seen him personally?" Munson asked.

"I haven't, but he's well known as being probably the greatest gun fighter in the Southwest, or he was before he was appointed a deputy U.S. marshal. It was Matt Jackson who killed Black Birney, the train robber. It was Jackson who cleaned out the Cave-in-the-Wall bandits. He run down the Pegasus Mine payroll thieves, too, and, single-handed, killed three of them and arrested the rest —"

"All right, all right," Munson growled sulkily, "you know who he is, so let's talk no more about it. I'm Matt Jackson. Just took the Munson name for this job. Figured my real name was too well known. Here" — he reached in a pocket and produced a wallet which he tossed on the table in front of Echardt — "my credentials are there. Take a look at them."

Montaldo laughed softly, though the gun in his hand didn't waver an inch. "It seems we are both being unmasked, Matt."

No one heard the words. All eyes were intent on Echardt, who was delving within the wallet, inside which was pinned a gold badge of office. Echardt unfolded and glanced quickly through certain papers. His jaw dropped. "My God!" he exclaimed. "You are Matt Jackson!"

"All right," Jackson said grouchily. "I told you that. No need to get excited about it."

"Then what in the devil," Echardt persisted, "is the idea of arresting Sundown — an operative for the Artexico Cattlemen's Association? I can't see —"

"WHAT!" The single word was very much in the nature of an explosion. Matt Jackson's eyes bulged from his head; his thin lips parted in amazement and his jaw dropped. He stared unbelievingly at Sundown. "You? You an Artexico man? No — no! Don't try to put that over, Mallare. You can't be! Why, you —"

Sundown's soft laugh interrupted Jackson's amazed voice. "Jackson, you sound as if you'd got your trails crossed somewhere along the line. Sure I'm an Artexico man. Now, maybe, you'd like a look at *my* credentials."

Sundown put one hand in a pocket, produced a wallet and tossed it on the table.

Still wary, backing away a trifle, his gun held level, Matt Jackson said, "Luis, you take a look — and watch out for tricks."

A trifle reluctantly the Mexican holstered his gun and approached the table. He flipped open Sundown's wallet and extracted certain papers it contained, studied them a few moments, then carefully folded and thrust them back into the wallet which he shoved across the table to Sundown.

"Señor Mallare," he said courteously, "I'm asking a thousand pardons." Then he turned to Matt Jackson. "Matt, you and I comprise a very thick-headed pair of prize idiots."

Jackson swallowed hard. "You — you mean to say, Luis, that he really is an Artexico dick?"

Montaldo nodded and showed a flash of white teeth in a wide smile. "And a very good one, I gather from his papers," he replied.

Slowly, still staring at Sundown, Matt Jackson

209

lowered his six-shooter. There was a rasping of metal against leather as Sundown put his gun away, and he faced Jackson with a broad grin.

"I reckon I'm a prime fool, Mallare," Jackson said slowly, and while his tones were still harsh, they held a friendly note now. "I don't know how this mistake was made, but I reckon we'd better compare notes and talk this business out a mite."

"That should clear up matters." Sundown chuckled, proffering his right hand across the table. "You know, I've been suspecting you and Montaldo too. Maybe we're both prime fools."

He commenced to laugh as Jackson and Montaldo gripped his hand, and the laughter was taken up by the others. The mess shanty resounded with roars as, the tension relieved, the men gave full vent to their feelings. Jackson's whole body was shaking, and momentarily all signs of the relentless man hunter had vanished from his features as he lowered himself to a seat at the table.

"What a boneheaded play I made," he bellowed, holding his sides. "I should be kicked clear from here across the Rio Grande! I'll never live this one down. The drinks are on me. Meanwhile, Echardt, could I get a cup of coffee? After a blow like this, I've got to have some kind of stimulant!"

"Biscuits!" Curry Echardt bellowed. "Put on the coffeepot!"

"It's already on," the cook snapped from his

kitchen doorway. "I ain't as slow as some folks to get an idea. And there's a bottle of Old Crow here, too, if you want I should bring it on."

"T'hell you're not slow," Echardt scoffed, "or you'd have realized that bottle is already needed here. We all want a stimulant!"

Fighting Men Needed

The chuckles and laughter died down after a time. Coffee was served and drinks poured from a bottle. The Lazy-E men were eying Matt Jackson with interest. Here was a man whose gunfighting exploits were known throughout the Southwest country. Cigarette and pipe smoke floated above the table around which the men sat and made spiral patterns through the shades of the hanging kerosene lamps.

Matt Jackson took the lead in the conversation. "I imagine you're working on the rustling game in the basin, aren't you, Mallare?"

"That's what I was sent here to do," Sundown replied.

Jackson nodded. "Made any progress?"

"Some. I'd like to tell you what I've —"

"And I'm anxious to hear," Jackson said, "but first, maybe we'd best tell what we've been doing here — or trying to do. Luis Montaldo has been working for the Mexican Government —"

"Secret-service man?" Echardt asked.

"Something like that," Jackson said. "He's got credentials, too, if you want to see them, but if you'll take my word for him, we'll save some time maybe."

"You word's good with us," Sundown replied. "Go on."

"We knew there was a deal of rustling taking place in the basin," Jackson commenced, "but that's not what brought us here. We had other fish to fry —"

"Speaking of fish" — Echardt beamed — "someday I'm going to head for California and —"

"Yeah," Jackson said, "we've heard about you planning to go on a fishing trip out to the Coast. Fact is, it's one of the first things we heard about you when Luis and I hit the basin. But, like I say, we're interested in another type of suckers — the kind that has been breaking the law and think they can get away with it." He settled into his story. "In short, we're on the trail of a gang of border scum — thieves, killers, raiders of small towns, and so on, that have been making things miserable for decent Mexicans for quite some spell now. Luis, why don't you tell these gents your part of this business?"

Montaldo nodded. "As Matt says, my government has for some time been troubled by a gang that's been operating along our side of the border. This gang would raid small towns and get pretty rough with some of the women. They stole horses continually and robbed money where they could find it. Finally, they planned and successfully executed a couple of bank robberies. My government assigned some army troopers and cavalry to tracking them down, but the army never got any place. They'd be hot on the trail, only to find the bandits had apparently vanished into thin air some place in the vicinity of the Terrera Bruta Range, on the Mexican side. So the army was called off, and I was detailed to see what I could learn through under-cover methods."

Montaldo drew deeply on his cigarette, exhaled a cloud of gray smoke into the air, and continued, "To cut a long story short, I wasn't a great deal more successful than the army per-sonnel had been, but I did hear rumors that one Zane Balter was at the head of the gang. I learned also that rustled cattle from the basin were being sold in Mexico and I finally came to a conclusion that there must be some sort of secret pass through the Terrera Brutas, running from the United States over to my country. I put in a good many hours riding the range, looking for the opening of that pass, but I had no success there, either. I finally concluded it might be easier to find from the States' side of the border. To receive permission, and help, to come to the basin, I wrote to your government at Wash-ington. Certain formalities were necessary, but eventually Deputy U.S. Marshal Jackson was assigned to help me. . . . Matt, you can go on from there."

Matt Jackson cleared his throat. "Figuring my name of Jackson might be recognized, I took the name of Munson when Luis and I arrived in Holster Basin. We did a lot of riding, but we've not yet been able to find any pass through the Terrera Bruta Range. We knew Zane Balter was heading the bandits, but when we tried to trail him to the pass, he just seemed to slip away from us. Probably made the journey at night — if there is such a pass in existence —"

"There is," Sundown said. "I can lead you there, I think."

"T'hell you say!" Matt Jackson exclaimed. "This looks better and better — but I'll get on with my story. We saw Nort Windsor with Balter a lot, so we figured Windsor was crooked too. Luis and I knew that folks in the basin looked on us with suspicion, but that was what we wanted. We figured the rustlers working hereabouts would figure we were crooks and would invite us to join 'em. In that way we could discover their hideout — but that plan wouldn't work. Nobody — rustler or honest — wanted anything to do with us, apparently. So that left just one thing for Luis and me to do. Every day we picked one man from each outfit and trailed him, spied on him from the brush, watched where he went, and so on. Trouble was, that got to be quite a job for just two men, and we never seemed able to find anything crooked. Of course we were right certain we had something in Balter and Windsor, but they never did anything suspicious in daylight, and, like I say, it's hard to watch a man in the dark —"

"And," Sundown interrupted, "about the time I hit Holster City and you heard I was looking for a job, you and Luis planned to offer me said job, helping you to trail?"

"That's right." Jackson nodded. "I figured you as honest when I first saw you. Later, I made my mistake and had an idea you were tied in with Windsor and Balter, but it was my first impression of you that made me take your part against Balter in the Royal Flush Saloon that night you arrived. Later, I got to feeling that was all an act staged to fool honest men, and that Balter had brought you in to help on his dirty schemes."

"And when Balter and I threw lead at each other," Sundown asked, "did you still think I was crooked?"

Matt Jackson frowned. "For a time that sort of shook our theory up, but then we got to thinking you'd hit him through accident. Either that, or you and him had had some trouble and you and Windsor were set to take over the leadership of the gang. That idea was strengthened when Luis and I trapped you when you and Windsor followed us that day."

"We thought we were trailing crooks" — Sundown grinned — "though by that time I was commencing to suspect Windsor too. But I wanted to learn what he was up to, if possible, and I thought there might be a chance he had some sort of tie-in with you."

"A very muddled affair all around." Montaldo smiled.

"It sure was," Jackson agreed. "If it hadn't been for Luis, I'd have arrested you and Windsor

216

that day. I'd been feeling right along that you were faking your blindness, but why I couldn't figure out. Now, of course, I realize you are blind. Anyway, Luis protested the idea of arresting you, figuring that if we gave you and Windsor a loose rein you might lead us to something. So from then on we trailed you. Day after day we watched you riding along the foothills of the Terrera Brutas. And then one day we saw you peg out your pony on a long rope near a small water hole in the foothills back of Windsor's Window-Sash a few miles. You left that pony there about four days and didn't go near him, as we figured it, unless it was at night, but we couldn't find any sign where you'd visited him at night."

"I didn't." Sundown furnished the information. "During those four days and nights I was snooping around that hidden valley. You can't ride a horse in there, because the hoofbeats make too much noise in the pass and the guard would hear you coming. I started in there one night, but after I'd traveled just a short distance on Coffee-Pot I knew we'd be heard, in case they did have a guard stationed, so I turned back."

"You mean you traveled afoot?" Rawhide Lacey sounded horrified at the very thought of walking.

Sundown nodded. "It's only about three miles through the pass, and the rustlers keep a guard stationed at either end — U.S. side and Mexican side. So you see I had to walk. You can't very well sneak a horse past a guard."

"I'll be damned! So that's what you were doing," Matt Jackson said, his eyes widening a trifle. "Luis and I were holed up in that shack just a short way from the water hole, keeping an eye out for you. We figured eventually you'd have to show up for your horse, but we couldn't figure where you went to. We just noticed your horse there one morning at daybreak, but no sign of you —"

"What shack you talking about?" Sundown demanded.

"That one among the trees, on the slope above the water hole a mile or so. We watched with our field glasses —"

"I don't know of any shack there." Sundown frowned.

"I know where it is," Rawhide put in. "Naturally, being blind, Sundown might miss it. It's been there for years. Nobody ever uses it — at least I didn't know it if they did."

A strange look had come over Jackson's harsh features. "You say you didn't know anything about that shack, Mallare? That you've never been there?"

"Never," Sundown replied promptly. "Didn't even know it existed."

Jackson's eyes narrowed, and he shot a short look toward Luis Montaldo in whose face had come a sort of perplexed expression. Jackson put one hand in his pocket and drew out a silver finger ring, set with a triangle of black basalt, which he tossed on the table in front of Mallare. "I suppose you've never seen this before, either," he said, then, "Oh, I forgot you can't see. It's a ring —"

"Where did you get this?" Sundown asked sharply. He'd picked up the ring and was turning it over and over in his fingers. "It's many a month since I've held this in my hand."

"You admit it is yours then?" Jackson said.

"It was mine." Sundown nodded.

Montaldo said, "Inside the band of the ring it is engraved 'S. D. Mallare.' "

"I know that, too, naturally," Sundown said. There were tight lines around his mouth. "Where did you get it, Jackson?"

"Found it on the floor in that shack we were just speaking of," Jackson said. "It was lying in one corner, half covered with some old newspapers and other rubbish. Somebody's been living in that shack, on and off, because there were a few supplies there. The place is thick with cobwebs though. But what about that ring, Mallare?"

"It used to be mine," Sundown said slowly. "Steve Wyatt — the Artexico man who was killed sometime back — was always crazy about this ring, so one day I gave it to him. He was wearing it the last time I saw him, so I think this proves he was in that shack at one time. The rustlers probably held him prisoner there, or I miss my guess. Likely some time when they had him untied, maybe to eat, he removed this ring and tossed it into a corner, hoping to leave a clue if anything happened to him. And it did, damn the luck. I imagine Steve figured he was done for and I might be the one sent here in his place. All the Artexico men have seen Steve wearing this ring."

Matt Jackson looked relieved. "I'm glad that's explained," he said. "For a minute there I was afraid you'd deny knowledge of the ring and tangle us all up again. It had me worried. Well, like I say, after we'd found this ring, we waited for you to return for your pony at that water hole. Eventually you did show up, got in the saddle, and headed in this direction. Luis and I talked things over a spell and then we decided you were guilty as hell and the best thing to do would be to come here, get you, and put you under arrest. Then we planned to put on some pressure and make you tell what you knew of the rustlers and bandits. We were afraid the Lazy-E crowd would object to our taking you away, so we acted as we did when we arrived. And naturally we didn't want to tip anybody off as to what we were doing here, for fear talk would get around. That's our side of the story, Sundown; now tell us what you know."

"And you won't have to put on pressure to make me talk, either." Sundown smiled. From that point he continued, and told how he had discovered the hidden pass to the secret valley of the rustlers. "And the bustards are there," he concluded, "just waiting for us to drop down and round them up."

"I'll be damned!" Matt Jackson said admiringly. "You've done more than Luis and I put together. Blind like you are, I don't see how you managed it."

"Cripes!" Rawhide exclaimed. "Sundown don't need eyes. When you've known him the way we have and seen the progress he's made just through feeling and hearing, you'll understand it."

"It's just too damn' bad we're not all blind," Echardt said. "In that case, we'd likely had the rustlers long ago."

"I don't see yet," Montaldo put in, "how you found that hidden pass in your condition."

"There was a lot of luck there," Sundown admitted. "I was out one night, just riding along the foothills of the Terrera Brutas, and was about to come home, when I heard the bawling of cows. At first it sounded like it was coming right from the heart of the mountains and was far off, but I knew it couldn't be that far, so I guessed there was a pass some place. I scouted around a long time before I found a place where some cows had passed. Then I sort of felt out the sign in the dark, and it led me to where the pass opens —"

"Probably rustled cows you heard," one of the hands put in.

"There's no doubt of that," Sundown said, "otherwise they wouldn't have been taken through the pass. So I sort of marked the place by instinct, you might say, it being dark and all. But it was mostly luck. As far off as those cows were, when I first heard 'em, they might have been missed by ordinary ears. But ever since I got that clout on the head that made me blind, my hearing has been a heap keener. Anyway, I started to follow on Coffee-Pot, but his hoofs made too much noise, so I turned back and slept out on the range, trying to figure some other way to get through that pass. I climbed to the peaks, and spent days maneuvering around, then crossed the range by horse and dropped down into Mexico. Eventually I recrossed the range to the States' side and decided I'd have to make my way through the pass on foot. It was then I tethered Coffee-Pot at that water hole while I made my way through the pass on foot, sneaked past the guard, and spent those days in the valley, uncovering the set-up I've just been telling about."

It was almost uncanny the things Sundown had accomplished. The men noted the light reflected from his smoked glasses, and even then found it difficult to believe he was actually blind.

Matt Jackson said finally, "Well, it looks like the time has come to round up a bunch of crooks and cow thieves. Handled right we can clean out the rustlers who've been pestering the basin and settle Luis's job and mine at the same time. Sundown, how much of a force has Balter got

222

working for him in that valley? In brief, how big is this gang?"

"Offhand," Sundown answered, "I'd say there was twenty-five or thirty men there. There might be a few more."

Jackson pondered a moment. "Hmmm," he said in his harsh voice, "it looks like some fighting men are needed — more than we got here. Echardt, can you get some men we can trust to keep their mouths shut, until we get organized and on our way to that secret pass?"

Echardt nodded. "Chris Newland and his hands will want to be in on this. Rawhide, you ride to the Flying-Box-9 and tell Chris to have his men ready by —" He broke off, then, "Sundown, what time do you figure to hit that pass?"

Sundown said, "We'd best plan our moves so we can enter the valley just about daybreak. That means we want to reach the entrance of the pass during the night. We can't get started tonight, so it will have to be tomorrow night." He turned to Rawhide. "Tell Newland we'll stop for him and his men tomorrow afternoon."

Echardt nodded. "Most of the men we need had better meet here at noon tomorrow. I'll send word in to Deputy Dave Beadle and tell him what's afoot, so he can round up some riders for us." He turned to Cal Sawyer. "I'll give you a note to take in to Dave, Cal."

One by one the Lazy-E men were given assignments to ride to the smaller ranches outside the basin. "We've got to make it clear to the little outfits," Echardt explained, "that if the big men in the basin are wiped out, the little ranches will get a dose of the same later."

Montaldo said, "What about Nort Windsor's crew? We're pretty certain they're not in with Windsor in the crooked work."

Echardt frowned. "No matter how honest he is, no cowhand likes to fight against the man who's been paying his wages. I don't know what to say, Luis."

Sundown said, "We can stop at the Window-Sash on our way to the pass. If Nort's there, we'll grab him. If he's not there, he'll either be with Balter or in Holster City. Curry, you might station one of the hands along the trail between the Window-Sash and town, so if Windsor goes to Holster City, we'll know about it. If we don't hear anything from the hand, we can pick him up on our way to the pass."

"Right," Echardt agreed. "Joe," to Joe Saxon, "that's a job for you. And no matter who you see, keep your mouth shut. We don't want word of this raid to get out."

Eventually plans were all laid, and the Lazy-E hands headed for the corral to rope out ponies and ride to various points on their errands. Sundown offered to ride any place Echardt saw fit to send him, but Echardt scoffed at the idea. "You'd best roll into your bunk, son, and get a well-earned rest. Matt, I reckon you and Luis had better stay here too." He swung around and went to the door of the mess shanty, his voice carrying to the saddlers' corral where the Lazy-E hands were mounting. "Everybody you talk to," Echardt bawled, "tell 'em to bring six-shooters *and* Winchesters, as there's a fight ahead. And tell 'em to bring plenty ammunition. It's sure to be needed!"

A few moments later hoofbeats drummed out of the ranch yard.

Echardt returned to the table and sat down. "Plans are started at last," he stated grimly. "There's a cleanup coming that will be remembered for many a year in the Holster Basin."

By ten o'clock the following morning riders had commenced to arrive at the Lazy-E. Deputy Sheriff Dave Beadle, lean and lanky, and with drooping black mustaches, had arrived, bringing seven well-armed riders with him. By twos and threes other men came loping in, with six-shooters at thighs and Winchester rifles in saddle-boots. All showed plainly their surprise at finding Montaldo and Matt Jackson on the side of the law enforcers. There was some quiet laughter as Jackson's true identity was revealed, but for the most part the men stood about grim-faced and smoking, but saying little. Biscuits Benmore placed platters and huge coffeepots on the table as noontime approached. By the time everyone had eaten, there was a band of nearly thirty men ready to ride.

Curry Echardt stood outside the bunkhouse in the warm noonday sun, talking to Sundown,

Montaldo and Jackson. "Ain't a man I sent word to," he announced with some satisfaction, "that ain't responded to our call. Everybody's here I expected would come."

Sundown said, "In that case, we might as well get started, Curry."

Echardt said awkwardly, "Look here, Sundown, slipping around at night and feeling out things is risky, but not as risky as riding into a fight with the lead slugs humming around you when you can't see. Why don't you stay here and sort of keep an eye on 'Ginny and the ranch?"

Sundown laughed. "After all I've accomplished so far, are you figuring to keep me out of the big showdown, Curry?"

"Hell, I suppose not," Echardt growled. "Nobody's got more right to go with us than you but I wish I could keep you here."

"Don't worry about me." Sundown smiled. "Anyway, you got to have me with you, to lead you to the pass."

Echardt sighed. Montaldo and Jackson added their protests to Echardt's but it did no good. "Jeepers!" Sundown said, "let's have no more arguments. I'm going, and that's settled."

"All right, dammit," Echardt growled, "it's settled, so we'll be leaving soon. But first you'd best go up to the house and say a few words to 'Ginny. She told me to tell you before you left that she wanted to see you and *habla* a mite."

"Anyway," Sundown chuckled, " 'Ginny

didn't have any doubts about my going." He started off toward the house, then hearing Rawhide Lacey's voice a short distance off, called to him, "Rawhide! Saddle up Coffee-Pot for me, will you? I've got business elsewhere a few minutes, and time's getting right precious now."

"I'll do that, cowboy," Rawhide called back. "Make your time count."

Deputy Dave Beadle emerged from the bunkhouse carrying a Winchester. Echardt said to him, "Find a rifle to your liking, Dave?"

Beadle nodded. "Same model as my own rifle. It was just my luck to have my own gun loaned out at a time like this."

"You're welcome to that, Dave, and you'll likely be using it plenty too."

The next time Rawhide came near, Echardt called to him. "Look here, Rawhide," Echardt said worriedly, "I don't like the idea of Sundown coming on a job like this, but there's no way to stop him. So I'm counting on you to stay near him and sort of guide him away from the thick of the action. Being blind, he won't know where you're taking him."

"I'll do my best," Rawhide said dubiously, "but so far Sundown has managed to outguess everybody in anything he tries, so I can't make any promises."

"I'll be near to help you, anyway," Echardt said.

Sundown had found Virginia on the long gallery of the big ranch house. Range-bred though she was, the girl found it difficult to keep from persuading Sundown not to take the trail with the others. And yet she knew it couldn't be otherwise; Sundown would play a man's part in the trouble that lay ahead.

Gradually, while they talked, Sundown convinced the girl he would return to her, although deep in his heart he wasn't sure of that. He said other things, too, things the girl had waited long to hear, and a sense of security and happiness rose in her breast.

The minutes flew past all too rapidly. Almost before the man and girl were aware of it there came a pounding of hoofs from the direction of the corral, and the body of riders came dashing up to the front of the house. Rawhide slowed down as he led Coffee-Pot toward the gallery.

"Here's your bronc," Rawhide called, "if you're aimin' to ride with us."

Echardt, too, had dismounted at the gallery to say good-by to Virginia. "Now don't you get to worryin' about us, 'Ginny. We'll be back, right side up and kicking, almost before you realize it. Whyn't you go sit a spell with Tom Leslie and Biscuits? Tom kicked like a steer at being left behind, but didn't want you left alone, neither. You can sort of console Tom and also give Biscuits that new receipt you found for making apple dumplings."

A moment later he and Sundown climbed into saddles and with Rawhide dug in their spurs to catch up with the others, waiting a short distance beyond the house. The cavalcade of horsemen swept through the gateway that fronted the house and, gathering speed at every jump, struck a trail running toward the south, those in the rear swerving their ponies wide to one side to escape the dust of the leaders.

Night-Hawking

The men rode steadily across the sun-bathed range and reached Chris Newland's Flying-Box-9 late in the afternoon. Newland and five punchers, fully armed, were waiting before the ranch house, their saddled horses near by. "Thought you never was going to get here," Newland greeted. "Rawhide didn't tell me much, and we've done a heap of wondering." He spoke to Sundown and several others, then moved forward to shake hands with Montaldo and Matt Jackson. "Guess we all sort of misjudged you two," he said, "according as Rawhide tells it."

Echardt broke in, "Here's the idea in a nutshell, Chris," and he proceeded to explain what had been learned about Balter, Windsor, and the rustling gang. He cut short Newland's amazed exclamation at news of Windsor's duplicity, and briefly outlined their plans.

While they talked, the other men dismounted to rest and water their horses. Newland turned to Sundown. "By Gawd, Sundown, you've done a real job. And you're an Artexico operative, eh? I'd never dreamed it. Well, me'n my hands are ready to go any time you give the word. There

don't seem much sense of waiting any longer."
He gave a nod to his Flying-Box-9 punchers and
stepped up to the saddle of his waiting pony.

Once more the body of riders swept off, riding
due east now. One man, Ferd Calkins, left the
body of horsemen and headed his pony in a
slightly northeasterly direction with instructions
to pick up Joe Saxon, who'd been assigned to
watch for Windsor on the trail between the
Window-Sash Ranch and Holster City.

The sun dropped lower in the western sky as
the men pounded across the grassy range. Now
and then small bunches of Hereford cows were
to be seen; some of them bore the Flying-Box-9
brand, but as the riders traveled farther east
Window-Sash cows commenced to predomi-
nate. The sun had touched the distant rocky
horizon to the west when Echardt called a halt
near a wagon-rutted and hoof-chopped trail
bearing northwest. He explained the reason for
the halt.

"This is the road from the Window-Sash to
town. We're just about a mile from Nort Windsor's house now. I told Ferd Calkins we'd wait
here for him and Joe Saxon." Once more the
men dismounted and allowed the ponies to crop
grass.

Three quarters of an hour passed, while the
men waited. The sun was gone now and the day
was fading. Rawhide said finally, "Here they
come," as he spied two riders across a rise of
land still some distance away.

In time Saxon and Calkins drew rein near the body of waiting men. Their ponies were somewhat lathered. Echardt said, "You been making time."

Saxon nodded. "We didn't want to get left out of this shindig. Afraid you might go on without us if we kept you too long, and Ferd and I weren't sure which way you'd be heading."

"There's no particular rush at this moment," Sundown put in. "And we wouldn't run off on you. We'll likely need every man we can get. Did you see Windsor?"

Saxon shook his head. "I've been waiting near the trail since early morning," he said. "Ain't no one passed me. I saw a couple of Window-Sash hands some distance off once, and hid behind a granite outcropping so they wouldn't spot me."

"Well," Sundown said. "If you didn't see Windsor, that means he's either at his ranch or in the hidden valley. C'mon, we'll get started for his house. I figure to drop down there just about the time they're eating supper."

Once more the men climbed into saddles. Darkness seeped almost imperceptibly across the Holster Basin. In the east the first few stars were commencing to wink into being. When the riders arrived at the Window-Sash, lights were shining from the windows of the combination bunkhouse and mess shanty. The noise of squeaking saddle leather and pounding hoofs brought a man to the doorway. He stood there, peering out, his dark form silhouetted against the lighted background. "Don't know who you are," he called genially, "but come on in."

"We aim to do that," Echardt called back.

"That you, Curry?"

"It's me," Echardt replied, and added in lower tones to Sundown, "That's Tim Carraway. A good man. But I don't know how he's going to take the news about Windsor."

Echardt, Deputy Beadle, Jackson, Montaldo, and Sundown entered the bunkhouse to find the men had just been eating supper. Tim Carraway was still standing. Four more hands were at the table, plates of food before them. The Window-Sash cook was peering inquisitively from his kitchen doorway. "Don't tell me I got more hungry mouths to feed," he started to grumble. "I can't see why —"

"Yeah, maybe you have, cookie," Echardt cut in, somewhat grimly. "We don't insist on it, but it might be wise for you to cook up a big batch of fodder." He turned to Carraway. "Where's Nort?"

"Damned if I know, unless he's in Holster City," Carraway responded. "I ain't seen him for two-three days now. Figured he might have gone on a bust. What's up?"

"He's not in Holster City," Echardt interrupted, "but I reckon we know now where to find him."

Carraway glanced suspiciously at Montaldo and Matt Jackson, and said again, "What's up?" His lean, weather-beaten form had stiffened belligerently at first sight of the Mexican and the deputy U.S. marshal.

"Don't worry about those two, Tim," Echardt said, jerking his head toward Montaldo and Jackson. "They're on our side in this. It's a long story that you'll be hearing presently. Meanwhile" — Echardt drew a long breath — "we're starting on a rustlers' roundup. We've located the thieves, Tim. They're in a hidden valley in the Terrera Brutas."

"I'll be damned!" Carraway exclaimed. "I want in on this. And so will these other boys" — nodding his head toward the four Window-Sash hands at the table. He turned toward the kitchen. "Cookie, hurry up with some chow. Don't bother peelin' potatoes. Open some cans and other stuff. Shake a laig." He swung back to Echardt. "I wish to hell Nort was here. He's going to be sorry to miss this."

"I'm sorry too," Sundown put in quietly, "but for the reason he is not going to miss this business."

"Huh? What you mean, Sundown?" Carraway asked.

Dave Beadle sighed. "Tim, you might as well know it now as any time. Nort's one of the men we're after."

Knives and forks clattered along the table. Jaws dropped. Eyes popped. Carraway's face flamed angrily. "You're crazy as hell!" he snapped.

"Calm down, Tim," Echardt said. "It's true.

We've got the proof of it. Ask Sundown. He knows."

"You can take my word for it," Sundown said. "That hidden valley Curry mentioned — Nort's there now, with Zane Balter."

Carraway's legs lowered him weakly to the bench alongside the table. He stared unbelievingly at the others. "It's mighty hard to take," he said in a slow voice. "Nort was a right good man to work for. I liked him. We all did."

"And so did we," Sundown reminded the man. "But you can't buck facts, Tim."

Tim slowly shook his head and gazed at the other Window-Sash hands. One of them said, "It fits in, Tim, like you and me were talking about a few nights ago."

"What's that?" Sundown asked.

Carraway said, and his voice sounded miserable, "Bob and me had been talking about Nort. Now that I look back and I can see things in a different light, maybe what you say makes sense, Sundown. Nort has been acting mighty queer for some time now. He's gone for two-three days at a time. After Zane Balter left this range we got to remembering how much he and Balter were together. And we always felt it mighty queer how he always sent us working the range to the north, east, and west of here, but never the south. He made it pretty clear we were to keep out of the foothills of the Terrera Brutas. I've told him more than once that I bet there was a lot of Window-Sash critters holed up in the draws and box canyons over that way, but he always said to pay 'em no mind, that we had plenty cows without 'em. And that wa'n't true. The Window-Sash stock has been on the downgrade for some time. But Nort never seemed to care. We just thought mebbe he was careless, but we done as he ordered. After all, he was payin' our wages."

"Either that," another Window-Sash puncher said, "like Tim says, makin' us work away from the mountains, or he kept us here at the ranch for days, whitewashin' buildin's that didn't need it, or mendin' harness, or buildin' up the water tank. It just didn't make sense sometimes."

A new thought struck Carraway. "I'm surprised you hombres trust us, Curry."

"We know you boys are straight," Echardt replied. "Each one of you has been trailed and watched, and no skulduggery found against any of you."

"Well, that's one thing to be thankful for, anyway," Carraway said. A frown creased his forehead. "I don't know — Hell! I hate to take up a gun against Nort. He always treated me fine, paid good wages. Curry, it just don't seem right —"

"I know how you boys feel," Echardt said, "that's why we're not insisting you go with us. And it won't be held against you, either, if you decide to stay."

Carraway's eyes sought his brother punchers' gaze. They sat there, looking troubled. Each man knew in which direction his duty lay, but there wasn't one of them who felt any desire to draw a gun on his employer.

"You've put us in a fix," Carraway said. "We want to do what's right, and yet, somehow —" He broke off, then, "Look here, is it all right if we go along and just do our warring against Balter and the rest of the gang? You see, I just can't bring myself —"

"Suits me," Echardt said promptly, "and I know the others will be satisfied."

"I'll be riding with you then," Carraway stated. He glanced at his companions and found agreeing nods at his decision. He turned back to Echardt. "We might even see if we could capture Nort before anybody shot him. He'd be held for trial, of course, but after his prison sentence was up, he could maybe make a new start. I can't figure him as all bad."

"I reckon that will be all right with us too," Echardt replied.

"But I'll sure as hell throw lead at Balter and his skunks if I get a chance," Carraway growled. "All right, we'll be sidin' you, Curry." He turned and yelled toward the kitchen, "Hurry up with that chow, cookie. You've got a passel of riders to feed and we don't want to waste much time."

The cook brought in some knives, forks, and spoons, threw them with a clatter on the table, then left to return with steaming platters and bowls. A great coffeepot was brought in, and cups went sliding the length of the long table. Echardt yelled to the waiting men outside and they commenced pushing into the big room.

"We don't have to rush too much," Sundown pointed out, "now that we're this near. Balter has a change of guards at the entrance to the pass. There's a relief guard comes on duty at midnight. We'd best wait until he gets on the job."

Within an hour all the men were once more mounted, having fed and watered their ponies, and were riding out of the Window-Sash ranch yard, the Window-Sash punchers, gathered somewhat glumly around Tim Carraway, riding with the rest.

It was totally dark now and the sky overhead was bright with stars. Sundown was riding up ahead flanked on one side by Curry Echardt and on the other by Rawhide. On either side of these two were Matt Jackson and Luis Montaldo. Deputy Dave Beadle was staying close to the lead too.

A faint light in the east proclaimed the rising of the moon. Gradually, as it climbed higher, the country became more broken. Reaching the foothills of the Terrera Brutas, the horsemen struck ascending ground. Dimly outlined against the dark sky, far above their heads, was a rugged, saw-toothed range of mountain peaks. Sundown spoke to Echardt, and the Lazy-E owner passed the word to the others. The horses slowed pace.

Sundown said to Echardt, "I could go a more direct route but with so many riders I'm afraid

238

the sound might carry to that guard in the pass, so I'm taking a sort of roundabout way to get there."

Higher and higher the ponies climbed. They were getting into timber now. Unerringly, Sundown led the way along a narrow shelf of rock that twisted and turned, sometimes with brush and trees on one side, sometimes around huge boulders and over stretches of scattered chunks of broken rock.

After a time Sundown led the way into a thick clump of stunted pine and scrub oak growing against the face of a great sandstone bluff which rose precipitously from the level below. Here, it seemed, the trail must surely end. The riders peered through the gloom but could see no outlet. The moon wasn't yet high enough to afford much light.

One of the Flying-Box-9 punchers whispered to Joe Saxon, "Do you reckon Sundown has made a mistake and lost his way?"

Saxon had been wondering the same thing. It would be so easy for a blind man to get confused in his directions. But Saxon remained faithful. "What? Sundown make a mistake? Are you crazy? Don't fret any. That waddie knows what he's doing."

And Sundown vindicated Saxon's judgment. Just as the men expected to find themselves riding squarely against the side of the high rock bluff, Sundown led the way around a gigantic upflung slab of sandstone, and there before them lay the opening to a narrow high-walled canyon. Although the bluff had appeared impenetrable from a distance, it was, in reality, one of two overlapping bluffs that the eye saw during the day. The pass between them was just about wide enough to allow the passage of three cows moving abreast. Here Sundown called a halt with the remark that he now had a bit of solo night-hawking to do.

"This canyon," he informed Echardt and the others, "runs along a couple of miles before it reaches the valley. It widens out about seventy-five yards from this point —"

"Cripes," a Lazy-E puncher put in, "it must be a job getting a bunch of cows up here!"

"There's an easier trail to arrive by," Sundown explained, "but, as I told Curry, I took a round-about way tonight. I was afraid the sound of the horses might carry through the pass if we came direct. About a mile from here, maybe a mite farther, the rustlers have a guard stationed. The canyon twists and turns so much it's a bit hard to judge the exact distance. I've got through the pass before without the guard knowing it, but this time I'll put him out of business so we can all ride through."

Even as he spoke he was slipping down from the saddle.

"Look here, Sundown" — Echardt sounded worried — "one or more of us had better go with you."

"Can't be done," Sundown refused promptly.

"This is a one-man job. More might make too much noise. I know the way, but I don't want to have to do any explaining, or guiding, to someone who doesn't, while I'm closing the distance between that guard and me. Savvy? And don't get impatient. If I'm not back by the time three hours have passed, then you hombres will have to act as you see fit. But I'm figuring to see you again before too long. *Adiós, compañeros!*"

And before anyone had an opportunity to protest further he had flitted through the gloom and disappeared around the corner of a big jagged side of sandstone that flanked half the entrance to the pass.

Rawhide turned bitterly to Echardt. "There you are, Curry. You see how it's done?" He snorted scornfully. "And you was tellin' me I was to keep close to him so's he wouldn't come to any harm. Fat chance I had, or you either. What in hell you goin' to do with a hombre like that?"

"Damned if I know," Echardt said helplessly. "He just sort of takes things into his own hands and leaves us here like we were dummies or something."

Matt Jackson growled, "Only that he made sense in what he said, I'd have insisted on at least one of us going along. But I reckon he knows best. We've just got to trust to his judgment, and God knows he's been correct in his actions so far. Me, I'm going to have a smoke. That three hours he mentioned might get to drag out some."

The men were dismounting now, loosening cinches and straightening out saddle blankets. Cigarettes and pipes were lighted. Here and there a man took a swallow of water from the canteen on his saddle. Tobacco smoke drifted through the night. When they spoke, the men talked in low tones, but there was little conversation. Each man in the group was thinking of the battle that lay ahead and was realizing that this could be his last night on earth. Unconsciously hands strayed to gun butts and fingers ran along the supply of cartridges in belts. There was no saying what the next sunrise might bring.

By this time Sundown was already deep into the pass. Hugging the brush that grew thickly along one wall, he made his way forward with all the silent stealth of a stalking Apache. Reaching the first bend in the pass, he halted in a crouching position and listened carefully before proceeding around the next turn.

The pass was wider now. Three more turns and more than a half-hour were passed before the way commenced to drop slightly as the canyon trail neared the valley beyond. Sundown moved more cautiously than ever. If he'd moved before with the stealth of an Apache, he was now proceeding with scarcely any sound whatever — no more than would have been made by that same Apache's ghost. Precipitous canyon walls rose on either side. A half-moon, riding directly above, was partly obscured by drifting clouds and shed but little light into the winding pass.

High brush and scrubby trees flanked both walls; here and there a spiny yucca jutted from wide cracks in the rock face, or clumps of prickly pear lifted their flat pads upward in search of light.

Eventually a faint cough reached Sundown's ears. At once he dropped to hands and knees and listened. Not more than fifteen yards away a man stood watch, leaning slouchily against a flat boulder, a Winchester rifle couched loosely in his left arm.

Sundown moved five yards nearer. He could hear certain movements from the guard now — a rustle of thin paper and the falling of tiny flecks of tobacco. Then the sound of a match being scratched reached Sundown's ears. The man had rolled and lighted a cigarette, this very fact evidence that he waited at ease, unsuspicious of approaching danger. Sundown edged nearer and ever nearer, working around to the guard's rear.

The guard had nearly finished his smoke and was taking the last "drag" on the cigarette when he heard the faintest of noises at his back. He started leisurely to turn, but at that moment the heavy barrel of a Colt's six-shooter crashed against one side of his head. He didn't even groan as his legs weakened and let him slump to earth.

Sundown gave a short grunt of satisfaction as he reholstered his gun and bent over the unconscious guard. Drawing a couple of short lengths of rope which he'd carried thrust through his cartridge belt, he quickly bound the guard's hands and feet, then dragged him into the brush near by.

"You may come to, and yell, hombre," Sundown said grimly as he stood a moment looking down on his victim, "but I don't reckon it would do you much good. You're all taken care of for a spell."

He turned and started back in the direction of the waiting riders, making much better time on the return trip.

Something under two hours and a half had passed before Sundown rejoined his companions. He gave a soft whistle as he drew near, and then called, "It's me — Sundown."

Echardt and the others heaved vast sighs of relief as he hove into sight through the shadowy lights filtering from the trees. There were many welcoming greetings. Echardt said, "Thank God you got back here all right. We were commencing to get worried, son." He peered closely at Sundown. "You don't look as if you'd had any excitement. What's the matter, wasn't that guard there?"

Sundown said, "Yes, he was there. He still is, but now he's all hog-tied, neat and proper. I got him hid in the brush in case some of his pals should come along, which same isn't likely." He turned to Deputy Beadle. "Joe, I'll show you where the place is as we ride through, so you can pick him up on the return trip. We wouldn't want to leave the cuss there to starve to death."

"I'll be damned," Rawhide grunted. "Sundown, you beat anything I ever saw."

"Jeepers!" Sundown said, "there wasn't much to it. I knew approximately where he'd be, and just crept up behind and tapped him over the head with my gun barrel."

Matt Jackson said impatiently, "I reckon we'd better get into saddles, eh, Sundown?"

Sundown shook his head. "Let's wait a spell. We don't want to arrive there in the dark where we can't see what we're doing. I figure we should hit the valley just when it's starting to get light. Most of the gang will be at breakfast about that time and will be off guard some. That might make it easier for us."

"That sounds smart," Montaldo agreed. "We'll just have to wait, Matt. Remember, patience is a virtue."

Matt Jackson said shortly, "Nobody yet ever accused me of being overburdened with virtues."

Cigarettes and pipes were again put in use. Pinpoints of crimson dotted the gloom. Sundown dropped down crosslegged on the ground, one hand holding Coffee-Pot's dangling reins. No one spoke a great deal.

Time passed slowly. The moon swung far to the west. It became darker, and then false dawn commenced to gray the eastern horizon line. The stars weren't so bright as they'd been a short time before. The men lounged about on the earth in various attitudes of ease, though each was impatient to be in the saddle. Imperceptibly the tension increased.

"Judas Priest on a tomcat!" Echardt growled. "If I have to wait much longer, I'll go crazy. Ain't it about time to start, Sundown?"

Sundown laughed softly. "Not yet, but right soon, Curry. You heard what Luis said about patience being a virtue?"

"That's all very well" — Echardt sighed — "but this just don't happen to be my night for being virtuous."

Sundown turned to Chris Newland. "Chris, there's another guard stationed at the far end of this pass too — at the Mexico end. I don't know what he'll do when the shooting starts, but he may come in to help his pals. On the other hand, he may run for it to save his skin and head down into *mañana* land. I wish you'd designate two of your hands to go after him. We don't want a single man to escape."

"I'll take care of it." Chris nodded. He swung around and addressed two of the Flying-Box-9 punchers, outlining their duties.

The minutes dragged on. Finally Sundown rose leisurely to his feet. "Well, time's up, hombres. There's a job to do. I reckon we'd better start pushing through that canyon."

There were exclamations of relief as the men rose with alacrity, tightened saddle cinches, and climbed to their horses' backs. In an instant they were all mounted and ready to travel. Sundown guided Coffee-Pot to the head of the group. "I

246

hope nobody gets an idea I'm trying to run this shindig singlehanded," he said earnestly, "but as it's up to me to show the way, my place has to be in the lead."

"Go ahead," Matt Jackson said in his harsh voice. "I don't know of any better leader. Without you to show the way, as you've been doing right along, we'd be no place. Ride, cowboy! We'll follow you through hell if needs be!"

The Valley of Flaming Lead

In the graying light that seeped down into the twisting canyon the riders looked about curiously. They could see now that a great many cows had passed through here: the earth was beaten hard at spots. At other points the trail was littered with chunks of broken rock. The men pushed steadily on, past spotty growths of scrub trees, yucca, and prickly pear, the hoofbeats of their ponies resounding loudly against the steep canyon walls and echoing in the narrow confines beyond.

"I reckon Sundown knew what he was doing when he wanted that guard out of the way," a Flying-Box-9 puncher commented to the companion riding at his side.

"Sure did," came the answer. "That guard would have heard us comin' before we got anywhere nigh him."

The horses pounded on. It became still lighter after a time. As they reached the last bend in the pass, the riders saw spread out before them a long, gentle slope with a smooth green floor of grazing land at its bottom. The hillsides of the valley were thick with timber and brush, but down the center was all lush grasslands.

Here and there could be seen white-faced cows in scattered bunches. Most of them, now that it was nearly sunup, were moving leisurely toward a water hole at the right side of the valley. At the other side, a thin blue spiral of smoke was seen rising above the trees. A lone rider trotted out from the timber but as yet he hadn't noticed the body of men bursting from the canyon pass. A short distance below the point at which the smoke was ascending a pole corral held a bunch of ponies. Saddles were scattered loosely about.

Sundown called back, "They'll spot us any second now. We'd better touch up our broncs a mite. Let's go, men!"

At almost the same instant there came a startled cry from the direction of the corral. The next moment the angry *ping-ng-g-g* of a Winchester bullet was heard as it whined harmlessly overhead. There was more yelling, and a group of men spilled, running, from the trees and headed in the direction of the corral, shaking out their ropes as they moved. One or two halted long enough to throw shots from their six-shooters, but the distance was still too great for accurate aiming.

"They've seen us!" Echardt yelled. "Come on, waddies! And make every shot count!"

There came another burst of scattered firing from among the trees and much wild yelling.

"Sundown!" Echardt yelled, "you stay back. You can't see what you might ride into." Rawhide added his calls to Echardt's, but Sundown kept straight ahead, and was spurring down the long, grassy slope. Behind him the other riders were spreading out as they poured from the canyon mouth.

Sundown plunged on, the six-shooter in his right hand thumbing hot lead in the direction of the corral where some of the rustlers were now getting into saddles. Others had broken away and were taking refuge behind rocks and in the brush.

There was a good deal of breath being wasted in wild yells as the other men followed Echardt's and Sundown's direction, some using six-shooters, others rifles. Within a few minutes the rattle of gunfire was almost deafening.

Some of the Balter faction commenced firing through the brush and from behind boulders. One clump of low scrub oaks was fringed with crimson flame. Flying lead hissed viciously through the air.

The rustlers spread out as they left the corral, and Sundown's crowd did likewise. Small knots of men battled angrily at various spots over the valley floor. Six-shooters were cracking like mad. There'd come a sudden rush of hoofbeats, a sharp exchange of gunfire, then the victor would head off in another direction.

Luis Montaldo saw a rustler just throwing down on Matt Jackson. Raising his gun, Montaldo triggered once. The rustler went spilling from the saddle even as Jackson dropped another rider at whom he'd been aiming. A horse went down screaming and thrashing, and loosening his feet from stirrups, the rider plunged back into the battle on foot.

The sun was peeking above the eastern peaks now to look down on a haze of black powder smoke that floated lazily above the valley floor. Through all the noise came the frantic bawling of cattle as they bunched and commenced to leave the water hole on the run. Frightened by the firing, they started to stampede. Away they went, lumbering awkwardly up the valley, heading in the direction of the canyon from which Sundown and his companions had just emerged.

Two of the Lazy-E men swerved their ponies at a tangent to stop the progress of the frantic, terror-stricken animals. Echardt saw them and yelled, "Joe — Noisy — let them critters run. They can't do nothing but head back to their home range. It'll save us the trouble of driving 'em." The two turned eagerly to get back into the fight.

Something struck Rawhide's horse a terrible blow. The animal slowed pace, then suddenly went to its knees and crashed down. Rawhide just slipped from the saddle in time to avoid being pinned down by the weight of the dying horse. He rolled over a couple of times and rose catlike to his feet six-shooter in hand.

"By Gawd!" he yelled, "if I don't get the dirty, slobberin' bustard that killed my bronc, I'll —"

He had no time to say more. The "dirty, slobberin' bustard" was closing in on him fast, bending low from the saddle, six-gun raised to finish off Rawhide. Rawhide threw two quick shots from the vicinity of his hip, shooting by instinct rather than aim. The rustler gave a wild yell, threw both arms in the air, and toppled from his pony's back. The horse immediately slowed down and came to a stop.

"Let that be a lesson to you," Rawhide yelled as he started on a run for the riderless horse. As he passed the prone figure on the ground he threw in another shot for good measure, then gathering the pony's reins he climbed on its back. Reloading swiftly, he headed his new mount toward a point where two rustlers were crowding in on Ferd Calkins.

Echardt was riding past a clump of brush when a rifle spoke from close at hand. The owner of the Lazy-E swayed in his saddle, then drawing the horse to a halt half fell to the ground. A second shot spurted viciously above his head.

Montaldo and Matt Jackson came plunging up. "You hit?" Montaldo yelled, dismounting and running to Echardt's side. Jackson also dismounted and started running, his objective the point of brush from which had come another white flash of rifle fire.

"Come out in the open and fight, you sneaky bustard," Jackson taunted.

Nothing loath, the rustler stepped into view, raising the Winchester to his shoulder, finger curling around trigger. Jackson threw himself to the earth, shooting as he dropped. The rustler dropped his Winchester, clawed frantically at his chest, then his knees buckled and he crashed, face downward, to the earth.

Jackson got to his feet and joined Montaldo and Echardt. Echardt was already up. Jackson said, "You hit bad, Curry?"

"It's nothing much," Echardt panted as he stooped to get his gun which had slipped from his hand when he went down. "Slug got me in the fleshy part of my thigh, but no bones broken. Sort of paralyzed me for a minute — hit a nerve, reckon. Go ahead. I'm all right. Don't wait for me." He tied a bandanna around his leg above the wound, gathered up his reins, and remounted. "I got to find Sundown. It's him I'm worried about."

The three men rode off in search of further action.

The firing in the valley increased. Savage puffs of black smoke and white fire were to be seen in all directions.

Meanwhile, Sundown seemed to be bearing a charmed life. He made no attempt to conceal himself as the bullets hissed and whined past his ears. A gun had no sooner cracked from some nearby point than he had answered it with a volley from his own weapon. Sometimes he scored hits, sometimes he missed. His gun emptied, he knee-guided Coffee-Pot while he reloaded, and again started thumbing bursts of flaming lead from the muzzle.

Hoofbeats drummed behind him, closing in fast. Sundown had started to whirl his horse when he heard Rawhide's voice. "Thank the Lord," Rawhide said, "you're still all right. I got so busy I lost track of you for a spell. Look out, Sundown!"

A rustler, mounted, was endeavoring to ride down Sundown's pony. The man lifted his gun, pulled trigger. At almost the same instant Rawhide fired. The rustler spun halfway around and fell from the saddle, his right foot caught in stirrup. The horse pounded madly on, dragging its former rider along the uneven rock-spotted earth. The man screamed once and then was silent.

Rawhide turned toward Sundown. "Damn' if that coyote didn't nearly get you."

Sundown's smoked glasses were hanging by a single bow to his left ear. Sundown smiled thinly. "Close, all right. His slug just cut off one bow where it joins the lens frame. Cripes! There's another pair of glasses gone." He ripped off the damaged spectacles and tossed them away.

"But won't the sunlight be too strong for your eyes?" Rawhide cried in some alarm. Looking into Sundown's wide-open gray eyes, he still found it difficult to believe the cowboy was blind.

"I'll make out all right." Sundown shrugged.

"But he didn't even hurt you in any way?" Rawhide persisted.

"Never even scratched me." Sundown laughed.

There weren't so many rustlers in view on the valley floor now, but there was a great deal of firing still taking place on the brushy slopes, as Rawhide and Sundown spurred their ponies back into action. Powder smoke drifted thickly in the sunny air, and here and there the cries of wounded men could be heard. There were several dead horses to be seen. A good many men lay face up to the sun, or in huddled heaps in the grass. One of the hill slopes was a point of concentration now, as Deputy Beadle directed a merciless fire toward a group of rustlers who were taking cover among the trees. Gradually the firing commenced to die away, except for short, sporadic bursts at widely varied points.

Suddenly a yell of surrender was heard from among the trees; other voices begged for mercy. Then came Curry Echardt's voice: "They've give up! Hold your fire! They're quittin'. Dammit! I said no more shooting," as several detonations of six-shooters interrupted the words. "We've got to take *some* prisoners back with us."

"I'm blasted if I know why," a Flying-Box-9 puncher growled. "We should wipe out every one of the scuts."

"Now that ain't no Christian spirit," a puncher named Tug chided him. There was smoke grime on Tug's face and an angry scratch ran along one cheekbone.

Echardt again directed his voice toward the

hidden outlaws. "Come out, you thievin' bustards. We're holding our fire."

But only a scant handful of men appeared — five in all, one of them waving a very dirty white handkerchief. They were quickly made prisoners. Some of the punchers were starting to bandage wounds. Rawhide and Sundown cantered up, followed by Matt Jackson and Luis Montaldo. Others of the Sundown faction commenced to gather, some on their own ponies, others forking mounts captured from the enemy. Chris Newland pushed up to Echardt's side. He said, "Curry, you better tend to that wound in your laig." Echardt said he'd get to it presently. Newland turned to Sundown.

"My two punchers that went to the Mexico end of the pass to grab the guard brought him in a spell ago. The guard didn't put up any fight. He says that Balter passed him, riding like a bat outten hell, a short while after the fighting broke out here."

Sundown frowned. "Damn! I hate to see Balter escape. I haven't seen Nort Windsor yet, either."

Deputy Dave Beadle put in, "We'd better make a check-up."

Orders were given and riders scattered about the valley to survey the casualties. When the check-up was completed it was learned that two of Beadle's men were dead, one of Newland's; three other punchers had made the supreme sacrifice. Several men were wounded, some but slightly, a few more seriously. The Lazy-E crew had fortunately escaped with but minor injuries. It was now that Sundown and his men learned that they had been fighting against odds: the previous night some twelve additional men had arrived to join Balter's gang. However, that had apparently made but slight difference in the result. Dave Batler had only a few men to make prisoners; the remainder of the rustling outfit had been killed outright. The prisoners who had been taken were a sullen-faced, unshaven, hard-bitten group of men, but at present only too anxious to do anything possible to lessen the fate that lay ahead of them. All of them cursed bitterly when they learned that Zane Balter had run off and left them to fight without a leader.

"But there was Nort Windsor," Sundown said. "We haven't found him yet."

"Windsor and Balter had an argument," one of the prisoners supplied the information, "and Balter shot him just before you hombres dropped down on us."

Another prisoner pointed up toward a clump of trees. "Windsor was layin' in that shack up yonderly still alive last time I saw him."

Rawhide squinted up the slope. "I see the shack. Come on, Sundown, I'll guide you up there."

Sundown laughed. "I reckon I could make to find the place myself, waddie. You forget I've been up there before."

Dave Beadle came riding up and spoke to Sundown and Echardt. "If you ain't no objection, I'll start these prisoners back to town. There's some wounded should go along, too, that needs medical attendance. There's a couple of wagons over near the corral. I reckon we can hitch up and fix the beds of the wagons up comfortable so them that's hurt bad can ride comfortable as possible."

"Good idea, Dave." Echard nodded. "I'll have some graves dug, too, if I can locate a couple of shovels. There's some bandaging of minor wounds to be attended to, likewise. By the way, Dave, when you ride back through that pass, don't forget to pick up that guard that Sundown knocked on the head last night."

"I'll take care of it," the deputy promised. "That hombre is lucky he escaped being killed in this fight. Damn' if this ain't a lesson to any cow thief who thinks he can rustle the Holster Basin. There's a lot owing to you, Sundown, for arranging this business. "

"There's something owing to every man who came with us too," Sundown said quietly. He turned as he heard Tim Carraway's voice.

"We've found Nort," Carraway said soberly. "He's not suffering much pain, but I don't figure he can live much longer. He's in a cabin up on that slope" — pointing to a clump of trees halfway up the side of the hill, where the outline of a small building could be seen dimly through the overhanging foliage of live-oak trees.

Sundown nodded. "Yeah, we heard about

him. Rawhide and I were just about to start up there."

Echardt said, "I'll follow on up in a few minutes. Got a couple of things to attend to here first."

Gone Wrong

Accompanied by Tim Carraway and Rawhide, Sundown made his way up the slope, picking a path among brush and loose chunks of rock, though there was a sort of trail to be followed. Arriving at the cabin, they found that the door stood wide open. Sundown entered, followed by the others. One of the Flying-Box-9 punchers stood within. Stretched on blankets spread on the floor, with another blanket rolled under his head, lay Nort Windsor.

Rawhide glanced at Windsor's white face and closed eyes. If it hadn't been for the man's labored breathing which parted the pallid lips, Rawhide would have thought him dead.

Sundown said, "Sounds to me as if he'd been shot through the lungs. Hear that soft scraping sound he makes with each breath?"

The Flying-Box-9 puncher said sorrowfully, "Through the lungs and belly both. Damn that Balter bustard! Say what you like, Nort was a good man to work for."

"Has he been conscious at all?" Sundown asked.

Tim Carraway nodded. "For just a couple minutes when we first found him. We got some water and made him as comfortable as we could."

Rawhide and Sundown stooped beside the wounded man. Rawhide produced a flask of whisky and poured some down Windsor's throat. The bite of the fiery liquor brought Windsor to consciousness. In a few moments he opened his eyes.

He tried to smile as his gaze fell on Sundown and Rawhide. "So it was you fellers made all that shooting a spell back that I heard. I couldn't be sure what was happening, though. I been passing out — on and off. Well, so you finally caught up with us, Sundown. I figured it was only a question of time. I just got what was coming to me — I reckon."

While he talked, small flecks of crimson foam appeared on his lips.

Sundown said, "Listen, Nort, I guess it's no secret that you're done for — and I admit I hate to say it too. But I want to know a few things. Balter's gang is all busted up. Tell me, who killed that Artexico man, Steve Wyatt?"

"Zane Balter," Windsor said, "damn him! If it wasn't for Balter —" He broke off. "Hell, I guess I got only myself to blame, but when Balter came to me with his schemes, I was just a damn fool to fall for 'em —" His breath gave out and he paused to regain some strength.

"Hang it, Nort," Rawhide put in, "I still don't see how you ever took to throwin' in with a bustard like Balter. You're a white man, and —"

"I was at one time, maybe," Windsor said in halting tones. "It didn't seem so bad at first, when Balter came to me with his story. He told me the government planned to buy up the outfits in the basin, so it could dam up Verde River and make a big lake in the basin. I believed him —"

"There was such a plan at one time," Sundown broke in, "but the government dropped the idea sometime back."

"I didn't know that," Windsor said weakly. "Balter's scheme was for him and me to buy up the basin outfits and then sell at a big profit to the government. Curry Echardt was always saying that he had enough to retire on and go fishing in California, so we figured we could rustle his cows a mite and irritate him into selling out. With the money we got for the cows and a loan on my outfit, I was to make him a down payment, then when I made the profit from the government, I'd finish paying Curry. It all sounded harmless enough when I went into it."

His voice was failing again. Rawhide asked, "What about the Flying-Box-9?"

Windsor explained after he'd had a few minutes' rest, "We figured with Echardt out of the way Chris would sell cheap. Balter had been stealing his cows for some time. He already had quite a gang working for him when I joined in on his plans. It was Balter who found the secret pass from my land into this valley. I reckon he was always afraid I might find it, so that's why he wanted me in on his plans. My herds was run down and sort of scrubby so I threw in with his ideas." He paused, and his dimming eyes sought Sundown. "Sundown, are you an Artexico man?"

"I've been an Artexico operative for a good many years," Sundown said.

"Always had an idea you might be," Windsor said feebly. "Balter was almost sure you was, but never quite certain. Neither of us worried about it after you was blinded, though. It was Balter shot you that day and hit you with that running iron. We both thought you was dead at the time. It wasn't needful to hit you that way. I had an argument with Balter about that too. I always liked you, Sundown, even if we were on opposite sides."

Sundown laughed awkwardly. He was feeling sorry for Windsor. "You had the makings of a mighty good hombre yourself, Nort, only you took the wrong course —"

"There was nothing else for me to do," Windsor said, "after Balter killed Steve Wyatt. Wyatt had discovered the secret pass, too, but we captured him, held him prisoner in an old shack on my property. Balter promised me he wouldn't hurt Wyatt, and — and then the bustard shot him right before my eyes. And I was in so deep I had to swear an alibi for Balter. Damn his dirty hide!" A pale resentful fire burned momentarily in Windsor's eyes. "Did you get him in your raid, Sundown?"

"He escaped us, Nort, but we'll catch up with him yet."

"He always looked after his own skin," Windsor said bitterly. "But watch out for him, Sundown. He hates you. Since that day you outshot him, he'd done little except practice with his six-shooter. He's terrible fast nowadays. I never saw a man so fast with a gun. I should have known better than to draw against him —"

"How did that happen?" Sundown asked. "What did you fight about?"

Another drink of whisky was necessary before Windsor could make a reply. He gave a few gasping breaths and answered, "Balter was getting impatient — wanted more money faster. He hit on the idea — of kidnapping 'Ginny Echardt, and then holding up Curry for a big ransom."

Sundown swore suddenly. He had gone white around the mouth. The two Flying-Box-9 punchers uttered angry exclamations. Rawhide checked the oath that rose to his lips and asked, "And you didn't fall in with the idea, Nort?"

Windsor said, "Hell, no," and even in their weakness his tones expressed disgust. "Stealing cows is one thing. Warring on women is something entirely different. Zane and me quarreled about it. One thing led to another. He grabbed his gun and invited me to draw. Like a fool I went for my six-shooter. Cripes, I never had a chance."

Sundown said, "Tell me, was it Balter that run the FlyingBox-9 brand on the Lazy-E calf to throw suspicion against Chris Newland?"

Windsor tried to reply, but his voice failed him. Again Rawhide applied the whisky flask. After a few moments Windsor's voice started again. "Yeah, that was Balter's work. God! You nearly finished Zane that day, Sundown. He didn't think he'd have so much trouble with a blind man. I wish you'd killed him. Yeah, that calf-branding business was a plant. Balter was trying to get rid of any suspicions that might be directed his way. He was tricky that way. Sundown, did you ever get a line on Munson and Montaldo?"

"His name's Jackson — not Munson," Sundown replied. "They're both law officers, Nort. They came on this raid with us."

A feeble smile crossed Windsor's pallid lips. "I was right about them, anyway. Always suspected they might be trying to run down Balter and me. Balter figured maybe they were cow thieves, but I pointed out that we were doing all the rustling. But they bothered me. That's why I wanted you to trail 'em with me that day they trapped us —"

His voice died to a whisper, and his eyes closed. Sundown reached for his wrist and found the pulse very thready. "Look, Nort," Sundown asked, "have you any idea where Balter might have gone from here?"

Windsor's eyes reopened, focused vacantly a moment, then became a trifle clearer. "Ain't sure . . . he might be riding to a little Mex town called Dotación — lot of white scum holed up there — men who've had to escape the States to avoid arrest and have got a price on their heads in this country. Balter might be plannin' to raise a regular army . . . of such scuts and return to — raid Holster Basin. He often . . . talked of doing that." The man's breath was coming more painfully every moment. When he spoke, it was only a gasp now. "Could you — roll — me a cigarette? Like a last — smoke."

Tim Carraway's fingers trembled as he twisted tobacco into a brown paper. He scratched a match and bent down to place the cigarette between Windsor's lips. Then he paused, his eyes widening. After a second he placed the cigarette in his own mouth and lighted it.

Sundown and Rawhide straightened slowly to their feet. "There's the end of a good man gone wrong," Rawhide muttered. "Damn! I liked Nort. I'm mighty glad he lived long enough to give us a line on Balter's actions — him and his gang of cutthroats."

Sundown's lips tightened at the thought. "Balter and I will yet have a final reckoning," he stated grimly. He turned to Tim Carraway and the other Flying-Box-9 puncher. "I reckon you two will want to bury Nort somewhere around here. Take care of anything you find in his pockets and so on."

"We'll take care of it." Carraway nodded. His eyes looked a trifle moist. He heaved a long sigh. "What a hell of an end for a good man."

Sundown and Rawhide made their way back

down the slope. They found Echardt sitting down, his legs bare. Joe Saxon was endeavoring to bandage the wound in his thigh.

Echardt said, "Did you find Nort?"

Sundown nodded and told what had happened. Echardt said, after a minute, "Well, that's likely best in the long run. It would have driven Nort crazy to be penned up behind bars. I figure this is the way he would have wanted it —" He broke off. "Dang it, Joe, go easy on that leg. It's right tender."

"Sorry, Curry," Saxon apologized, "but this wound is sort of difficult to bandage. I've got this rag tight —"

"Here," Rawhide offered, "let me do it, Joe. I've had a mite more experience than you."

Saxon stood back and thankfully gave over the job to Rawhide. Sundown stood waiting a minute, then whistled for Coffee-Pot. The horse had been standing with hanging reins a short distance away.

It was nearly an hour later that Rawhide asked Echardt, "Say, where did Sundown go?"

"You got me," Echardt replied. "He's likely around here some place."

At that moment Montaldo and Matt Jackson came trotting up. Rawhide asked if they'd seen Sundown.

Jackson nodded. "Luis and I were just riding around, sort of checking up to see that we hadn't missed any of those rustling bastards. We saw Sundown ride past and stopped to chew the rag a minute. He said he was going to ride down to the south end of the valley and scout around a bit."

"How long ago was this?" Rawhide asked sharply.

Montaldo shrugged. "Half or three quarters of an hour back, I imagine. What's wrong? You look bothered."

"You're damn' right I'm bothered," Rawhide snorted. "Do you know where I figure he's gone? He's riding on Balter's trail. Balter's only got two-three hours' start of him. He's aiming to shoot it out with the coyote —"

"Hell's bells!" Echardt swore. "Why didn't we think of this before? My God, blind like he is, he won't have a chance if Balter sees him coming —"

"Jeez!" Jackson said harshly. "I never thought of that. I'd almost forgot he was blind. He gets around as good as any of us. He wasn't even wearing his smoked glasses when we talked to him, and his eyes looked normal as hell —"

"His glasses were shot off in the fight," Rawhide snapped, "but that don't make him see any better just because his eyes look good. I —" He broke off and started away.

Echardt said, "Where you going?"

Rawhide spoke over his shoulder. "I'm following Sundown. I hope I can get to him before Balter does."

"I'll go too," Echardt said. He started to rise and sank back, wincing. "This damn' laig of mine," he gasped. "So stiff I can't make to get up —"

"You stay here and take care of that leg," Jackson said. "You've still a ride to get to the Lazy-E. Luis and I will go with Rawhide. With luck we can catch up before Balter has a chance to kill him."

They swung their ponies around just as Rawhide went loping past. Riding hard, the three men pounded along the valley floor, heading for the pass into Old Mexico.

Better Than an Even Chance

Zane Balter had left the valley by the southern end of the pass that entered Mexico even while the fighting in the valley was at its hottest. He slowed pace somewhat, after ascertaining that he wasn't being followed, and loped along in more leisurely fashion, his mind a muddled turmoil of thought. The raid on the valley had come so swiftly that until now he hadn't given himself a chance to analyze the business. How the secret pass had been discovered he didn't know, but instinctively he blamed Sundown Mallare.

"That damn' Mallare," he growled. "Someday I'll get a chance to square matters with him. I wonder how much of a chance my men had. Not much, I reckon. Mallare wouldn't come raiding unless he had a mighty big force with him. I guess it's the finish of the valley for a hideout, as far as I'm concerned, but what the hell! there's other, better games than picking up cows and bothering to forge bills of sale and all that truck. Me, I've just been wasting my time as I look back on things now."

His horse was traveling across fairly level country now, dotted here and there with clumps of plant growth. An ocotillo raised flaming red tips to the cloudless blue sky above. Mesquite trees offered scanty shade here and there, but the morning sun wasn't yet high enough to demand a halt. Far ahead, misty in the distance, was a low-lying range of purple mountains.

Balter slapped the horse with his quirt when his angry mind paused momentarily on Nort Windsor. Zane Balter had no regrets for killing Windsor. He felt certain the man had died. Balter laughed shortly. "Ain't no man goin' to live long when my slugs strike him," he boasted in a low mutter. "I was a fool to ever tie up with Windsor in the first place. Too chicken-hearted. First he bellyaches about me shooting Wyatt, then he crabbed when I hit Mallare over the head with a running iron. If it hadn't been for Nort I'd have kept on beatin' Mallare that day until his brains was mush. But no, Nort has to act like a fool and object to what I was doing. Damn him, anyway; I'm glad I finished him."

He drew the stub of a cigar from a vest pocket and lighted it, drew savagely on the tobacco a few minutes. "Yep," he told himself again, "I've just been wasting my time rustling cows. Down in Dotación there's plenty of good gun slingers just waiting for a chance to be organized. I'll put it up to 'em as a chance to get back at the law officers that chased 'em over the border. I'll pick up, say, seventy-five — no, a hundred, by Gawd — men, and sometime when Holster Basin has settled back to live peaceful, me and my crowd will drop down some night and really pull a cleanup. There's the bank at Holster City, then the Lazy-E. Once I get my mitts on that 'Ginny Echardt I'll not let go for lessen a hundred thousand bucks. And maybe more. She's always been too blasted cool to give a man a civil word. Maybe I'll teach her a lesson or two."

He paused in his cogitations to glance back over his shoulder. The distant peaks of the Terrera Brutas looked much farther behind him now. He continued his evil planning when he settled back to the saddle again, his thoughts broken only by the steady *cloppety-clop* of his horse's hoofs across the sandy wastes.

"Why should I," Zane Balter asked himself, "confine myself to raiding ranches? With a proper crew behind me I can hit towns all along the Mexican border. That's where the big money's to be had. And liquor and women. Then add more and more men to my gang. When we get big enough we can head down into Mexico, start a revolution, and take over the Mexican treasury. Jeez! There's no limit to what a man can do with money and the proper nerve. And I won't have any trouble picking up a gang, either. I'll get men with guts and shooting ability. You can find them all over Mexico, just waiting the right opportunity to get back at the law-abidin' white-livered skunks that chased 'em out of the States."

The horse loped steadily on its way. Ahead lay a vast expanse of sage-dotted sand and alkali country, with here and there clumps of mesquite, barrel cactus, and an occasional palo verde tree to break the monotony. Occasionally Balter was forced to guide his pony past huge sandstone boulders which looked as though they'd been hurled down helter skelter by some gigantic hand, to roll and land as they would. Now they were a third buried in drifting sand and eroded by the blasting winds of desert storms. By now the sun had climbed much higher, and Balter drew his bandanna across his mouth and chin and huddled in his saddle.

"That damn' Mallare," he growled. "I'll put that blind son-of-a-she-wolf out of the way if it's the last thing I ever do. I ain't forgetting that slug he put in my shoulder. That was sure a mighty lucky shot for him. But I'll square that. I'd like to get my mitts on him just once. By the time I got through with him, he'd think blindness was a blessing. He'd be craving death! Shoot me, will he? I'll cut his damn' ears off and feed 'em to the buzzards, then he won't be hearing so sharp. And those hands of his, too, always feeling out brand markings. Chopping off his fingers one by one would be too good for him. I'd teach the bustard it don't pay to buck Zane Balter. Not nowise!"

An hour passed in this manner, while the horse started to climb slightly ascending terrain that reached to the mountain range in the south. Balter had long since pulled the pony to a slower gait, and it plodded patiently across the sandy stretches, while the sun beat down with an increasing fury. Balter sat hunched in his saddle, muttering and cursing to himself. Every once in a while his eyes lighted fiendishly as he planned some new torture for his enemies when they fell into his hands. Occasionally he took a few sips of lukewarm water from the canteen on his saddle.

The way became more thickly strewn with huge boulders and jutting outcroppings of sandstone. Spanish dagger raised its sharp, spiny tips in all directions and there was more mesquite to be seen now.

Suddenly, warned by some inner sense that he was being followed, Balter twisted in his saddle and glanced around. Somewhat to his consternation he saw a rider approaching some distance back. The man, whoever he was, was traveling fast, his horse kicking up a steady flurry of dust as it moved across the alkali flats to the rear.

"Might be one of the boys, escaped from that valley fight," Balter mused. "I don't know, though." He drew his horse to a halt and reached for the field glasses that hung from his saddle horn. Placing the binoculars to his eyes, Balter focused them on the approaching rider for a moment. The next instant a curse was torn from his lips, and his features went wax white as he recognized the rider who was following him. The glasses nearly dropped from his trembling hands. He realized, abruptly, that now he was actually in great fear of Sundown Mallare, and all his threats and muttering to the contrary had merely been a futile attempt to bolster flagging spirits.

"Damn that hell-ridin' blind sneak," he half gasped. See-sawing violently on his pony's reins, he urged the horse to motion as the binoculars dropped to the sand. The horse, unaccustomed to such treatment and startled by the vicious stabbing of cruel spurs, reared on hind hoofs and then commenced plunging. This abrupt shaking up brought Balter to his senses. He managed to quiet the horse, and after a few minutes reached to the rifle boot under his right leg.

"Hell!" Balter told himself. "I'm acting like a scared fool. All the advantage is with me. I can see him, but he can't see me." He swung his mount around to face the approaching Sundown. "I'll wait until he gets almost here, then let him have it. He'll be riding right into his finish and he won't know what hit him."

Mallare's horse was rapidly closing the distance between the two men now, but the nearer he came, the more nervous Balter became. Abruptly he raised the walnut stock of the Winchester to his shoulder and took aim — as careful an aim as his shaking hands would allow. His finger slowly curled around the trigger — tightened.

The rifle barked sharply, as a spurt of white fire darted from the muzzle. At the same instant Sundown threw up his arms and toppled from his horse, rolling over and over as he struck the earth. Coffee-Pot shied off and ran a short distance before coming to a halt.

Balter levered another cartridge into firing position and triggered a second time as Sundown staggered to his feet. This time the dust spurted two feet away from Sundown.

Balter cursed. "Missed, blast the luck! Why can't I hold this gun steady?"

He levered another load into his chamber and again raised the weapon. He could see Sundown staggering blindly about, searching futilely for cover. A few yards away from the cowboy was a big sandstone boulder. Whether Sundown sensed that the rock was there, or whether it was just blind chance that carried the cowboy in its direction, Balter wasn't certain. He only knew that he wanted to kill Mallare before he had an opportunity to reach the shelter of the rock.

A third time Balter's Winchester cracked out. Through the drifting powder smoke Balter saw Sundown crash forward on his face. Most of his body fell behind the boulder, but his booted feet, toes down, projected plainly in view.

"Got him, by God!" Balter exulted.

Laughing crazily with relief, Balter spurred his horse closer to throw in a finishing shot if it were necessary. He could see Sundown's boots still moving spasmodically. There was a sort of drumming in the movement of those feet, a drumming that drove the toes deep into the sandy soil. Finally all motion ceased, and the boots became quiet.

"I sure hope he ain't quite dead when I get

there." Balter spoke aloud, his eyes glittering insanely. "I want him to know who did this. I want to tell him Zane Balter can't be beat. I want to shoot him again."

Thrusting the rifle back into its boot, Balter leaped from the saddle a few yards from where the motionless boots showed around the corner of the big rock. No, there'd been no further movement. Cautiously Balter drew his six-shooter and approached nearer. Even now he didn't intend to risk any needless chances. He drew closer, walking softly through the sand, then when he had reached the rock he timorously stretched out one foot and kicked at the nearest boot.

To Balter's shocked amazement the boot fell on its side as though it were empty, as though it no longer encased a foot and lower leg. Balter frowned, his mind churning with confusion. Even now it wasn't quite clear to him. He came a step nearer, six-shooter held ready — and saw nothing before him except a pair of empty boots on the sand. A sudden terrified choking rose in his throat as he realized he'd been deceived. He started to turn, but in this also he was too late.

"You'd better raise 'em high, Balter!" The words held all the cold chill of a Texas norther. Sundown had completely circled the big boulder in his sock feet and had come up behind his would-be killer!

Blood rushed to Balter's head. Shaking with fear, the gun dropping from his hand, he swung clumsily around, both arms lifting in the air. There, before him, stood Sundown Mallare, a grim smile on his face, a leveled Colt's gun in hand.

"Looks like you took sucker's bait, Balter," Sundown said, his tones hard and relentless. "I figured you'd bite. This isn't the first time I've worked this stunt on sidewinders. It takes a heap of practice to kick boots off that way. And it's not the first time I've used that fake fall from a horse, either. You'd better learn that when you draw a bead on a man you can't afford to miss. Must have been right shaky, weren't you? This is the showdown, Balter. Your game's up. Your valley gang of thieves is wiped out. You're all through."

"Wha— what you aiming to do ab— about it?" Balter's tongue licked at dry lips. He was sparring for time. His gun was on the ground where he'd dropped it near his feet, but there might still be a chance. He gazed fearfully into Sundown's gray eyes that now seemed to be flickering with tiny lights of cold flame — almost as though he could see.

Balter was remembering now that Sundown had always had to "shoot by ear," had to have some sort of sound to get his direction. *The game wasn't up then!* Not yet! All that was necessary was to bend carefully down and retrieve that gun from the earth. It was well within reach. No steps would be necessary. Carefully, slowly, moving with extreme caution, Balter lowered one arm, then his knees started to bend as he reached for

278

the six-shooter. His hand was about to touch the walnut butt.

"Don't try it, Balter!" Sundown said sharply. The six-shooter in his grasp tilted a trifle.

There was a churning at the middle of Balter's stomach now as he straightened up, dismay plain in his ashen features. He was certain, he *knew*, he hadn't made the slightest sound, and yet Mallare had been instantly aware of his movements. How . . . ? Comprehension swept suddenly through Balter with jolting force. His eyes dilated with terror, and there came an icy clutching at his heart.

"My God!" he almost screamed the words. "You aren't blind. You can see! *You can see!*"

"Yes, I can see," Sundown admitted quietly. "See as good as you. I reckon, Balter, there's a heap of things I can see in cleaner light than you do — but you wouldn't understand that."

"You can see!" Balter exclaimed again, unbelievingly. "You've just been bluffing me."

"Put it that way if you like." There was no humor in Sundown's voice as he added, "You might call it a sort of blindman's bluff."

Balter moved back a pace, fighting to regain control of his nerves, trying desperately to find a way out of the trap in which he found himself. Momentarily he pulled himself together. "All right," he said sullenly, "so you got away with your bluff. But you don't dare kill me. What you aiming to do?"

"I dare, but I'm giving you your chance too," Sundown stated, level-voiced. "Maybe you've guessed by this time that I'm an Artexico man, Balter. You killed one of us a spell back — Steve Wyatt. Remember?"

"I didn't. I swear I didn't!"

"Don't lie, Balter. It won't do any good. This is a showdown. I thought a lot of Steve Wyatt, and I can't forget it was your bullets that ended Steve's life. I ought to take you back to face trial for that murder."

Balter's eyes darted from side to side like those of an animal caught in a trap. "Do you call that giving me a chance?" he whined. "Why — why, they'd hang me."

"Not a bit of doubt of that," Sundown nodded, his tones curiously flat and emotionless. "But I said before I'd give you one last chance — which same is more than you gave Steve. Balter, pick up your gun and shove it in your holster."

Balter didn't understand, but, tremblingly, he stooped and retrieved his weapon from the sand and holstered it: "What — what you aiming to do now?" he queried, his arms hanging at his sides.

Sundown stepped back a few steps and suddenly shoved his own gun into its scabbard. Now his hands, too, were hanging at his sides.

"It's an even thing, Balter," he said, steady-voiced. "You can draw when you're ready."

Balter stiffened slightly, then looking into

those cold steel-gray eyes his nerve deserted him. "My God, I can't do it. You —"

"*Your* God, Balter? Who are you to appeal to God? All you've ever worshiped is your own black heart, a heart blackened in the devil's furnace. Go on, draw! It's your chance."

"I can't do it. I can't do it." Balter half-sobbed, cringing away. "You — you'd kill me —"

"Either go for your gun or I'll take you back to be hanged," Sundown said sternly.

"No, no, Mallare! You can't ask me to fight you now. I'm shaken, unsteady. You'd have all the advantage. Let me go. I'll get out of the country, out of Mexico. Give me one more chance." Saliva was drooling from the man's trembling lips; stark fear was mirrored in his eyes.

Sundown gazed at the man contemptuously, feeling a trifle nauseated before this display of groveling cowardice. Finally he reached a decision and spoke with a certain deadly intent in his tones. "Balter, living's too good a thing like you. I said I'd give you an even chance. You were too low to take it. All right, I'll give you better than an even chance."

Sundown paused a moment, then flung both arms high in the air, away from his holstered six-shooter. "Now will you draw, Balter? I've heard you were fast. Let's see your speed!"

Balter's eyes widened a trifle; unbelievingly he stared at Sundown. By God, this was his chance!

Some last remnants of courage, brought to life by sheer desperation, took hold on Balter. He cursed triumphantly as his right hand darted to gun butt, unbelievably swift.

Even so Sundown's draw was but a split instant later. The men fired almost simultaneously. A leaden slug cut viciously through the neckerchief tied about Sundown's throat. A second bullet passed harmlessly between Sundown's right arm and body.

Balter crumpled suddenly, even as his gun blazed a third time. Sundown felt something like a red-hot hammer smash through the bone of his right leg, and he was hurled off balance.

Both men were down now, facing each other in huddled positions across the intervening yards of sand. Drifting powder smoke lifted lazily between them.

A sort of crimson haze undulated before Sundown's eyes, making everything blurry, confused. He was conscious of a torturing pain, a pain so sharp that it brought his vision into focus again, and he saw Zane Balter bracing himself on one hand while the other lifted a six-shooter. Smoke and white flame erupted from the muzzle. Fire tore savagely through Sundown's ribs and he felt himself sinking forward.

Thrusting out one arm to break the fall, Sundown thumbed two shots close together. A puff of dust spurted from Balter's vest as the first bullet found its mark. Through his fast-fading senses, Sundown glimpsed Balter's wide-open mouth. He guessed the man was yelling or screaming. Almost magically a round black hole appeared beneath Balter's left eye — a black hole that instantly turned to scarlet. . . .

And then Sundown was prone, feeling harsh sand particles against his face. He experienced a sort of floating sensation as a black curtain of velvety oblivion slowly overcame his consciousness.

Overhead three buzzards circled nearer the earth, drawn by the scent of blood seeping quietly into the hot desert sands.

Conclusion

Weeks passed before Sundown's mind was completely clear again. Days and nights passed swiftly in a bewildering kaleidoscopic muddle of sounds, extreme thirsts, bitter medicines, and probing pains. And there were long periods of sleep, and then short awakenings, and a memory of Virginia's cool tones and a window with a curtain through which sunshine streamed or cool night winds blew. And a time came when Virginia told him he was in her bed, in her room, the most airy in the Lazy-E ranch house, but he was too weary at the moment to ask, or even care, how he had gotten there. And still later he spoke a few sentences and dutifully swallowed food that the girl proffered him on a spoon. And there was an occasional man's voice, too, but he was too exhausted for talk.

Until there came a morning when his body felt good and he opened his eyes to see Virginia entering the room. Her eyes lighted at his sudden grin, and she said, "Hi-yuh, cowboy. You look sane at last."

"Cripes," he replied, struggling to get higher in the bed. "I always have been sane —"

"That's what you think. We thought you never

were going to get over being delirious." She put an arm around him and pillows behind his shoulders, smoothed out the bedclothing. A balmy breeze fluttered the curtain at the window.

Sundown asked suddenly, "Did I get Balter?"

Virginia's usually placid brow creased to a slight frown. "If you've asked that once, you've asked it a thousand times. Yes, you did get Balter, as I've told you a thousand times. They found you there —"

"Who found me?"

"Rawhide, Matt Jackson, Luis Montaldo — oh, fiddlesticks!" Her lips lightly brushed his, then she stood up, despite his protests. "Dad and Rawhide are just outside the door, waiting to talk to you. I'd better let them in."

She went to the door and opened it. Rawhide and Curry Echardt entered. They both asked how Sundown felt, and he said he felt fine. He asked about Echardt's wounded leg, and Curry said that was fine too. Virginia left the room while the three men talked. Sundown said he'd like to know just how they got him to the ranch house. Rawhide launched into explanations.

"When we caught up with you — Luis and Matt and me," Rawhide said, "Balter had been dead for some time, and there you was, slowly bleedin' to death — and with your boots off. You roused to consciousness when we picked you up, and I asked what your boots was doin' off, and you sort of snickered, lightheaded, and said you took 'em off 'cause you didn't want to die with your boots on — some such damn-fool statement. And then you prompt passed out again. Matt bandaged you up as well as possible and then we tied you into Coffee-Pot's saddle and started through the valley —"

"I reckon we never would have got you here, neither — not alive," Curry Echardt interrupted, "if it hadn't been for 'Ginny." Sundown broke in to ask what 'Ginny had done. Echardt explained. "You'd lost so damn' much blood, it was like you was drained. Anyway, 'Ginny hadn't been able to stand the suspense of staying home no longer, so she persuaded Tom Leslie to hitch up a wagon and she got her horse and they reached the valley about the time you did, with you nigh dead —"

"How in the devil," Sundown wanted to know, "did 'Ginny and Tom find that canyon pass?"

"That was pure luck. 'Ginny and Tom ran into Dave Beadle just as he emerged from the pass with his prisoners, and Dave showed 'em the way. 'Ginny had had sense enough to put bandages and medicines in the wagon, so we were able to fix you up a mite more, and then make a bed in the wagon. Rawhide rode ahead to Holster City to get Doc Pearson and have him at the house here by the time you arrived. And — and that's about all, except that you had a close shave, son. It was sure nip-and-tuck for a spell as to whether Doc could save you — Doc and

'Ginny's nursing —"

"Sa-a-ay," Rawhide interrupted, "what's all this about you being able to see again? 'Ginny says you told her about it before you left the house, the day we went raiding that valley. Sundown, did your sight really come back?"

"It really did." Sundown smiled. "And I'm all through shooting my ca'tridges blind. I reckon I can thank Zane Balter for my recovered sight. It was him blinded me in the first place, and then that day he shot at me, at the Flying-Box-9, his slug just skinned the bone that was pressing on a nerve and making me blind — sort of jarred the bone back in place, or something of the sort. Anyhow, that's the way I figure it. I plan to ask Doc Pearson what he thinks —"

"You mean" — Rawhide's eyes were wide — "that you were no sooner shot than you could see again?"

Sundown shook his head. "Far from it. The wound was all healed and things remained as black as ever. Then one morning when we were on beef roundup I awakened and there'd been a change — instead of black, I could see a bit of grayish light. I couldn't believe my luck at first, but from then on my sight gradually improved. My sight was completely restored by the time we left on that raid."

"Whyn't you tell us?" Curry asked.

"First, I waited to make sure my sight was actually back. Second, I figured I'd run into Balter someday, and the other crooks, and I

287

didn't want them to know. If I'd told you hombres and the rest of the boys, the word might have leaked out someway. So long as the crooks believed I was blind, they wouldn't pay any particular attention if they saw me riding in the vicinity of their hidden pass. Anyway, like I say, it was Balter who blinded me, but his bullet restored my sight."

"The yellow bastard," Echardt growled.

"Yellow, yes." Sundown nodded. "But he sure fought like a cornered wildcat when the showdown came. He was almost too much for me."

The door opened, and Virginia entered. "Time's up," she stated. "I can't have you tiring my patient. Besides, Tom Leslie and the other boys will be coming up to see Sundown too."

Echardt and Rawhide departed under protest. Virginia took a seat on the bed at Sundown's side. He asked suddenly, "Are Montaldo and Matt Jackson still around?"

Virginia replied, "No, they had duties to get back to. But they've promised to return for the wedding."

"Wedding?" Sundown asked blankly. "Whose wedding?"

Virginia eyed him sternly. "You know very well whose wedding, you long-legged, red-headed lug. Why do you think I had you brought here?"

Sundown snickered. "Had you fooled for a minute, didn't I? Come closer, I want to kiss the bride."

There was a long, long silence. Virginia finally twisted away, her face flushed. Sundown said, "Hey, did you notice a sort of floating sensation then, like we were both riding a cloud?"

Virginia said with mock severity, "You'd better go back to sleep. You're getting delirious again." And after a moment's hesitation, "maybe I don't care though," she murmured. "I think I like you when you're delirious. Let's see if it really was a cloud. . . ."